YHWH

'Ancient, almost secret stories, which will fascinate and feed, educate and enrich, inform and improve understanding and universal knowledge. A twenty-first-century treasure trove of challenging, simple, historic but utterly relevant lessons from the past.'

Gerald Coates, author, broadcaster and founder of Pioneer Christian Community

'Fascinating and powerfully written, *The Flood, the Fish & the Giant* captures the imagination and tells the human saga in the midst of God's story. A triumph.'

Chris Coppernoll, author of *Screen Play* and *Providence*

'With creativity, G.P. Taylor and Paula K. Parker take ancient stories with timeless principles and bring them to life. A refreshing experience to read.'

Canon J.John, author and communicator

'A walk through the garden was never so pungent, so earthy as the stroll you will take with G.P. Taylor and Paula K. Parker in the pages of their masterwork *YHWH: The Flood, the Fish & the Giant*. Smell the loamy earth, see the light glint from the scales of the serpent, taste the sweet-tart fruit of doom as the juice drips down your chin. Then wipe your mouth and turn the page and listen as the raindrops fall and the hammer pounds the nail into the cypress wood and the smell of pitch rises from the page to greet you. G.P. Taylor and Paula K. Parker have taken our Sunday school stories off the felt-board and created a world so vivid, so tactile and real, that you and your children will gasp, wide-eyed at the stench of meat on the lion's breath and feel the sway of the ark itself. This book is a masterpiece. Step into its pages and you will forget you are learning and simply experience the wonder and the miracle of God's word, reminded again and again that you, too, are part of the story.'

Melanie Wells, author of *My Soul to Keep*

'Employing their great skills as storytellers, G.P. Taylor and Paula K. Parker imaginatively recast the major stories of Scripture for a modern-day audience. *The Flood, the Fish & the Giant* will be enjoyed by youngsters and adults alike. It closely follows the original biblical material, whilst bringing alive its ancient near-eastern setting and customs, drawing out a clear and immensely faithful message. The pace is bracing, the read dramatic and exciting, which will both delight and engage readers young and old, enticing them to re-read and be enlarged by the stories in their original scriptural setting. As 2011 is the 400th anniversary of the King James version of Holy Scripture, reading this book would be an excellent way of marking the English Bible's 400th birthday!'

Revd Canon David Wilbourne, Assistant Bishop of Llandaff

'What an absolute delight! Rarely have I seen stories so vividly portrayed – portrayed in a way that makes them come alive the way a good campfire story comes alive. And the source, the greatest stories ever told, but in a way that makes them accessible as they have not been before. You can walk through the gardens, feel Noah's confusion, experience Abraham's anguish, but in all we see unquestioned faith. We've heard or read the stories before, but what G.P. Taylor and Paula K. Parker have done is make you "feel" the stories in a new and profound way.'

Mitchell Galin, film and television producer of *Journey to Everest, Apostles of Comedy* **and** **Stephen King's** *The Langoliers*

'In this wonderful book they have unearthed some great, lost treasures of the Bible and polished them with their own extraordinary gift of storytelling, causing them to sparkle again for a generation that has so often forgotten these brilliant gems. This book is a treasure chest. Cup your hands and dig deep.'

Dr Mark Stibbe, author and founder of **the Father's House Trust**

'In a world where the Bible is often a dusty book at the back of a cupboard, we need new ways of engaging with the Bible's characters and stories. G.P. Taylor and Paula K. Parker keep to the text but retell the story in a modern idiom, holding the attention of the reader and renewing the story once again. This book could bring the Bible alive again for children and remind them of the treasures in store in the actual Bible.'

Revd Dr Peter Phillips, Director of Research, Centre for Biblical Literacy and Communication, St John's College, Durham University

YHWH

The Flood, The Fish & The Giant
Ancient Mysteries Retold

G.P. Taylor
&
Paula K. Parker

Authentic

15 14 13 12 11 10   7 6 5 4 3 2 1

First published 2010 by Authentic Media Ltd
Milton Keynes
Company Registration No: 7101487

www.authenticmedia.co.uk

British Library Cataloguing in Publication Data
A catalogue record for this book is available from the British Library

ISBN: 978-1-86024-800-9

Cover Design by www.steve-oakley.com
Printed in Great Britain by J.F. Print, Sparkford

Contents

1

The Fall

In the early light of morning, by the Tigris River that ran through the valley of Gan-Eden, a long, black serpent slithered in and out of the eucalyptus trees. The creature was followed at a distance by a small and fearful rat. Wherever the snake went, so the rat followed, but always far enough away so the bright white teeth that were hidden in the snake's mouth could not strike it. The cobra cared for nothing but itself. It neither ate nor slept, but just slid through the undergrowth as it sought a place to hide from the sun. The serpent raised itself up and puffed out its hood, then stopped and tasted the air as it flickered its blood-red tongue. Every creature in the garden sensed the advent of death and all were silent. Sensing warmth nearby, the snake edged closer to the body of a man that lay as if unconscious in the clearing of the forest.

As the first rays of sunlight broke against the tall trees, the snake sniffed the face of the bearded creature. He smelled different from any other beast of the forest. It was then, with no human eye to see, that the snake began to slowly transform. Inch by inch, the scales of the creature quickly disintegrated and took the form of pure, white skin. As if it were being peeled, the snake changed in appearance. Its head grew and took on the countenance of a man. As the snakeskin peeled back, the rest of the body emerged. It was distinctly human, the only trace of what had been the cobra were the slitted eyes and two sharp fangs that edged his ruby lips.

Soon, the snake was no more. Its transformation was complete. The creature was angelic, tall, with long thin fingers. Waves of white hair were brushed back to reveal a chiselled face – the beauty of which no one on earth had ever seen.

'Wormwood . . . do you always have to stay in that form?' the creature asked the rat as it crawled over the stump of an old tree and looked up at him.

'*HE* . . . might not see me like this. I feel safe if *HE* can't see me,' the rat replied, as it brushed its face with clawed hands that looked quite human.

'*HE* sees everything. There is nothing in the universe that *HE* can't see,' the man replied angrily.

'But Lucifer, *HE* was your friend and master,' the rat answered without thinking.

'As *HE* was yours, Wormwood. Then the Creator cast us out – just for thinking we were His equal . . .' Lucifer answered as he looked about him, knowing he was being overheard. 'And now, not only does the man Marah inhabit this place, but the Creator in His wisdom has made that – a friend for Marah; the man created from dust – blood and gall – now has a companion.'

Lucifer pointed to the body of a woman who lay on the ground in a deep sleep. She was covered in eucalyptus leaves, her long black hair trailing in ringlets across her dark skin.

'She is . . . very beautiful,' Wormwood answered as he looked down at the woman. 'Is she an angel?'

Lucifer looked at Marah. He traced his finger along Marah's naked skin and dug the nail into his flesh until he came to a long wound in his side.

'Interesting . . .' Lucifer mused as he traced the wound. 'It looks as though *HE* has taken a rib to form this other one.'

'Shall we kill them?' Wormwood asked. 'We killed many angels in heaven until Raphael put an end to our war.'

'Not yet,' Lucifer answered. 'I think that here will be a fine place to wage our war on the Creator. If *HE* has one weakness, it is compassion. If I were King of Heaven, I would not have allowed us to live. All *HE* did was cast us down to this place. Even with our rebellion, *HE* showed kindness. How foolish is *HE*?' Lucifer asked the rat.

Wormwood did not speak. He stared at the woman and watched her breathing. Lucifer reached out and touched her face.

'What will we do with them?' Wormwood asked.

'There will be time; after all, we have all eternity,' Lucifer answered quickly as he heard footsteps in the forest.

Suddenly changing back to the shape of the serpent, Lucifer slithered quickly into the undergrowth. Wormwood darted to the cover of the trees.

Gan-Eden was still. The scent of death had vanished. Marah lay on the ground as if asleep. Around him, bushes covered in blossoms were once more humming with bees. The trees shadowing him were alive with birds singing, building nests and pecking at the ripening fruit. Animals walked up to gently sniff at the sleeping humans and then wander into the brush. The footsteps drew closer and closer. From amongst the trees and bushes, a breath as warm as sunlight and deep as eternity flared the nostrils of the man as the voice echoed, *'Marah . . . awake.'*

Marah's eyes shifted under closed lids and gradually opened; without turning his head, he looked around, taking in the sights, sounds, and smells of Gan-Eden. Yawning he stretched, extending his arms, and touched . . . something.

He turned to see a figure sleeping on the ground. It was like him . . . but it wasn't.

'Creator,' Marah asked, '. . . what . . . is this?'

The voice that had awakened him echoed in response, *'She is woman. She will be your companion and your helper. Your wife. All the animals in the garden were made male and female. It was not good for you to be alone; in the entire garden, there was none equal to you. I caused you to fall into a deep sleep and took one of your ribs and, from that rib, I created her.'*

Marah rose to his knees to inspect the sleeping woman. He brushed away the leaves that covered her body. Her skin was soft as a butterfly's wings and thick dark lashes brushed cheeks the colour of peaches. Hair the shade of a raven's wing flowed from her head, covering her to her thighs. Her lids fluttered and then opened. The eyes inspecting him were almond-shaped, their colour reflecting the grass beneath her. She looked at Marah curiously and reached to touch his face. She laughed; the sound was as light and fresh as the mist that arose each morning.

Taking her hand, Marah helped the woman to stand. *Wife*, he thought. *A companion and a helper. Like me, but not like me.*

'You are bone of my bone,' he told her, 'and flesh of my flesh.'

Her brow wrinkled, as if not understanding.

Marah cupped her cheek. 'You are "woman",' – then he touched his side – 'for you were taken out of "man".'

The woman opened her mouth, working to shape full lips. 'Mmm . . . aaahhh . . .'

Touching his chest, he told her, 'I am "Marah".'

'Marah,' she spoke as if tasting the word.

Pointing to her, he said, 'Havva.'

That is good,' the voice of the Creator echoed through the trees.

Havva looked around for the source of the voice and then looked at Marah, her brow furrowed in question.

'That is the Creator,' Marah said.

Havva looked at him and smiled. It was as if she knew all of what Marah spoke.

'The Creator . . . good,' Havva answered.

Marah smiled. 'Yes, He is.' Taking her hand, he said, 'Now come . . . let me show you Gan-Eden.'

Together they walked through forests and meadows, up hills and down into valleys, enjoying the feel of soft grass beneath their feet. Marah led Havva to a river; releasing her hand, he jumped into the water, laughing. Turning, he extended his arms. 'Water.'

'Water,' she laughed and jumped, gasping as the cold water hit her skin and filled her mouth and nose.

He held her hand as they waded through the water. Fish darted between the man and woman, tickling their legs and feet with brightly coloured fins. Marah showed Havva how to drink the water with cupped hands and wiped her dripping lips. Then they left the river and walked to a nearby tree. Plucking fruit from a laden bough, Marah handed one to Havva.

'Peach,' he bit into the ripe flesh, juice spurting and dripping to his chest. 'Mmmm . . .' he nodded.

She bit into her peach; her eyes widened at her first taste of food. She nodded and laughed as the juice ran down her chin. After eating several more peaches, they plunged back into the river to wash their skin and then laid down on the bank to rest in the sunlight.

As the sun slipped down the sky, changing from golden to orange, to disappear beyond the horizon, Marah led Havva to a spot beneath a massive oak. He showed her how to pull up armfuls of tall blades of grass and lay them on top of each other. When the pile of grass reached their knees, Marah sat down and reached up to pull Havva down next to him. He lay on his back, with his hands cushioning his head. After a moment, Havva lay next to him and placed her head on his chest. As the sky darkened the moon arose, creamy and full, and stars scattered like diamonds across the expanse. The man and woman's breathing slowed and before they fell asleep, they heard, *'That is very good,'* whispered across the night sky.

Through the days that followed, Marah showed Havva the length and breadth of Gan-Eden. As they wandered, they tended the plants. Marah showed Havva how to use a sharp stone to cut the pips and seeds from the fruit they ate; they stuck the seeds in the ground. 'From these, the Creator will make more grow.' They would climb the trees to toss down fruit for the animals that couldn't reach it. And in the evening, the Creator would come. Not that they saw the Creator; they felt His presence as the moonlight washed over their skin and heard His voice whispering through the sky. They would talk about all they had done and the Creator would instruct them about the needs of the animals and plants in Gan-Eden.

'Be fruitful and increase in number,' the voice of the Creator whispered in their hearts, *'fill the earth and subdue it. Rule over the fish of the sea and the birds of the air and over every living creature that moves on the ground. I give you every seed-bearing plant on the face of the whole earth and every tree that has fruit with seed in it. They will be yours for food. And to all the beasts of the earth and all the birds of the air and all the creatures that move on the ground*

— everything that has the breath of life in it — I give every green plant for food.'

One golden day when the warm wind blew in from the west, Marah and Havva followed the bank of the Tigris to where it met with the Euphrates to form the Great River. The waters rolled and cascaded, frothing over rocks. On the bank of the river, stood two trees. Both were gigantic, taller than any other tree in Gan-Eden and laden with ripe fruit, filling the air with spicy sweetness. As they looked across the waters, the Creator spoke. The voice echoed across the sky.

'This is the centre of the garden,' the Creator spoke above the sounds of the rushing water. *'The trees in the middle of the garden are the tree of life,'* the wind blew, ruffling the leaves on the tree on the right, *'and the tree of the knowledge of good and evil.'* The leaves on the left tree waved in the breeze. *'You are free to eat from any tree in the garden; but you must not eat from the tree of the knowledge of good and evil, for when you eat of it you will surely taste death.'*

'Marah,' Havva asked, 'what is "death"?'

'I do not know,' he told her. His face had grown solemn and thoughtful. He was not laughing now. 'But we do not need to know. It is enough that the Creator tells us not to eat from the tree.' He took her hand and looked into her eyes. 'We will obey.'

She nodded hesitantly. 'We will obey.'

As they turned to go, Havva caught sight of an animal she had not met. From a distance, it looked like the branch of a tree it curled around, but its skin glistened like a lizard.

'Marah, what is that?' she pointed to the snake as it bowed from the branch.

He looked. 'That is Serpent.'

'Why does it not come and greet us?'

Marah shrugged. 'I know not.' He took her hand. 'Come, I saw pomegranates. Let's eat some.'

As they walked away, Havva felt an itching sensation between her shoulders. Looking back, she saw the serpent watching her; it looked as though it was smiling.

Time passed slowly in Gan-Eden. Havva had grown accustomed to the land. She knew where to find the best pears and apples, when to pick the raspberries and how to choose the ripest tomatoes. All was well. The Creator walked in the land by the river and they listened to His voice as the sun set and the moon rose out of the mountains.

One morning, the sunlight streamed into her eyes and woke Havva. She looked over at Marah; he was sleeping on his side, with a large leaf covering his head. She smiled at her husband, who snorted and rubbed his nose, and snuggled into their bed. Havva stood up to gather food for Marah and herself.

Wandering, she plucked an apple from a nearby tree; the fruit was sweet and crunchy. She washed the sticky juice from her fingers. She pulled a large leaf from a tree and used it to gather fruit for Marah and herself: more apples, raspberries, dark red cherries, peaches, a small melon. When she came upon the pomegranate tree, she found herself standing near the Great River and the two trees the Creator had told them about.

The fruits on both trees were unlike any she had seen before: larger than any Havva had gathered, and their fragrance made her mouth water and filled the glade with its essence.

'Havva,' a voice said from deep within the glade.

She turned. There, slithering towards her, was the serpent. As it neared, she could see that it began to slowly change and stand up on two legs. It looked like Marah – its eyes were tilted slits, the mouth wide. The creature shuddered joyfully.

'How do you know my name?' she asked.

'We all know that Havva and Marah are favoured by the Creator,' Serpent spoke, hissing out each word. 'I see you are gathering food,' it said. 'Have you come to pick fruit from these trees?' It walked towards the tree on the left.

'But not fruit from the tree of the knowledge of good and evil,' Havva answered.

'Is it true that the Creator really said, "You must not eat from any tree in the garden"?'

'No,' Havva said. 'We may eat fruit from the trees in the garden, but the Creator said, "You must not eat fruit from the tree that is in the middle of the garden, and you must not touch it, or you will die."'

'You will not surely die,' Serpent said. 'The Creator does not want you to eat it, for He knows that when you eat the fruit, you will be wise like Him, knowing good and evil.' Plucking a fruit, it bit into the flesh. Serpent closed its eyes and hissed, 'No other fruit tastes so good.'

Havva took a step closer to the tree. The fruit was large and plump, its aroma filling her head. She dropped the leaf filled with the fruit she had gathered. *None of the fruit I picked looks or smells as good as this,* she thought. *Surely becoming as wise as the Creator is a good thing.*

Slowly lifting her hand, she reached up and – hesitantly – touched the nearest fruit. It was firm and ripe; one slight tug and the fruit fell into Havva's hand. She sniffed it; the aroma was sweet and set her mouth watering. She extended her tongue and licked it. She waited . . . nothing happened . . . no death . . . it tasted like the dawn. She took one bite – then another and another. She consumed the fruit, grabbed another and ate it. Hand over hand, she ate several pieces of fruit, unable to assuage her hunger.

'Havva!' shouted another voice. She whirled around, a fruit in one hand and a half-eaten fruit in the other.

Marah stared at her, stared at her hands. 'What have you done?' he whispered.

Havva stepped towards her husband. 'Marah . . . I woke before you . . . wanted to gather food . . . the serpent told me that the Creator didn't want us to be like Him . . . I ate one . . . the fruit is unlike any we have eaten before . . . nothing happened . . . I'm the same –'

'No,' he shook his head, 'you are different . . .'

'I am like the Creator . . .' She lifted the uneaten fruit to his mouth. 'Don't you want to . . . be like Him?' She lifted the other fruit and took a bite. 'They are wonderful.'

Marah stared at his wife . . . opened his mouth . . . and took a bite.

The ground was soon littered with fruit, some eaten, some just bitten into. Other fruit was just thrown to the ground and smashed underfoot in their haste to grab more. No matter how many they ate, their hunger remained.

'Marah . . .' she said, her voice anguished. 'Something is different.'

'What do you mean?' Marah asked, his mouth full of fruit.

'I do not know. We should know,' Havva's voice was rough and sharp as a stone. 'We ate the fruit . . . the serpent said we would be wise as the Creator and know everything.'

'Havva . . .' Marah said, 'the serpent is not the Creator and we did as he told us, not as the Creator told us.'

Havva grabbed her waist. 'Marah . . . something is different . . . in me.' She doubled over, crying out in pain. 'Something is twisting inside.'

Running to the river, Havva retched as she coughed up the half-eaten fruit of the tree of the knowledge of good and evil. It twisted her guts and stuck in her throat as she retched and retched. Again and again she tried to rid herself of the pain in her stomach and her heart. She was distantly aware of Marah kneeling next to her. She heard his cries of anguish and pain as he emptied his stomach of the fruit.

Reaching out, she pulled a leaf from a nearby bush and wiped her mouth. *Not enough.* She grabbed another and, opening her mouth, wiped her tongue. *Still not enough.*

Pulling leaf after leaf, the man and woman tried to clean the feeling from their mouths, their bellies, their hearts. Shivering, Havva took fig leaves and knotted the ends, until she had formed a covering for herself. Noticing that Marah was also trembling, she formed a covering for Marah.

'Marah . . . Havva . . .'

They looked at each other, hearts pounding.

'The Creator,' Marah whispered. 'He is coming.'

'He will see us . . . He will know.' Havva said. Turning, she ran down the path, stumbling over rocks and stumps, scratching her legs on bushes, until she found four trees that leaned towards each other. Several small bushes growing at their base formed a small shelter. Dropping to her knees, she crawled inside. A moment later, Marah crawled in beside her. She could hear Marah's heart beating in fear.

'Marah . . . Havva . . . *where are you?*' The leaves on the bushes trembled . . . '*Marah?*'

Marah looked at Havva and shook his head. 'I must answer . . .' Taking a shuddering breath, the man stuttered, 'I-I am in here . . .'

'*Where is Havva?*'

Havva looked wide-eyed at Marah, who nodded.

'I . . . I am in here with Marah.'

'*Why are you in there?*'

'We heard You in the forest and we were afraid You would see . . . us . . . as we are . . . naked . . . so we hid from You.'

'Who told you that you were naked?' the Creator spoke in a sad whisper. *'Have you eaten from the tree that I commanded you not to eat from?'*

The pain in the Creator's voice tore at Marah, the knowledge of his disobedience too heavy to confess.

'The woman you put here with me – she gave me some fruit from the tree, and I ate it.'

'Havva.' The woman cringed under the weight of His voice. *'What is this you have done?'*

Havva's thoughts were as rapid as her heartbeat. *What can I say? How do I explain?*

'It was Serpent. He told me it would make me like You . . .' her voice dropped to a tearful whisper, 'and I ate.'

The leaves at the door to their shelter began trembling, shivering, as the wind began blowing, howling. The presence of the Creator rose above the earth, His voice swelled to cover all creation.

'Serpent, because you have done this, you are cursed above all the creatures of the night. You will crawl on your belly and you will eat dust all the days of your life. I will put hostility between you and the woman, and between your offspring and hers; he will crush your head, and you will strike his heel.'

'What will He do to us?' she whispered.

'Havva.' The woman wrapped her arms around her legs and laid her head on her knees. *'You will give birth to children and they will bring you pain. Your desire will be for your husband, and he will rule over you.'*

'*Marah.*' The man turned from his wife, as the Creator spoke to him. '*Because you listened to your wife and ate from the tree about which I commanded you, "You must not eat of it": cursed is the ground because of you; through painful toil you will eat of it all the days of your life. It will produce thorns and thistles for you, and you will eat the plants of the field. By the sweat of your brow you will eat your food until you return to the ground, since from it you were taken; for dust you are and to dust you will return.*'

A sudden, sharp sound rent the air. It was unlike anything that Marah or Havva had ever heard before. It pierced their ears and tore at their hearts.

'*Marah . . . Havva . . .*' The Creator's voice sounded as painful as their hearts. '*Come here.*'

Marah dropped to his knees to crawl from their hiding place; after a moment, Havva followed. Standing, they looked around. Nothing seemed different about the land . . . yet it was. There, by a bush, was a slaughtered sheep. Its throat was cut, blood issued from its fleece, mixing with the dust of the earth.

The voice of the Creator rose above the trees again, '*The man has now become like one of us, knowing good and evil. He must not be allowed to reach out his hand and take also from the tree of life and eat, and live forever.*'

The ground under the man and woman's feet trembled and shook, as the sky grew blinding white. In fear, they watched as a figure descended from the clouds to stand in front of the two trees. It had the shape of a man, with wings like the mighty eagle. His face was terrible to see. In his hand was a flaming sword.

Looking at Marah and Havva, the angel lifted the sword and opened his mouth, *'GO.'*

The word echoed from one end of Gan-Eden to the other. Fire flashed from the sword; a tree near the humans erupted into flames.

Grabbing Havva's hand, Marah began running, screaming, as first a tree and then a bush exploded before them.

They came to the edge of the river where Marah had first showed Havva how to drink and swam across the river, choking on the water that filled their nose and mouth. They crawled out of the water and collapsed on the riverbank, panting. After his heart and breathing had slowed, Marah rolled over and pulled himself to his knees. He looked up and gasped.

Havva grabbed his ankle, too afraid to look. 'What is it?'

'They're gone,' Marah's voice was ragged.

'What's gone? The serpent?'

'No,' Marah dropped to the ground next to his wife. 'The tree of life . . . it is gone. Gan-Eden has disappeared.'

Turning, Havva looked behind them. Across the river, beyond the far bank, was . . . nothing. There were bushes, forests, and hills; but they were not those of the garden. Arching her neck, Havva looked in one direction and then turned to look in the other. Straining her eyes, she could not see the massive tree of life or the tree of the knowledge of good and evil. They were . . . gone!

'Marah, where is it? Did the Creator destroy the land?'

'I don't think so. I think Gan-Eden is hidden from us. Maybe one day, He will let us return.' He reached down and took Havva's hand and pulled her up. '. . . For now, we must find shelter . . . the night is coming.'

2

The Flood

In the foothills of Gan-Eden, just above a line of acacia trees, an old man stood by the door of his house and looked out across the valley. It was more of a shack than a house. The walls were planks of wood that had all been neatly cut, hewn by hand from gigantic cypress trees, and nailed side by side. They had been daubed in thick black resin that stained the timbers to keep out the rain. It was well built by skilled hands. Each door was craftsman carved and every window fitted perfectly. A collar of stone girdled the house five layers deep. On the lintel above the door was the word: NOAH. It spoke of the man who had built the house, timber by timber, many years ago. Underneath his name were carved those of his sons, Shem, Ham and Japheth.

Now, much older than the day he had dug the foundations and carved each name as the children were born, Noah stared out across the land that had been handed down to him from generation to generation.

Instinctively and somewhat impatiently, he groomed his long beard with the tips of his fingers and pulled his flowing coat tightly around him as he looked at his son. He sensed something in the wind. For the first time in many months, the sky looked cold and long clouds cut between the mountains.

'Japheth,' Noah said to the young man who stood on the far side of the dusty road that wound its way up the slight hill from the lakeside. 'Now that you're to be married, we need to begin building a room onto the house for you and Mari.'

The man turned to his father and smiled. He looked up to the sky and raised his hands in welcome as the wind blew across the water from the far mountains.

'I'm ready to begin today, Father,' Japheth grinned as beads of work-hard sweat trickled across his weathered face.

A voice came from the doorway: 'It will be good to have another daughter added to the family,' Noah's wife, Ana, smiled as she set the basket of bread on the table. 'And may the Creator bless them with children.'

'Yes, my dear,' Noah laughed as he shrugged his shoulders and looked at her. 'May the Almighty bless all of our sons with children in His time.'

'Amen to that, Father,' Shem grinned at his wife, Racu, as she placed a platter of figs near the bread and watched her husband step outside the house and stand with his father and brother.

'Betel and I agree,' Ham laughed, hugging his wife.

She slapped his hand as he reached for the cheese. 'Children would be wonderful,' Betel said with a smile. 'They're easier to raise than husbands.'

Ana clapped her hands joyfully and laughed. She looked at the family gathered around her and in her heart she thanked the Creator.

'Since grandchildren would mean more building, we'd better get started,' Noah said as he put his arms around Japheth and pulled him closer. 'Japheth,' Noah whispered. 'After we have finished breakfast, you gather the tools and make sure the saw is sharp. I will go to the cypress grove and mark the trees we will use.'

'I'll go right now,' he said, blushing as his brothers laughed.

'Sit down, son,' Noah smiled. 'You haven't eaten and you'll need your strength for the work. First, we must give thanks to the Creator.' Noah smiled as he looked at his wife, their sons and daughters-in-law, and then to the table laden with food. 'He has given us many blessings.'

Ana took Noah's hand softly. 'He has indeed.'

The family ate quickly and no one spoke. After the last crumb was eaten, Noah sent Shem and Ham to work in the wheatfields.

'Now Japheth,' Noah said, turning to his youngest son, 'after you get the tools, meet me near the stream in the cypress grove. We'll begin to make plans for your room.'

Noah left the house and walked along the well-worn path towards the ancient grove of cypress trees. Noah paced each yard with a prod of his staff and looked at the thunderous sky.

The grove of majestic trees that towered over all the other plants, stretched for several miles. They blotted out the morning sun that broke through the mountain clouds and covered the dust in long, cool shadows.

For as long as Noah could remember, his family had harvested the trees for building what they needed. The cypress wood was long-lasting and, when crafted, would shine with a silver radiance.

The cypress grove was Noah's favourite place. He had walked the path from his house to the grove every day of his life. It was a special place where he could go to sit amongst the shadows and listen to the wind as it whispered through the branches.

As he walked through the grove, Noah used a small hammer and chisel to mark several trees to use for Japheth and Mari's room, and then sat down to wait for his son. He looked back along the path and, leaning his head against the trunk of a tree, he closed his eyes.

'*Noah,*' a voice whispered. '*Noah . . .*'

Noah opened one eye to look around; no one was there. *Am I dreaming?* he thought, closing his eye and settling back against the tree.

'*Noah,*' the voice came again, spoken as if it was all around him.

Noah sat up; his hand trembled. He looked around the tree, trying to see the source of the voice.

He could see no one. *Perhaps I heard the wind rustling the trees . . . perhaps I was asleep . . . perhaps . . .* Yawning, he leaned back once more.

'*NOAH!*' The voice shook the ground.

Noah jumped up, his heart pounded. *That was not a dream or a whisper or the wind.*

'Who's there? Show yourself,' Noah said feebly, lifting the small chisel and hammer to protect himself. 'Where are you?'

There was silence. Noah walked around the trunk of the tree, looking in all directions, but no one was there. He was alone in the cypress grove.

Suddenly and from right in front of him, the voice spoke again: *'Noah, don't be afraid.'*

'Who are you? . . . Where are you?' Noah asked as the voice echoed through the forest.

'I am the Creator. I saw you before you were born. I know your words before they fall from your lips. I am the One who made Marah from the dust of the earth and gave him Havva.'

Noah fell trembling to his knees; the hammer and chisel dropped from his fear-numbed fingers. Noah stared at the dirt, fearful to raise his eyes from the mud of the earth. He tried to speak. The spittle had dried in his mouth and his tongue cleft to his lips like a dried snake. 'Here . . .' he said, 'here I am, Lord . . . Speak to Your servant.'

'Noah . . .' the Creator's voice swelled, echoing through the grove. It rattled the branches of the trees and swirled dust about his feet. It shook the trees and trembled the breeze. It fell silent. Noah waited, unable to move. Then, slowly and peacefully, the Creator spoke again: *'Noah . . . I am going to put an end to all people. The earth is filled with violence and wickedness. I am going to destroy people and their world.'*

Noah held his breath. *Destroy all the people on the earth? Ana . . . my sons . . . their wives? Why?*

The Creator heard his thoughts and answered. *'I will bring floodwaters on the earth to destroy all life under the heavens. Everything on it will perish. But . . . I will spare you . . . and your family. I will establish my pledge with you.'*

Noah gasped for breath and gripped the dust of the earth with his fingers. 'Me . . . me . . . Lord? Your pledge? A covenant with Noah?'

'Of all the people on the earth, I have found you to be a good man. You are going to build an ark of cypress wood for yourself, your sons and their wives, and for the animals I will send to you.'

'An ark, Lord . . . how?'

'Here is how you are to build it.'

Noah's trembling increased as he listened. The Creator spoke in the cypress grove, whispering on the breeze and shouting in the wind. Noah could do nothing but listen.

'A boat how big? Three levels? With a roof running the length of it? I am used to building things, but this . . . this ark . . . it would take years, decades . . . or more . . . to build such a thing . . . and possibly require every tree in the grove. Lord, how can I undertake such a task? I am but an old man and I only have three sons.'

'Is anything too great for ME?' the Creator asked as the wind shook the trees and moved the stones across the path. *'I will be with you and will help you. When you have finished building the ark, you are to gather the animals.'*

Noah's eyes grew wide as he continued to listen. Then there was silence.

It was an hour before Japheth came to the cypress grove in search of Noah. His father was hacking furiously at the trunk of a cypress tree with the hammer and chisel. Wood chips flew with each hammer strike, catching in Noah's hair and beard. When he saw Japheth he dropped the tools to the dry ground. He stared at his son with a crazed look.

'Ah, Japheth, there you are,' he said quickly as he reached for one end of the saw. 'Hurry . . . hurry now . . . help me with this tree. We have much work to do before the rain.'

'Work? Rain?' Japheth stumbled over the words not knowing what his father said. 'Father, what do you mean? What is . . . *rain?*'

'I know not,' Noah said, pressing the saw's blade into the trunk where he had been hacking. 'But the Almighty assures me that rain is coming, much rain . . . torrents . . . to wash away the earth.'

'Why, Father? Why would the Creator do that to the world?'

'Since Marah, our race has turned its back on the Creator. They seek power before grace and forget the poor. It is as if they think of nothing but themselves and how full their stomachs are,' Noah answered.

'I heard there were giants to the north who had taken our women as wives,' Japheth answered wide-eyed.

'The Nephilim – giants. People said they were demons or fallen angels; for myself, I know not. I saw one once when

I was a boy. Bigger than a man by the length of an arm. It had red hair flowing from its head and a beard like a thorn bush.' Noah said as he stretched out his arms in wonder.

'But why should the Almighty end the world?' his son asked.

'The ways of the Creator are not our ways. Our minds cannot understand. In faith I take all that is said as the truth and in that I put my trust.' Noah again took the handle of the saw and looked at Japheth. 'We have to work. There is an ark to build.'

Days, weeks and months rolled ever on. Many, many years passed as Noah and his sons worked on the ark, pausing long enough to build a room on their home for Japheth and Mari and to celebrate the couple's marriage.

In his long life, Noah had built a house and barns – and even a boat for fishing on the Great Sea – but he had never built anything the size of this ark. It measured 150 metreslong, 25 metres wide and 15 metres high. The walls stopped 50 centimetres underneath the sloping roof, creating a window in the side of the vessel.

There was a door so gigantic that when it was let down, it could be used as a gangplank to enter the boat.

Ana and the women helped too. Without them, the ark would not have been built and their labour was valued by the Creator in equal measure to that of the men. In addition to their housework, each day they would care for the livestock and the crops, so the men could build the ark.

The Creator blessed their efforts. The cows and goats thrived, the corn grew in the field and the harvest was plentiful. Ana laughed as Betel showed the men the growing mountain of cheese. Ana and her daughters-in-law stored basket after basket of vegetables and fruit in the winter cellar. None of it spoiled. As if by divine providence, all was kept as if it had just been picked.

When they weren't tending to the housework or the crops and animals, the women carried buckets of tar to seal the cracks between the boards on the ark. As they worked, the ark grew in size until it was bigger than any ship that had ever been built before.

Once the outside of the boat was constructed, the men moved inside to work.

'Three levels?' Shem asked, dropping the basket of tools on the floor of the ark; the sound echoed throughout the ship's hull. 'The Creator said *three* levels?'

'He said three,' his father nodded. 'With rooms on every deck.'

'And tell us again what the Creator said was going to be in these rooms?' Ham asked, wiping the sweat from his face.

Noah took a cup of water from Ana and drank it all before answering. He smiled, trying to stop the laughter that twisted in his stomach. 'We're going to live in some of the rooms; the rest are for the animals and to store food.'

'Our animals?' Japheth asked. 'The goats, chickens, cows and sheep?'

'Not all of our animals,' Noah replied. 'The Creator told me just to take two of every type of animal that inhabits the earth. We have to preserve their kind.'

'Father!' Ham erupted. 'This is impossible! Yes, we can put our own animals on the ark, but what about the wild animals? Do we throw a rope around a lion's neck and lead him inside? And if, by some miracle, we do gather them, how are we going to keep the lions or cobras or any of the other predators from attacking? What the Creator is asking of you is impossible.'

'And the Creator is going to destroy all life?' Shem's wife asked. She looked at Racu and Betel. Her eyes clouded with tears. 'What about our families? Our fathers and mothers? Our brothers and sisters?'

Noah placed a hand on his son's shoulder.

'Mari,' he said, looking at her and then the other girls. 'Racu, Betel. I'm sorry. I can't answer your questions. All I know is that the Creator is good and He has called us to this task. I don't know how all of this will happen, or when, but I *do* know that He will not abandon us, and – as we obey – He will help us. Do you believe me?'

Noah looked at each of his family; one by one, they all nodded their heads.

'We believe you, Father,' Shem answered.

'Good. Now, we have all worked hard, why don't we stop work on the ark for today? Go, Ana, you and the girls prepare the evening meal. Shem, you and your brothers clean and sharpen the tools for tomorrow. Go, now. I want to be alone to pray.'

When they had all gone, Noah wandered around the ark. With every step, he stopped to check the wooden joints, testing the tar to see whether it was dry, pushing against the wood to see if it could hold back the creatures.

The size of the boat still amazed him. It was higher than the cypress trees and covered in rich, black kopher. The hardened pitch shone like a black diamond.

'I didn't think we could do this, Almighty Creator,' Noah prayed. 'But, *we* really didn't do this, did we? Nothing more than a hammer and saw built this ark. Like them, we are just tools in Your hand. Soon it will all be finished, according to Your instructions, Lord; then what will you have us do? Whatever it is, Lord, we will obey.'

His words trembled on his lips and shook in his heart. They were not the ramblings of a magician, but the yearnings of a man speaking to God. Noah sighed as he spoke the last words; they hung in his mind and haunted him like a distant echo.

Noah stood up and looked about him. Many of the townspeople had come to laugh at Noah and his family. They had scorned the old man for being stupid. No one had listened to his warnings of the coming destruction. They thought him to be a mad man. Yet, Noah knew that if he stayed faithful to the Creator, then the promise of protection from the coming flood would be fulfilled.

Early the next morning, Noah went to the ark to pray. In the darkness of the boat, Noah knelt. He had barely finished his prayers, when he heard urgent footsteps on the gangplank.

'Put that bag of grain there, Japheth . . . next to the cheese . . . The water barrels go over there, Shem . . . Ham, take the stalks of straw into the other room,' Ana said. 'Girls, the clothes and bedding go in our rooms. Would someone please comfort our animals; this boat scares them.'

Noah watched Ana direct their children in storing their food and belongings. A large section of the boat near the family rooms was set aside for food storage. The moans of the animals floated up from the floor below. Noah stroked his beard as he looked into room after room of grain, produce, cheese, barrels of water, and food for themselves and for countless animals.

He shook his head and smiled. *It would take years to eat so much food.* The smile froze on his face, *Lord, how long are we going to be on the ark?*

'Noah . . . Noah?' He turned to see Ana standing, surrounded by their sons and daughters-in-law.

'Yes? What is it?'

'It's done.'

'What? What is done?'

'Everything, Noah,' his wife swept her hands out. 'The food is in place, our possessions are in the rooms and our animals are on board. Everything you told us the Creator said to do . . . it is finished.'

Noah looked around. 'It . . . is . . . finished,' he murmured as he smiled at her.

'What do we do now, Father?' Shem asked.

'Do?' Noah looked at his family. 'We wait . . . to see what the Creator will do next. Come, let's go to the house. It's time to –'

'Father Noah . . .' Racu said as she stepped out suddenly in front of him. Her face was pale, drawn and fearful.

'What is it, Racu? Are you ill?'

'Noah,' Ana whispered, her eyes wide, 'don't . . . don't move.'

Noah froze. *Why?* he mouthed to his wife in a whisper.

'Lion,' Shem whispered. 'Behind you . . . a lion.'

The blood froze in Noah's veins. He inched towards the side of the ark. The sunlight streaming through the door-way cast a giant shadow of the lion that stood at the top of the plank. The creature roared, shaking its mane. Then, turning, it started to slowly walk towards Noah.

'Don't move,' Noah spoke softly. 'If we are still, maybe it won't attack us.' He heard one of the girls whimper. 'It's all right . . . be still.'

Noah's heart was pounding in his ears as the lion lumbered up to him. The beast's muscles rippled as it shifted its weight and, standing on its hind legs, placed massive paws on Noah's shoulders. Its breath was hot and stank of raw meat. As it lowered its mouth to Noah's head, it licked his cheek. Then with a heavy sigh, the lion dropped to the floor and lay down at Noah's feet, panting.

'Father,' whispered Japheth watching as the lion began licking its paws, 'did that lion taste you or . . . did it kiss you?'

'I . . .' Noah swallowed hard as he wondered if it had been a dream, 'I think it kissed me.' Noah froze again as the lion lifted its head and roared.

A moment later, another lion – a female – stepped through the door, padded over to Noah and flopped down next to the male. Leaning over, she began grooming her mate.

'Noah,' Ana pointed, 'look . . .'

In the doorway stood two gazelles. They glided past the lions to nuzzle Betel. Suddenly, every kind of creature began entering the ark. Noah saw tigers, water buffalo, horses, crocodiles and monkeys. Looking out of the door, he saw the area surrounding the boat teeming with animals. Looking up, Noah saw birds of every size and colour swooping through the opening to land on the floor or perch in the rafters.

Noah turned to his family, staring at the menagerie around them. 'Well, Ham,' he smiled as he spoke slowly, 'I think the Creator has answered your question. It appears we won't have to gather the animals.'

For days, the animals – many that Noah recognized and many he had never seen before – kept arriving. Noah and his family were busy from dawn to dusk, herding the animals into the pens on the ark's lower floors and filling the troughs with food and water. In each case, after eating a huge portion of grain or straw – even the predators – and drinking deeply, the animal would lie down on the hay-strewn floor and go to sleep. By the end of the seventh day, every pen in the ark was packed with feathered, furry, sleek and leathery creatures . . . all asleep.

'How long do you think they will sleep, Father Noah?' Mari asked, handing him a cup of wine.

Noah drained the cup and wiped his face with his sleeve, he looked around. 'I know not, Mari. I know there are creatures that go into a deep sleep through the winter. If all these animals sleep like this, we could stay on the ark . . . for months. We have to trust that the Creator will –'

He stopped speaking as if his words had been stolen from him.

'What was that?' Betel asked, walking towards the opened door. Noah and Mari followed. Ana and their sons joined them.

The sky was dark – even though it was midday – the air felt close. In the distance was a deep, ominous rumbling. Thick black clouds rolled in from beyond the Great Sea. The mountains to the west disappeared in a thick mist.

'I have never seen a cloud like it,' Betel said as she pointed to the distant mountains that were being quickly engulfed by the mist.

'That isn't cloud,' Shem answered. 'It is . . . it is . . .'

'Noah!' Ana screamed as she took her husband's hand, her voice trembling. '. . . What . . . is it?'

Noah stepped out on the plank to look. 'I don't . . .'

He jumped back as the wood under his feet trembled. As they watched, the trembling increased and the plank began rising, moved by an unseen hand – hinges screeching – and suddenly slammed shut. The lower decks of the ark were immersed in darkness. Light filtered in from the narrow window on the upper deck.

Noah stumbled across the darkened floor until he found the stairs. Grasping the rail, he ran – pulling himself hand over hand – up the stairs to the top floor. The distant rumbling they had heard now sounded like giant beasts stampeding towards the ark. Noah ran across the floor to the ladder nailed to the wall and climbed up to peer through the window.

The sky was angry, dark with black, boiling clouds that twisted and turned in ever quickening spirals. Noah watched in amazement as lightning streaked in jagged white lines across the sky, leaving a white glow on his vision. Another white line streaked to the ground, erupting in dirt and rocks. The wind began howling.

Thump. Something hit the roof.

Thump . . . thump . . . thump . . .

Noah shifted to stick his arm out of the window, reaching as far as he could. After a moment, he drew his arm back in and studied his hand. It was wet. *Is this rain?*

'Noah . . .' Ana asked, 'what is it?'

'Father . . .' Shem asked, 'Father, what is it?'

Noah turned and extended his hand to his family as water seeped through the open window to the floor.

'God's judgement . . . has begun,' Noah answered slowly.

In the six hundredth year of Noah's life, in the second month, on the seventeenth day, at that moment, all the

springs of the deep were released and the windows of
heaven were opened.

A sudden, deafening crash threw Noah to the floor, as
the storm's fury was unleashed. The once-dry land was
beaten with hail and thunder as the clouds opened. The rain
poured from the heavens and the earth erupted under massive earthquakes.

What was more frightening than the sound of creation
being ripped apart, were the terrified screams of people
pounding on the base of the ark. They shouted and begged
to be let in. Dying hands grasped at the ship as the deluge
beat down, flooding the valley.

Betel, Racu and Mari ran down the stairs to the lower
deck. Noah and his sons followed and watched as the
women pushed against the massive door, screaming out,
'Mama! Papa! NO . . .'

As the ark lurched and rolled over the floodwaters, the
brothers pulled their wives away from the door and carried
them to the upper deck.

Ana moved from one grieving girl to the other. She
wrapped them in blankets, urging sips of water, cradling
each in her arms and rocking them until they finally
cried themselves into a fitful sleep. The men sat, staring
at the women and each other. Their faces were edged
with fear as they realized the reality of the Creator's
words.

'Will everyone be drowned?' Shem asked his father when
he knew the women were asleep.

'The Creator wanted to rid the world of wickedness and, if that is what needs to be done, then who are we to ask questions?'

'Surely not everyone was evil. I knew many good people,' Ham answered.

'A new world washed of evil – that is all I know,' Noah answered.

'And will it happen again when the Creator tires of us?' Ham asked.

Noah shrugged his shoulders and rubbed his wrinkled brow.

The rains fell without ceasing. Only a shifting of light separated night from day. The ark tossed from wave to wave as the storm grew.

Noah scratched notches on the wall to mark the storm's duration. Days turned to weeks, weeks turned to a month. And still the rain continued.

'Forty days,' he announced, setting the hammer and chisel on the floor next to the bed.

'Forty days?' Ana repeated. 'I can't stand it any more. When will it end?'

'I know not, my love,' Noah climbed into bed and wrapped his arms around his wife. 'I know not. We must not give up hope. The Creator has promised we would see an end to this, and what the Creator promises, He fulfils.'

He held his wife long after she went to sleep and stared into the darkness. In his heart he had no doubt that what the Creator said would come true. Yet, as he heard the rain lash against the side of the ark, he wondered if they too would perish.

'Noah . . .'

'Hmmm . . .'

'Noah, wake up.'

'What is it, Ana? Noah turned on the bed.

'Listen . . . the rain has stopped.'

'What?' Noah's eyes popped open. He sat up and stared at Ana smiling as sunlight streamed through the window. The sounds of laughter floated in from the other rooms.

The days without rain were longer than the days with rain, but the eight humans in the ark did not care. *They were alive!* They had survived the destruction God had brought on the earth. Thankfulness poured from their lips as each evening they prayed.

As the boat stopped rocking from the angry waves, the animals began waking. Not all at once, but enough to keep the family busy. The women moved from pen to pen, providing the creatures with food and water. The men cleaned out the pens and hauled soiled straw up to the upper level to toss out the narrow windows. At the end of each day, they ate supper, yawning as Noah offered the evening prayer, and then fell into bed. In the morning, the sunlight woke them to begin again.

The notches on the wall increased. One hundred and ten days after the rain had ceased, the ark lurched to a stop. Noah climbed the ladder to peer outside; the ark was grounded on a small island. Water was everywhere. In the distance, he could see other islands poking up through the water.

Noah and his family ran down the stairs to push on the door. It held fast.

'When the Creator is ready for us to leave,' he said, 'He will open the door.'

Seventy-five days passed. More islands – the tops of mountains – became visible as the waters receded.

Forty days later, Noah carried a raven up the ladder to release it through the window. He watched as it flew around the boat, around the mountaintop, afraid to settle on the barren rock yet afraid to fly back to the ark.

Seven days later, Noah released a dove and climbed down the ladder as the bird flew away. Later that evening, it hopped back inside the boat, holding a twig in its beak. Plants were growing again on the earth!

A week later, Noah released the dove again; it flew off and did not return.

Each time a bird was sent out, the family would try the door; each time it held. 'The Almighty will open the door when it is time,' Noah would remind the others. 'In the meantime, we work.'

'Three hundred and seventy days,' Noah announced, chiselling the mark. 'We have been on the ark for three hundred and seventy days.'

'I can't remember what it's like to walk on grass,' Mari sighed over breakfast.

'Or walk through the wheatfields,' said Japheth.

'Once we leave this boat, I'll never complain about walking anywhere, ever again,' Ham's laughter was cut off as the boat shifted.

'What was that?' Betel asked.

'It sounded like . . . the door,' Shem said.

'The door!'

Noah, Ana and their children stumbled down the stairs and stopped. The bottom deck – which had been bathed in darkness for over a year – was lit by sunlight streaming through the open door. They looked at each other for a moment and then ran laughing into the light, down the gangplank, to fall to their knees in the soft grass.

Noah and his family soaked in the sights of the new earth: the grass lush and green, the distant mountains a deep purple. The sounds of the animals caught their attention.

'Those poor animals,' Ana laughed. 'They're tired of being in that ark. Let's go and set them free.'

Several hours later, Ham and Japheth guided the last elephant down the ramp, while Shem scattered the last of the grain for some birds. The whole area around the ark teemed with creatures as they discovered the new earth. The girls stroked the soft noses of deer who nuzzled them. Noah stood and called to his family.

'We must make sacrifice and thank the Creator,' Noah told his family. 'We must thank Him for keeping His promises, for protecting us through the flood, and for restoring the earth.'

Together they knelt as Noah offered the sacrifice on the altar. As the fragrance of the smoke arose, a voice was heard amongst them:

'Never again will I curse the ground because of man, even though every inclination of his heart is evil from childhood. And never again will I destroy all living creatures as I have done. As long as the earth endures, seedtime and harvest, cold and heat, summer and winter, day and night will never cease. And this is the sign of my promise . . .'

Overhead, stretching from one end of the sky to the other – in ribbons of red, orange, yellow, green, blue, indigo and violet – was a rainbow.

3

The Tower

As the last velvet edges of darkness were banished by the rising sun, two men walked the high balcony that overlooked the lush, green gardens. The old man in a long cloak followed the warrior, who pulled at his curled beard as he walked ahead. At each side of them were the grim statues of grotesque demons that formed the pillars of the roof above and shone like silver in the fresh light. Before the men was a great city. Its buildings were built one on the other and glowed, in the coming dawn, as if they were made of gold. Nearby was the base of a massive construction; square at the base, it reduced as it reached upwards into the clouds. Beyond the city was the desert that went as far as the mountains on the horizon. All was quiet, and peace filled the land.

'Nimrod,' the old man said as they stepped from the balcony into a room filled with noblemen, 'I do not believe your noble ancestor, Noah, would be pleased.'

The other men, who had been waiting for the king and his shaman, took a step back. No one ever addressed the king without his title and no one ever – ever – disputed him. Except the old sage, Mikel, whose wrinkles and grey hair awarded him the protection of age. The others, however, were younger than the ancient counsellor and none were taking chances with the anger of King Nimrod.

Nimrod walked up the steps of his throne, planted his sandals wide, straightening up to remind everyone that no one in Babylon was taller. From piercing black eyes, flared nostrils and set chin, anger lined his face. His hands clenched and unclenched in a struggle to keep them from the sword at his side.

'What,' the king spoke softly to Mikel, but no one doubted the controlled rage within, 'what . . . did you say?'

If the fury of the warrior king frightened the elderly advisor, he gave no sign.

'I said, I do not believe your noble ancestor, Noah, would be pleased.' His steps reverberated throughout the throne room as he crossed to stand in front of the king's dais. 'The Creator commanded your ancestor and ours to fill the earth,' the old man said, spreading his hands wide. 'How can people obey that command when you have declared yourself king and have begun building a fortified city that prevents anyone from leaving without your permission?'

Nimrod's eyebrows lowered even further and his hand grasped the hilt of his sword, whitening his knuckles. 'Be careful, old man,' Nimrod seethed. 'You go too far. You forget who I am.'

'You are the son of my friend, Cush, and you are of my family. I watched you grow as a child. Don't YOU forget . . . I am not afraid of you, Nimrod. It is difficult to be afraid of someone who, as an infant, wet his swaddling clothes when I held him. The Creator made you to be a mighty hunter; *YOU* made yourself king.'

A muffled snigger erupted in the room and quickly died away as Nimrod whipped his head side to side, like an angry bull, trying to find the source of the laughter.

Advisors and soldiers lowered their heads, refusing to meet each other's eyes; no one wanted to experience the king's wrath. When Nimrod could find no one to unleash his fury on, he turned back to Mikel.

'I'm not one to be afraid of a *god*,' Nimrod sneered. 'And I have no desire to live as a nomad, following herds and milking goats.' His sneer spread to an ugly smile when several people in the crowd openly laughed at the joke. 'We have built a mighty city. Babylon will be known in the earth long after our children's children are dead. Now we are going to build a mighty tower, one that will reach into the heavens. It will be a gateway to God. Then I will talk with the Creator face to face, and He shall listen to me.'

No one tried to stifle their gasps as they heard what the king said. This time, even Nimrod was shocked at his words.

'Did I just proclaim myself as equal with the Creator?' he whispered to himself as he glared at Mikel. Rage seethed in Nimrod. *Does Mikel think to frighten me? How dare he?* He forced his hand away from his sword. He would not run Mikel through . . . not today.

The old man looked down and shook his head. He raised his hands slightly as if giving up on a wayward child. He turned and walked to the door of the throne room. Placing a hand on the door, he paused and looked back.

'Nimrod,' Mikel said. 'As a boy, you were strong and handsome and showed wisdom in your decisions. I do not know what happened to that boy. Babylon – and this tower – might indeed be spoken of for many generations. But I do not think you will care for what will be said. It is a foolish man who falls into the hands of a mighty God.'

The sound of the door shutting echoed through the throne room and drowned the words of the old man. No one dared speak – no one dared breathe – all waited for the king's wrath to descend in torrents.

'Dedan!' Nimrod barked.

The captain of the king's guard strode to the foot of the throne and bowed, saluting with a fist to his chest.

'Yes, Your Majesty?'

'Mikel is never – *never* – to enter my presence again,' the king's words dripped venom. 'Relay that command to all the household guards.'

'Yes, Your Majesty.' He saluted again and, pivoting, left the throne room.

'Now that the *crazy old man* has left,' Nimrod sat down as laughter flitted through the room, 'let us return to our discussion. Eliasaph, I believe you were reporting on the tower.'

'Yes, Majesty,' the master builder stepped forward from the crowd, bowed, took out his square and compass, unrolled the parchment and scanned it to find his place. 'As I said, the tower is soon to be finished. The goldsmiths are completing the overlay on the altar on the top of the tower.' Eliasaph dropped the scroll and looked at the king, 'This tower will be a magnificent tribute to your reign. Already many call the tower of Babylon "The Gate of God".'

'But will it reach the sky? I cannot see the top for the clouds – how high will it be?' the king asked furiously.

'Nothing on earth has ever been built to touch the heavens. Your tower is taller than the highest mountains. It can be seen from the Great Sea.'

Nimrod rubbed his hands together. 'Excellent. Excellent.'

Eliasaph bowed and stepped back into the crowd.

'Ocran, have the priests finished the arrangements for the ceremony of dedication?' the king demanded.

The chief priest minced forward. Bald head and painted eyes, Ocran wore a white linen robe wrapped around his skeletal body. He placed his hands, with long nails painted gold, together and bowed.

'My King, preparations are finished. The knives used for the sacrifice have been sharpened and they – along with the bowls to catch the blood and entrails – have been sanctified. Seven hundred goats, sheep and bulls have been selected for sacrifice. The sacred incense has been mixed and the anointing oil prepared. In two days' time, when Orion the Hunter is overhead, the celebration will begin.'

'Excellent.' Nimrod gloated as he spoke. 'Zohar, what about the plans for the celebration?'

The governor of the city walked forward and bowed, hand on his heart. The simple robe he wore belied the power of his position. Unlike the others in the room, Zohar had been one of the king's boyhood friends. He was a humble man who some said was a sheep amongst wolves. All knew he had the king's best interests at heart. Zohar did not use friendship to increase his own power or wealth.

'Sire, the food for the celebration will be unmatched. The ovens in the Street of Bakers have not cooled for days. The vineyards have produced the finest wine in years. There will be an abundance of cheese, olives, dates and figs, enough to feed the entire city for a week. For entertainment, there will be acrobats, jugglers, dancers and musicians. A decree has gone out that all work will be stopped during the celebration. By the end of the tower's dedication all the people of Babylon will honour your name.'

'Good.' Nimrod nodded, stroking the throne's armrest. 'Excellent, excellent! You have all done well.' He stood. 'In two days' time, the dedication and celebration will begin. This tower will make the name of Babylon known throughout the earth as a great and powerful city. It will be spoken of by man forever.'

Someone in the crowd cried out, 'All hail, King Nimrod . . . the king of all kings.'

The throne room echoed as the chorus rose and all joined in, 'Hail, King Nimrod . . . the king of all kings.'

Nimrod stood smiling, basking in the adulation. All around him, the people fell to their knees, their faces against the stone floor.

Nimrod left the throne room and strode to his personal chambers. As the slaves removed his sword and sandals, a door in the wall of the outer room opened and his wife, Astarte, entered.

Tall and slender, her robes swished as she glided across the room. Her almond-shaped eyes were painted with kohl and gems twinkled in her hair, on her arms and in the folds of her gown.

Several slaves bearing platters of food and pitchers beaded with condensation followed the queen.

'Ah, Nimrod, I arranged for our meal to be served here.' She nodded to the slaves, who began arranging the plates on the low table.

When all was ready, Astarte and Nimrod reclined on either side of the table. Nimrod lifted a golden goblet and took a long drink of wine. When he had drunk his fill, he set the goblet down and tore a piece off a loaf of bread. 'Being the king makes me hungry for many things.'

'I am certain it does,' Astarte answered as she bit into a grape. 'From your look, can I assume that all the preparations are complete?'

Nimrod nodded as he chewed the bread.

'In two days' time, the tower will be dedicated and Babylon will become known as the greatest city on the earth.' His brow furrowed and his expression darkened.

'Yet something's happened,' his wife observed.

'Mikel,' he growled.

Astarte's laughter sounded like crystals. 'That crazy old man? What did he do?'

'Before all my counsellors, he pronounced the building of the tower was disobedient to the Creator, as was my becoming King of Babylon. He would have us scattered throughout the earth, being ruled by our fathers.'

Astarte's hand froze with the goblet at her lips. 'He said this to you?'

The king nodded.

'And where is his lifeless body now?'

Nimrod tossed the bread onto the golden plate and snatched up his goblet to drain it. He held it out for the slave to refill.

'I cannot harm him, you know that,' he said. 'He is an elder in our family. To harm him would bring disgrace, even for the king.' Nimrod frowned as the wine hardened his thoughts. 'Yet, something must be done. He is respected among the people; they listen to his ramblings.'

The queen sipped her wine and then set the goblet on the table. 'What if he suffered . . . an accident?'

Nimrod and Astarte looked at each other. 'It cannot be traced back to me,' he said.

She picked up a knife and plunged it into the heart of a blood orange. 'It won't be.'

'I now know why I married you,' Nimrod laughed as he spoke.

'And I know why I married you,' she replied as she wiped the juice of the orange from her fingers.

On the morning of the dedication, Nimrod and Astarte stood on the platform erected at the base of the tower. Crowds of people surrounded the platform and the tower.

'More of a mountain than a tower,' Mikel whispered to himself half in prayer, hoping the Creator would hear.

The tower rose level upon level, each layer smaller than the last, with a smooth circular path along the outer edge. Those standing near it could not see the top, no matter how far back they tilted their heads. It went higher and higher until it reached the clouds and then burst through as if it touched the outer rim of light that surrounded the world.

Those who stood at the back of the crowd could see the altar – glinting golden in the light – on the top of the tower. It shone like a second sun and was brighter than the moon.

Babylon was dressed as a bride, her streets picked of their dirt, the walls washed and garlands of flowers draping windows. The roads swarmed with crowds – all dressed in their finest – jostling to get a better view of their king and queen; rooftops of nearby buildings were packed with people. The air was on fire with anticipation.

Nearby, the priests of Orcan stood ready to lead animal after animal up the flower-strewn path to offer their lives as a sacrifice and dedicate the tower. A woman dressed in a flowing red gown sat astride a white bull that had been tethered to six others. She gulped wine as she shouted praise to Babylon.

Nimrod breathed in satisfaction as he looked over the city – *his city.*

'Today, the mighty tower will crown Babylon as the queen of all earthly cities and I will receive glory as its king,' Nimrod whispered to his wife.

Staring over the crowd, Nimrod frowned; near the end of the Street of Bakers, he saw Mikel. The elderly advisor was speaking first to one person in the crowd and then another. *He's probably condemning the tower and me.* Nimrod thought.

'Why the frown?' Astarte whispered in his ear. He turned and saw his wife smiling. Without changing her smile, she said, 'Smile at your people.'

Lifting a hand, he waved at the crowds, who cheered in response.

'Mikel is in the crowd,' he said through a tight smile.

The queen's eyes widened slightly. She lifted a hand and waved. 'Where?'

'To your left, by the Street of Bakers.'

Astarte turned to the other side and waved. Her eyes narrowed when they swept over Mikel. She turned slightly and nodded.

'Do not worry,' she said, through clenched teeth. 'I have made arrangements. Mikel will be . . . removed, and it will not be traced back to us. Now, let us dedicate your tower.'

Nimrod spread his arms wide and smiled. The crowd roared in response. He relished their adulation for a moment and then gestured for them to calm down.

'My people, since the Great Flood, our family has wandered across the land. We had no homeland and no one to lead us. Then we came to the plain of Shinar, to this beautiful valley. We decided to stay here – to build a home here. And then, you chose me to be your king –'

'Nimrod, the Mighty Warrior of God,' a voice in the crowd cried out.

The king's smile faltered slightly. Nodding, he said, 'Yes, I was a warrior – brave, strong, a perfect choice to lead this people. We built this beautiful city and put up tall walls to protect us. And now we have built this mighty tower, a tower that reaches to the heavens, so that we may make a name for ourselves and not be scattered over the face of the whole earth.'

Nimrod turned to gesture to Ocran, when a voice arose from the crowd.

'Nimrod!' cried Mikel. The crowd shifted, moving away from the old man. He noticed none of this and stood, pointing at the king. 'You built a mighty tower to reach into heaven, but the Creator came down to see this city and this tower that you and the people have built. God said, "If as one people speaking the same language they have begun to do this, then nothing they plan to do will be impossible for them." Now, the King of Kings will pronounce judgement upon you and upon the people.'

'You dare speak against the king?' Ocran screamed from one end of the platform. He raised a hand, indicating the city. 'A king who built the mighty city of Babylon?' He half turned and pointed to the tower. 'A king who built the Gate of God?' He pointed towards Mikel. 'Get out of this city, *old man*, lest the gods prevent you from ever speaking again!'

Mikel shifted his hand to point at the shrivelled priest. 'You have spoken lies since the day you were born, Ocran. You are a whitewashed temple full of dead men's bones. You stink like a corpse and have the face of a camel. Today, your own words will come back upon you and upon the people. Today, the Almighty will confuse your language and you will not be able to understand each other. Today, you will leave Babylon and wander the earth.' Mikel raised both hands towards the sky. He grasped the air as if he were taking hold of an invisible staff. 'This is the word of the Creator of Heaven and Earth.'

All eyes followed Mikel's hands skyward. They waited, listening for the sound of thunder, the rumble of an earthquake. They heard – nothing. One man chuckled, then another. Soon the crowd erupted into laughter.

Suddenly, a wind swirled around the tower. It blew dust in from the desert and covered the sky with darkness, blocking out the sun. As quickly as the wind came, it had vanished and again all was still.

Watching from the platform, Nimrod looked at Astarte and smiled. *We could not have planned this any better.* Turning, he raised his arms and gestured for quiet.

'My people, let us take pity on this crazy old man –'

'What is he saying? He sounds like a donkey,' a small boy in the front of the crowd cried out. 'The king is speaking like an animal.'

Several people around the child laughed, while others frowned or scratched their heads. Some reamed out their ears, certain a blockage kept them from hearing clearly.

'What does this child mean?' Nimrod asked.

'Agto benus lafthed be rappado?' a man called out.

Nimrod frowned, anger building. He turned to his wife, 'What does this mean?'

'I do not know,' Astarte replied. Turning to Dedan, she said, 'Bring that man to us.'

The captain of the king's guard had a quizzical look on his face. *'Eno wapo, mia gusta. Hathata beena yelta?'*

'What are you saying?' Nimrod asked. 'Are you drunk?'

'Nimrod,' Astarte grabbed his arm, pointing over his shoulder. 'Look.'

Turning, Nimrod looked. The crowd that had packed the streets was divided into small groups. Each was speaking . . . gibberish and yelling at another group that was speaking . . . gibberish. Here and there, he heard snatches of real words.

'What happened?'

'It's a sickness.'

'We've been cursed.'

A large man took hold of a child, shaking him, and raising his voice, as if by yelling his gibberish, he might be understood. The child freed himself and ran away. He called out in gibberish to several people, who followed him.

In the midst of the confusion stood Mikel. He looked on, undisturbed by what he saw.

Nimrod turned and grabbed Astarte's hand.

'Come, we must get out of here.' Nimrod said as he dragged her through the madness of the crowd toward the tower. At the base of the ramp stood Zohar. Nimrod dropped Astarte's hand to grab his friend. 'Do you understand me?'

'Yes.'

'Do you know what is happening?'

'No, but the crowd appears to be growing wild. Go to the palace. It will be safe there. I will take the guard and report to you later.'

Nimrod and Astarte hurried to the king's chariot. The chariot driver was fighting with a soldier, each yelling at the other in gibberish.

'They have all gone mad!' Astarte's eyes were wide with fear.

Nimrod shoved the two men out of the way and lifted his wife into the chariot and jumped in after her. He grabbed the reins and slapped them against the horse's rump. The chariot lurched wildly as the horses galloped down the street; Astarte clung to Nimrod to keep from falling out.

At the palace, they stumbled out of the chariot and ran past hysterical servants all crying out strange words, until they reached their chambers. Nimrod bolted the main door while Astarte ran to bolt the door that connected to her chamber. Then as one, they crossed to the window to look out on the chaos below.

Everywhere they looked people were fighting, screaming or crying. Groups of men were running from others who brandished knives or swords. Looters were breaking into homes and shops, carrying off whatever they could find. The king and queen stood spellbound for hours, watching as their kingdom fell apart.

Knocking at the chamber door startled them. Striding over, Nimrod yelled through the thick wooden panel, 'Who is it?'

'It's Zohar.'

The king sighed in relief as he unbolted the door and pulled his friend inside. He looked in the hall before closing and locking the door again to keep out those he could not understand.

'Zohar,' Nimrod said. 'Have you learnt anything about this gibberish?'

The governor of the city lifted his hands in a sign of failure.

'Your Majesty, I do not think it is gibberish. When one man speaks, someone understands. A woman calls out and her children come to her. Yet their neighbours do not know what is being said.' He took a deep breath. 'It is almost as if they are . . . all speaking different languages.'

'Different languages?' the queen asked. 'How can that be?'

'I know not, Your Majesty,' he replied. 'Those that appear to understand each other are banding together and leaving.'

'Leaving?' Nimrod asked. 'What do you mean, leaving?'

'They are leaving Babylon. Some on horseback, some in wagons, others on foot. Many are leaving behind everything and fleeing with only the clothes they are wearing.'

'They cannot leave!' Nimrod cried. 'That is the reason we built this city. So we would not have to wander. So we could be known throughout the earth.' He grabbed Zohar's robe and shook him. 'You must go to the city gates! You're the governor. Tell them to come back.'

'Your Majesty . . . Nimrod . . .' Zohar whispered. 'They wouldn't understand me.'

Nimrod turned from his friend and walked to the window. The king stood at the window, staring out into the night. The tower – the Gate of God – rose up from the earth like a tall, dark sword. All around its base were fires dancing in the streets. In the heavens, the stars of Orion shone brightly in the night sky and shimmered in the rising smoke.

'Is there not one man who can tell me why this has happened?' Nimrod asked.

'Nimrod,' Mikel said as he stepped in to the room.

'You came back?' Nimrod asked.

'I would never leave,' Mikel answered.

The king stared at the old man for a moment and then turned to look out of the window.

'They're still leaving,' Nimrod said. 'In the dark, some carrying torches, some not. They're leaving.' Sighing, he crossed the marble floor to sit on a low couch. He spread out his hands in front of him, inspecting them. He searched each line as if he thought they would tell him his future. 'I was a mighty hunter. No one could shoot an arrow or throw a spear further than I. Many thought being the strongest meant I should be king.' He dropped his head into his hands. 'Now I am a king over a nation of how many . . . ten? Fifty? How can I be king over so few?'

Mikel walked over and sat next to Nimrod. The old man reached out and put his arm around his broad shoulders.

'You don't need to be king over so few. But you can be their leader. You disobeyed the Creator, but He has not given up on you. No one understands this land like you, Nimrod. Find those fifty and lead them from this city. Be what the Almighty created you to be. You are like the stars that shine down on us. Listen to the Creator and He will restore everything to you. He has a plan for your life to prosper you – as He has for us all . . .'

As Mikel spoke, the ground thundered as an earthquake rocked the tower. Stone by stone, it began to fall. As the sun rose in the east, all that was left of the Gate of God was a pile of smouldering rubble and twisted, broken beams of cedar.

4

The Dagger

The road from the valley was harsh and barren. Little grew by the wayside and circling high overhead was an old eagle. It called, the sound echoing through the deep ravine as the sun edged its way higher over the jagged ridge. The air was still and the wind had gone. Every cloud had vanished many days before. It was as if the heavens were a looking glass and, even at that time of morning, the full moon tipped the far horizon.

In the distance, far below the eagle, an old man rode a donkey along the dusty track. A young man followed behind on another beast that plodded steadfastly, despite the rider kicking his heels to make it walk faster. In the shadow of the mountain, their servants followed, dragging more donkeys laden with tents and food.

Finally, the young man convinced his donkey to pick up speed; Isaac bounced as his donkey trotted up the road, to ride alongside Abraham, his father. Isaac was certain that something was wrong with his father. These trips were time to enjoy being just the two of them, but this one was different. His father would usually talk and talk, telling Isaac stories of when he was a boy. Their laughter would echo around the hills, but this time, there was just an uncomfortable silence. Abraham seemed strangely preoccupied, keeping his thoughts to himself.

Isaac could not draw a smile from his father. The old man would not even look at him face to face. Abraham had been solemn since they left their encampment in Beersheba two days before, and today he was even quieter and stared blankly at the barren countryside.

As they turned a sharp corner in the mountain path, Abraham suddenly pulled back the hood of his cloak and spoke.

'Isaac?' Abraham's voice always surprised strangers. He was an old man, but his voice was deep and strong. 'Have I ever told you about your birth?'

Isaac laughed, 'Yes, Father, I've heard it at least twenty times, for you always tell it on my birthday.'

Abraham's laugh was soft and almost bittersweet. *Something's wrong*, Isaac thought.

'Then you shall hear it twenty-one times.'

'And I will enjoy it as if I have never heard it before, Father.' Isaac answered hoping his father's mood would lift.

The old man grew silent, as if he were looking backwards through time. Isaac shifted, trying to find a comfortable position on the saddle. His father would tell the story when he was ready.

'After your mother, Sarah, and I married, we tried for many years to have children. All our family, all our friends, were having lots of children and we couldn't have even one.' He shook his head, his expression still grieving from the pain he and his wife had endured. 'That is hard on a couple; there were many nights when your mother cried herself to sleep. We kept praying and hoping . . . but, as the years went by, it looked as if our prayers were not going to be answered.'

'The Creator is always faithful,' Isaac said in a whisper.

'When I was ninety-nine years old, three men – three strangers – came to our tent one day. It was not uncommon to have travellers pass by and, in the tradition of our people, I asked them to stay for supper. I ran and told your mother,' Abraham laughed and looked at Isaac. 'She wasn't happy about having unexpected guests, I can tell you. Let this be a warning, son; women don't like surprise guests, especially if they have been cleaning and doing laundry all day and don't think they are fit to be seen.

'But Sarah quickly made a supper, which I brought to them, while she stayed in the tent. After they had eaten, one of the men looked up at me and asked, *"Where is your wife, Sarah?"*

'I pointed to the tent and said, "There, in the tent."'

The donkey lurched as Abraham spoke. Isaac laughed.

'And then, Father?' he asked.

'Then another of the strangers said, *"I will return to you about this time next year, and Sarah, your wife, will have a son."*

'I was curious as to how he knew we didn't have children. There was something about him that was different, almost strange. I was about to ask, when the third man said, *"Why did Sarah laugh and say, 'Will I really have a child, now that I am old?' Is anything too hard for the Lord? I will return to you at the appointed time next year and Sarah will have a son."'*

'Where were they from?' Isaac asked.

'I began to wonder whether these men had lost their senses in the desert sun – I had not heard anyone laugh – when Sarah stumbled out of the tent and fell on her knees in front of the men. She was trembling. "Lord," she said, "I did not laugh."

'The third man looked at her and said, *"You did laugh, Sarah."*

'I was angry. How dare this man – crazy or not – call my wife a liar. I opened my mouth to tell them to leave when Sarah started crying. "Lord," she said, "I heard you when I was inside the tent. I heard you say that, after all these years, we would have children. I laughed and thought, *After my husband and I are old*, now *I will have children?* I did not realize it was *You*."'

Isaac had heard this story so many times; he even knew what his father would do next. He watched . . . and smiled as his father's eyes grew wide. *He's going to say, 'It was the Lord Almighty,'* he thought.

Abraham turned towards him, 'It was the Lord Almighty . . . Isaac, what are you laughing at?'

'Nothing . . . I love you, Father. I love your stories. Who could ask for a better father than you?'

'I . . . I love you also,' Abraham stuttered as he looked at his son, obviously not understanding the joke. His brow furrowed. '. . . Now where was I?'

'It was the Lord Almighty.' Isaac wanted his father to finish the story.

The narrow road twisted and turned up the mountainside. Isaac looked down at the deep ravine and wondered where his father was taking him. Abraham fell silent for a moment and then spoke, his voice faltering.

'Ah, yes . . . It was the Lord Almighty. I fell to my knees next to Sarah. The Creator of the Universe was standing before us; we were both so terrified that we couldn't say anything.'

'I would have fled,' Isaac said.

'He said to us, *"Is anything too hard for the Lord? As I said, I will return to you at the appointed time next year and Sarah will have a son."*'

Abraham turned to look at Isaac. 'And Sarah did have a son – you – born from a dead womb: the child of promise. God had promised that nations and kings would come through me, more descendants than there are grains of sand on the sea or stars in the heavens. He said he would establish an everlasting covenant with my descendants for generations to come.

'The Almighty told us that you would be named Isaac –'

'Which means, "laughter",' Isaac interrupted.

Abraham laughed, 'And it was an appropriate name. A good name, for you have brought joy and laughter every day of your life . . .' The old man's face fell. 'Every day . . . of your . . . life, you have lived up to your name.' Tears trickled along the wrinkles of the old man's face. He rubbed them away with old, work-worn hands.

'Father!' Isaac reached out to him. 'Are you unwell? What is it?'

'Nothing is wrong, my son,' the old man wiped his eyes again with the palm of his hand. 'I'm so very thankful to the Creator . . .' Abraham reached over to take Isaac's hand. 'You are everything I've ever wanted in a son.'

'Thank you.' The young man squeezed the leathery hand wondering why his father spoke this way to him. *It is as if it were the last time we will ever be this way*, he thought. 'You are a wonderful father.' Isaac was not going to be deterred. *Something is wrong.*

'Thank you, Isaac,' Abraham said, clinging to his son's hand.

'Father, if it's not you . . . is Mother all right? I noticed that her eyes were red before we left; she had been crying.'

'Sarah is fine.'

'Have you had bad news . . . from our family? Are the animals well?' Shepherds cared for their animals almost as much as they cared for their family. Abraham cared for his flocks like no other. He had prospered and grown wealthy with many fine animals.

'No, Isaac . . . there's no bad news and the herds are fine. We're all fine.'

Father's fine . . . Mother is fine . . . the family . . . the herds. . . Isaac thought.

'We've arrived,' his father said.

Isaac looked around. He had been so concerned with his father – and whatever it was that troubled the heart of this gentle old man – that he did not notice they had been drawing closer to a plateau near Mount Moriah.

The land was barren rock, with tufts of grass and brush that not even goats would eat. The sunlight created what appeared to be a face of a skull on the side of the mountain. A sudden and sharp mistral wind blew around them. Sand and dust swirled and ebbed as it bit their skin.

Abraham looked at Isaac as he pulled his hood forward to cover his face.

'Javan, Dedan . . .' Abraham gestured to the two servants leading the donkeys. The men walked up to the father and son, leading the beasts laden with baskets.

'Master?' Javan asked, bowing his head.

Abraham swung off his animal and began looking through the baskets on the donkeys. 'Stay here with the donkeys. Set up camp.' He handed a torch to Javan. 'Light this. Isaac and I will go up the mountain to worship and then come back here to you.' Swiftly reaching into the basket, he took out a long dagger. It was made of the finest bronze with a bone handle held in place with gold wire.

'Should you not rest before you go further?' Dedan asked.

'I have come here for this. The time is now.' Abraham answered, his words razor-sharp as the blade. 'Isaac. We need wood for a fire.'

Isaac gathered several armfuls of wood and tied them with a coil of rope. His father motioned for him to turn around. Abraham lifted the bundle of wood onto Isaac's back and helped loop the rope around the young man's chest. When Isaac adjusted the burden, several of the sticks shifted, their broken ends piercing his skin. Blood stained his robe. He turned, waiting for his father.

'Your hands are bleeding,' Abraham said to his son.

'The thorns have pierced my flesh, that is all,' Isaac answered. He grinned. 'Mother will not be happy with the blood on my robe.'

Abraham looked at his son for a long moment, then closed his eyes and took a deep breath. Then he picked up the dagger and took the flaming torch from Javan.

'Come, let us go.' Turning, he started up the slopes of Mount Moriah.

Isaac hesitated. Something in the way his father spoke made him fearful. Isaac had worshipped with his father many times. The ceremony was as predictable as when Abraham told the story of Isaac's birth.

Walking to the place of sacrifice, his father would confess the instances he had disobeyed the Almighty and encouraged his son to do the same. As they built the altar, they would consider the sacrifice of the lamb's blood. Each drop was an offering to pay the penalty for their sin. Afterwards, they would sing hymns in worship of the Creator's goodness and the joy of restoration.

As with the rest of this journey, Isaac noticed that something was missing. 'Father?' he asked.

'Yes, my son?' Abraham replied.

'The fire and wood are here,' Isaac said, 'but where is the lamb for the sacrifice?'

At first, his father did not answer. Abraham's eyes were heavy and sad as he spoke, 'God himself will provide the lamb for the burnt offering, my son.'

'But . . .?' Isaac asked, as his father walked ahead.

By the time they reached the place of sacrifice, the sun had cut the sky in half. The mountaintop was flat, covered with tall, sharp-rough rocks. In places, they were piled upon each other, several large enough to create a citadel of stone. The wind blowing over the mountaintop was sharp and mournful.

Abraham stuck the torch into a crevice between two rocks to protect the flame from the wind. He laid the knife on a nearby ledge and then turned to take the wood off Isaac's back. 'Let's gather the rocks for the altar.'

As Isaac hefted stone after stone, he kept expecting one of the servants to join them, leading the sacrificial lamb. When the last stone was in place, he put the wood in layers on top. He turned to find his father standing nearby, holding the coil of rope. The old man's eyes were sad and heavy.

'Father? The altar is prepared. The wood is ready for the sacrifice. But the lamb is not here; no one has brought it.'

'No, my son,' Abraham walked to his son. 'The sacrifice *is* here.'

'What?' Isaac frowned as he looked hesitantly about him.
'I don't understand.'

'Four days ago,' Abraham said slowly, 'the Creator called
my name. Unlike when He appeared to me before, this time
I recognized His voice. "Here I am," I replied.'

'And?' Isaac asked.

'Then the Almighty said, *"Take your son, your son, Isaac,
whom you love, and go to the land of Moriah. Sacrifice him there as
a burnt offering on one of the mountains I will tell you about."*'

Isaac shook his head. 'Father, you don't mean . . . *me*? No,
it can't be true.'

Abraham slowly nodded. 'Isaac, we must obey the
Creator. We are always asked to sacrifice the best and you,
my beloved Isaac, are to be the sacrifice.'

'But *Father* . . . the Creator would never ask for the life of
a man. It is forbidden.'

'Trust me, Isaac. He promised that the nations of the
world would be blessed through me – through you. The
Almighty always keeps His promises and we *must* obey.'

Isaac looked into the eyes of Abraham; he truly believed
what his father had said. He knew he would rather die
before he stopped trusting his father or the Creator – and
he knew he would die.

'Then not my will but yours,' Isaac whispered.

Isaac walked to the altar that he had just built, and stepping on the stones, climbed on top of the wood he had carried up the mountainside. Locking eyes with his father, the
young man placed his wrists together and extended his

arms. Abraham brought the coils of rope over and bound Isaac's hands. Isaac lay back on the wood. He watched as his father walked to the ledge to pick up the bronze dagger and crossed back to the altar.

Then with a trembling hand, Abraham leaned over and kissed Isaac's brow.

'I love you, my son,' he said softly.

The young man looked into his father's eyes. 'I love you too, Father,' he answered. His stomach tightened as his father raised the knife high over his head. The old man paused and, tensing the muscles in his arm, took a deep breath. 'Not my will but Yours . . .' Abraham whispered.

'ABRAHAM . . . ABRAHAM . . .'

A voice came from the wind rushing around the altar. Abraham stopped just as he was about to kill his son.

'Father,' Isaac said as a maelstrom of swirling gusts gathered the dry dust and spiralled it into the air. Abraham dropped the dagger and fell to his knees.

'ABRAHAM . . .' the voice came from all around.

'Here am I, Lord,' Abraham said.

'Do not lay a hand on the boy,' the angel said. *'Do not do anything to him. Now I know that you fear the Creator, because you have not withheld your son, your only son from Him.'*

Abraham stood, his body shaking with fear. He bent over to pick up the knife. He stared at the blade and then at Isaac. Quickly, Abraham stepped forward to cut the ropes that held his son. He set the blade down and helped Isaac from the altar.

Father and son stood looking at each other. With a groan, Abraham drew his son to his chest, weeping. Each buried his face on the other's shoulder. Abraham and Isaac embraced until the shadow of the sun fell behind the mountain.

'What of the sacrifice, Father?' Isaac asked.

'The Creator will provide,' his father answered.

Then, from the far side of the mountain, came a bleating. Following the sound to the other side of one of the tall stones, Abraham and Isaac saw a large ram struggling, its horns caught in a thorn bush.

'I will call this place Jehovah-jireh – the Creator provides,' Abraham said. They looked at the ram and then at each other. Abraham closed his eyes and prayed, 'Thank you, Almighty Creator. For you have provided the sacrifice.' Looking at his son, the old man said, 'Come, Isaac . . . NOW it's time to worship.'

5

The Quarrel

It had been several hours since the full moon had crossed the horizon and climbed slowly in to the dark sky. The moonlight and stars cast long shadows of the mountain peaks over the desert that reached towards a solitary encampment. In the narrow valley, next to a trickling stream, the flaps of one tent heaved in the wind. From inside, a woman's panting echoed in the night. The man pacing outside the tent did not see the sleeping serpent draped over the bough of a dead, brittle tree.

'They are fighting inside me . . . Mara . . . please . . .' the woman screamed as she clutched her swollen belly.

'It is near your time, Rebekah,' the older woman gave the labouring mother a sip of water.

'They have been the same throughout my confinement,' Rebekah moaned. 'It's as if they hate each other.'

'How can they hate each other?' Mara stroked Rebekah's hair. 'They are just children waiting to come into the world.'

Rebekah clutched Mara's hand. 'They fight; I can feel it. Night and day they twist and turn as if possessed.'

'They are unborn children and don't know the ways of this world,' Mara answered as she wiped the sweat from Rebekah's brow.

'I had a dream when they were conceived. I dreamed the Creator told me my twins would hate each other and the older would serve the younger,' Rebekah cried in pain. 'They will divide our nation – I know it . . .' She groaned in the agony of a contraction.

'They are here, I can see them,' Mara paused as the first child emerged. 'Look.'

'What is it?' Rebekah asked.

'They fight even now,' Mara laughed, lifting the firstborn to his mother. 'When this boy was born, the other twin gripped this child's heel.'

In the light of the fire, Rebekah looked at her son. The baby was thick set and covered in red hair as if he were an animal.

'He's ugly,' Rebekah said.

'Most babies are ugly at birth,' Mara smiled. 'Ah, this strong, ruddy boy will be a hunter.'

Quickly, Rebekah brought her other child to the world.

'Are they the same?' she asked.

'No, your second son is like his father, dark and handsome,' Mara answered, handing the new baby to Rebekah. 'He wouldn't let go of the heel of his brother.'

'He's beautiful,' the young mother sighed. 'I shall call him Jacob.'

'And his brother?' Mara asked. 'What will his name be?'

'Ask his father. I cannot think of a word to describe him.'

Mara raised her eyebrows, surprised at the mother's answer. She stepped out of the tent and reappeared several moments later. 'Your husband, Isaac, said the firstborn is to be called Esau.'

From the day of their birth, the parents each preferred a different son. Isaac loved Esau while Rebekah loved Jacob. Esau became a strong hunter who desired to chase the beasts and bring them down with his hands. His brother, Jacob, stayed close to home; his hands were soft and strangers to hard work.

Late one morning as the sun approached midday, Rebekah was teaching her sons of their ancestors. Jacob listened while Esau leaned against the cushions, his eyes closed.

'Esau . . . Esau . . .' Rebekah's voice rose in frustration. 'Esau!'

The young man startled awake. 'Wh-whhh . . .' he wiped his face and shook his head. 'What is it, Mother?'

'You fell asleep while I was telling of your grandfather.'

'It's boring . . .'

'Esau!' Rebekah crossed her arms. 'You are the first-born. One day you will be responsible before the Creator for the family. How can you lead if you do not know what was expected of our ancestors and what is expected of you?'

Esau yawned, stretching his hairy arms wide. 'Mother, you don't have to worry. If I forget anything, I'm sure Jacob will remind me.' Slapping his knee, Esau stood. 'In fact, Jacob is so good at learning, there is no reason for me to stay.' He walked to the tent flap and grabbed a quiver of arrows and a bow as tall as he that was leaning against the wall. 'Jacob can study. I'm going hunting.' With a laugh, Esau ducked through the opening.

Rebekah crossed to the opening – 'Esau, come back!' – but it was too late. Esau was across the camp, inviting several of the men sitting around a fire to join in the hunt. Soon the men were riding off, whooping and kicking up dust in their wake.

'Rebekah?' She turned to see her husband approaching, a staff in one hand and holding on to the arm of a servant with the other. 'Did I hear you call Esau?'

'Yes,' she replied. 'I was telling the boys about your father, Abraham, when Esau fell asleep. When I woke him, instead of being ashamed, he laughed. Then he left to go hunting and would not return when I called!'

Isaac smiled, shaking his head. 'You can't expect a young man like Esau to sit around and listen to stories,' there was a note of pride in his voice. 'He has to be out, doing things. Esau is a hunter. With him I am well pleased.'

Her husband's reply did not help.

'Isaac, how will he assume his family responsibilities if he is always – *out, doing things*?'

Isaac absently patted Rebekah's arm. 'Do not worry. It will be many years before that happens.' He turned to walk away. 'Maybe the Creator will grant Esau success in the hunt,' he called over his shoulder. 'Esau brings me what I want . . . isn't that right, Jacob?'

Rebekah stared at her husband.

'Mother?'

She turned to see Jacob standing in the doorway.

'Mother, don't let Esau upset you . . . I enjoy talking with you about our ancestors.'

Warmth washed over Rebekah. 'As do I, my son.'

'I don't know how my brother will lead this family if he does not attend to his studies,' Jacob commented.

'I do not know either,' Rebekah murmured. 'Jacob, let us stop for today. Esau always makes my head pound.'

'All right, Mother,' Jacob said, hugging her. 'I will find Beahnna and ask her to let me help her gather herbs.' He grinned. 'I have been thinking about a new way to prepare red lentils. Should Esau not have success on his hunt, perhaps Father will enjoy what I cook.'

Rebekah touched her son's cheek. 'You are a treasure, Jacob.'

He turned his head to kiss her hand and, stepping away, bowed, hand over his heart. Jacob walked towards the area where the cook had set her pots over the lighted fires.

Rebekah watched her son. He was tall and slender, with dark hair and a thin face. *Could two brothers be more different?* She thought as she grabbed a basket of dirty clothes and began walking towards the stream.

The land of Beersheba had been in Isaac's family since his father Abraham's time. The surrounding hills were wild, with scant vegetation and water considered a treasure. During the rainy season, however, the stream by the camp provided sufficient water to allow the women to wash clothes and even bathe.

Rebekah set the basket down and lifted out one of Isaac's robes. As she scrubbed it, she noticed a hole in an elbow. *I need to make him a new one. This robe is getting old . . .* she sighed as she thought, *just as he is.*

Rebekah was much younger than Isaac's forty years when they married, but she didn't care. The Creator had brought this kind and loving man into her life. She eagerly awaited children but, as the months passed, it became obvious that she was barren. Then, after they had been married nearly twenty years, the Creator heard their prayers and she became pregnant.

As she sat by the stream, she noticed a snake unfurl itself from the stem of a bush. *Jacob would make a better leader of our family than Esau,* Rebekah thought as she laid the clean garment aside and picked up another. *Lord, you told me the older one would serve the younger. Does that mean that Jacob will become the head of the family . . . how can that happen?* The sun passed over the hills as it flew to the western sky. The day gave way to evening. Rebekah carried the washing back to the tents.

'Beahnna, I think the stew needs a little more salt,' Rebekah heard Jacob say as she passed where he stooped over the fire, stirring a pot of boiling lentils.

Beahnna looked up from kneading dough and smiled. 'With the spices you put in that stew, I'm surprised you can taste anything,' she said.

'My father loves savoury foods. Should Esau be unsuccessful . . .'

'Did I hear my name?'

Jacob turned to see his brother striding up to the fire. His long red hair was wild from riding in the wind and his clothes covered in dirt, but not, Jacob noticed, in blood.

Esau dropped down next to the large rock where Beahnna was shaping the loaves of bread. He tried to snatch a piece from the stack of hot bread and got his hand slapped instead.

'Esau, those are for the evening meal!' Beahnna scolded. 'If you begin eating them, I'll never make enough.'

'Take pity on me, Beahnna,' he pleaded. 'I'm famished. Hunger consumes my bones . . .'

The cook was unmoved. 'You're always famished.'

Esau grinned. 'That's because I am a big, strong man . . . not like my *little* brother here.' He turned towards his brother. 'Something smells delicious. . . What is that, Jacob?'

Jacob ignored Esau's taunts. 'Red stew made from lentils, onions, garlic, tomatoes and spices.'

'That stew is spicy enough to burn the hide off a camel,' Beahnna commented.

'It sounds wonderful,' Esau said. 'Let me have some.'

'I thought you were bringing back meat for the evening meal,' Jacob said.

'We didn't kill anything,' Esau frowned. 'But unlike cooking and telling stories, hunting can make a man hungry. Quick, let me have some of that red stew. I'm famished.'

'Telling stories about our ancestors will be part of your life when you become head of the family,' Jacob retorted.

'I care nothing for our ancestors – all I care about right now is that stew.'

Jacob's anger was as hot as the fire. *He cares nothing about our ancestors? Does he care only for his belly?* 'First sell me your birthright.'

Beahnna gasped. 'Jacob! What a thing to ask!'

Jacob waved the woman to silence. 'Esau, you claim you care nothing about our ancestors. You do not care to learn about the responsibilities that come with the birthright. Then sell it to me . . . for a bowl of red stew.'

'Look, if I don't eat soon, I will die,' Esau laughed as he lay on the ground and closed his eyes. 'What good is the birthright to me?' he said, ignoring Beahnna's second gasp.

'Swear to me,' Jacob whispered, 'with Beahnna as witness, that you will give me your birthright for a bowl of stew.'

'Fine!' Esau answered, placing his hand under his thigh, as their father did to swear an oath. 'I, Esau, give you, Jacob, my birthright as the eldest, for a bowl of red stew.' Esau sat up. 'Now, give me the stew . . . and some bread.'

*　*　*

Jacob found his mother mending Isaac's robe.

'Esau sold me his birthright for a bowl of stew and a piece of bread.'

'He must have been joking,' Rebekah said. 'Even Esau would not scorn his birthright. He will deny it later.'

'He cannot,' Jacob said, 'he swore it before Beahnna.'

'Your brother always acts without thinking,' Rebekah bit the thread off and set the garment aside. 'Be careful around your brother, Jacob. This action will shame Esau before all in the camp, before your father. Esau will blame you.'

'Mother . . .' Jacob's eyes widened. 'This will make me head of the family after Father's death. I never thought he would actually sell me his birthright. I was merely taunting him. Now I will be the head – me, the younger brother!'

Rebekah whispered. 'Jacob, let me tell you a story. When I was pregnant with you and Esau . . .'

By evening, the entire camp had heard the news. Isaac wept, crushed that his favourite son had treated his heritage with such contempt. If Esau believed his father would not hold him to his oath, he was mistaken.

From that day, Isaac – and everyone else in the camp – deferred to Jacob as 'the heir'. He sat next to Isaac at feasts, received the choicest cut of meat, people listened when he spoke. All knew he would lead the tribe when his father died.

Esau simmered in his anger. He could do nothing to undo the consequences of his actions. His attitude towards his brother changed. Before, he had teased and taunted Jacob as brothers often do. Now, instead of acknowledging his own actions, Esau convinced himself that Jacob had tricked him into selling his birthright and was therefore

responsible for his fall from favour. Revenge became Esau's
bedfellow. As age dimmed the eyes of his father, so Esau
burnt with anger and rage. He saw how his mother looked
at Jacob. He heard their laughter and saw their mocking
glances. Not even the running of the wild deer could lift his
heart from the blackness that gripped his soul.

Late one evening, many months later, Isaac lay in his bed.

'Rebekah, are you there?' he asked.

'I am here.'

'Where?' the old man reached out, patting the air.

Since the day of Esau's disgrace, Isaac had grown weaker
and his eyesight was almost consumed in shadows. He spent
more time in his tent talking with Jacob, trying to instill
everything he would need to know as head of the family.
Rebekah knew that the time for his death was near and tried
to comfort him as best she could. She bathed his face,
brought him cool water, and would sit for hours talking
about their life together.

'Here.' She took his hand and put it to her face.

'Where is Esau?'

'Esau?' Her smile faded. 'He is tending his horse.'

'Call him to me. I wish to bless him.'

She pulled away from her husband. 'Bless him?'

'Yes, when I die, he will have a smaller portion. I would
also bless him.'

'But . . . what about Jacob?'

'Jacob has Esau's birthright; he will have a double portion of inheritance.'

'But, Isaac –'

'Rebekah,' the elderly man interrupted her. 'Call Esau.'

'Yes, Isaac.'

She walked through the tent flap, her mind whirling in grief. Giving a blessing – especially the head of a family – was giving one's soul. Whatever Isaac spoke, the Creator would surely grant. *Esau cared only for himself . . . why should he receive Isaac's blessing?* She paused beside a nearby tamarisk tree, thinking rapidly; after a moment, her face hardened.

Rebekah walked through the camp until she found Esau, grooming his stallion.

'Esau . . . Esau.'

'What do you want?' The fatigue and bitterness tinged his voice.

'Your father wishes to see you.'

'Truly?' Esau turned to her, sneering. 'Isaac wishes to see the son who disgraced him?'

'Esau,' she whispered, 'he will not live much longer.'

Esau stared into the distance, his throat working to keep back tears. 'I will go to him.'

Rebekah waited until Esau walked past the gnarled tree, and then ran quickly around the encampment to the back of the tent she shared with Isaac. *If anyone asks, I will tell them I am gathering herbs to ease Isaac's pain.* She pressed her ear to the tent wall and listened.

'Is that you, my son?' Isaac asked as Esau slipped into the tent.

'Yes, Father.'

'I want to give you my blessing before I die. It is the most important thing I could leave you. Go . . . kill me a deer and cook it for me the way I like; then I will give you my blessing.'

'But what of Jacob?' Esau asked.

'He has the inheritance, but the blessing will be honoured by the Creator.'

Rebekah hid in the shade of the tamarisk tree as Esau left the tent. She did not see the serpent coiled in its branches high above her. When Esau rode from the camp, she slipped from her hiding place and found Jacob, cooking with Beahnna.

'You want me to do what?' Jacob asked when she took him aside to tell him what she had heard through the tent wall.

'Shhh . . .' she looked around to watch for signs of people overhearing. 'You need to pretend to be Esau while he is out hunting.'

'You want me to trick my father into giving me the blessing he intends for my brother? Isn't it enough that I have the birthright?'

'Jacob . . . the Creator told me before you were born that you would be the head of a nation and that your brother would serve you.' When Jacob hesitated, Rebekah grabbed his arm. 'Son, this is important. No one will follow you without both the birthright *and* the blessing.'

'What if Father touches me? He would know I was tricking him. He would curse me.'

'Let the curse fall on me,' Rebekah hissed. 'Just do what I say.'

Jacob stared as she explained her plans. Then he took a deep breath and nodded.

Rebekah had thought of everything. She had two young goats prepared the way Isaac liked. Several days before, Esau had brought his best clothes to Rebekah to wash them and she still had them in her tent. After Jacob put on his brother's clothes, she tied the skins from the goats around Jacob's neck and hands. The coarse hair on the hide was like that which covered her eldest son and would make Isaac think he was with Esau.

When the food was ready, she carried it, along with some bread, to Jacob.

'The sun is setting,' she said. 'As Esau has not returned by now, he will wait until morning. Go to your father; the twilight will keep your face from anyone in the camp. Wear the goatskin and Isaac will think you are Esau. After he blesses you – it will be too late.'

By the time he reached his father's tent, Jacob's heart was racing. For a brief moment he almost turned around. *Mother is right,* he thought. *I need both the birthright and Father's blessing.* Taking a deep breath, he stepped inside the tent. He set the food down and smoothed the goatskin on his hands and neck.

'Father,' he pitched his voice lower.

'Yes . . .' Isaac lifted his head. 'Who is it?'

'Esau,' Jacob said gruffly. 'I have done as you asked. Please sit up and eat the food I prepared so that you may give me your blessing.'

'How did you find it so quickly, my son?' Isaac asked.

Rebekah had thought of an answer for this question. 'The Creator gave me success.'

'Come near so I can touch you, my son,' Isaac said, 'to know whether you really are my son Esau or not.'

Jacob hesitated, and then slowly crossed to his father.

Isaac reached over and touched the goatskin on Jacob's hand.

'The voice is the voice of Jacob, but the hands are the hands of Esau. Are you really my son Esau?'

'I am,' Jacob replied.

'My eyes grow faint and what I hear deceives me. Is it you Esau?' he asked.

'It is I,' Jacob answered.

'Then bring me some of your food to eat,' Isaac said, 'so that I may give you my blessing.'

Jacob helped Isaac sit up and then brought the food to him.

Isaac ate slowly and drank some wine. When he had finished, Isaac said, 'Come here, my son, and kiss me.'

Jacob walked to his father and nervously bowed towards the old man, fearful of discovery.

'Here I am, Father,' he said.

Isaac breathed in, smelling Esau's clothes.

'Ah, the smell of my son,' he said. 'It is like the smell of a field that the Lord has blessed. May God give you of heaven's dew and of earth's richness – an abundance of grain and new wine. May nations serve you and peoples bow down to you. Be lord over your brothers, and may the sons of your mother bow down to you. May those who curse you be cursed and those who bless you be blessed.'

When Isaac had finished, Jacob helped him lie down. Smoothing his father's hair, he whispered, 'Thank you, Father . . . I . . . love you.' Picking up the empty bowls, Jacob went back to his mother.

*　*　*

Isaac was dozing when he heard someone enter his tent.

'My Father,' said a deep voice, 'sit up and eat some of my game, so that you may bless me.'

Isaac frowned. 'Who are you?'

'I am your firstborn, Esau.'

Isaac began trembling. 'Who was it,' he asked, 'that gave me food? I ate it just before you came and I blessed him. And he will be blessed!'

Isaac heard a loud and bitter cry. He felt his son drop to the floor and grab his hand.

'Bless me . . . me too, my Father!'

'I'm sorry,' Isaac said. 'Your brother came and took your blessing. He lied – he said it was you.'

'He's rightly named Jacob, for he's deceived me these two times. He has grabbed at my heel all of my life and stolen what is mine.'

'My son,' said Isaac. 'Jacob may have stolen your blessing, but *you* sold your birthright.'

Esau dropped his head on his father's lap.

'Do you have any blessing for me?' he cried.

'I have made him lord over you and made all this family his
servants,' Isaac said, 'and I have sustained him with grain and
new wine. What can I possibly do for you, my son?'

'Anything, please, Father,' Esau cried. 'Bless me too!'

Isaac placed a hand on his son's trembling head.

'Your dwelling will be away from the earth's richness,
away from the dew of heaven above,' his voice was weak,
as of one about to die. 'You will live by the sword and will
serve your brother. But when you grow restless, you will
throw his yoke from your neck.'

Rebekah stood guard at the entrance to the tent where
Jacob – exhausted from the time spent with his father –
slept. She saw Esau storm out of the tent where Isaac lay
dying. He threw the food and wineskin on the ground and
raised his fists to the sky.

'When my father dies, I will kill my brother Jacob!' Esau
screamed at the moon like a baying dog.

What have I done? Rebekah raised a trembling hand to her
mouth. *What have I done?*

Rebekah entered her tent to check on Isaac. He lay trembling, but would not explain what had happened between
him and their sons. She wiped his face and gave him a drink
of goats' milk and then sat, holding his hand and talking of
news within the camp.

'I have heard that some of our men are marrying the women of this land; I know these women will lead them to worship false gods.' She peered at her husband. 'I couldn't bear it if Jacob takes a foreign wife.'

'What do you want me to do?' Isaac's voice was cold, emotionless.

'Send him to my family. They will help him find a wife,' Rebekah answered.

Isaac was silent for a long time. 'I will do as you ask.'

'Good.' She sat for several minutes, unsure what to say.

'Rebekah?' Isaac asked.

'Yes, Isaac?'

'What did we do wrong? We each chose to love one child over another, preferred one child over another. Now we have to send a son away to prevent his brother from killing him. In this we have destroyed two lives . . .'

The weight of what she had done pierced her heart. Rebecca fell on her knees next to her husband, weeping.

'Lord, forgive us. How can we make it right?'

'I think *we* have done enough,' Isaac smoothed a hand over his wife's head. 'We should never have tried to help the Creator; it has ended in hatred and division. We have to leave our sons to Him; only the Creator can restore our family.'

6

The Dreamer

The sun had set over the desert. Tall fingers of rock stood like knives on the far horizon. Not a single tree or blade of grass could be seen; all was an arid, desolate wasteland. Like a dead land, it stretched to the rim of darkness that cupped the earth. Ghostly swirls of spinning sand ebbed about the edges of the rock. As the light faded and the grim shadows lengthened, the flames in the campfire writhed and flickered. The blaze cast an eerie and haunting glow on the faces of those gathered around its light. It was as if they were all waiting for their lives to begin and the famine to be over.

An old man looked around the campfire at the expectant faces of his sons. In the silence of their eating, he counted them one by one, as they picked at the meagre grain. He had seen every one of them born into this world, and as they had cried their first breath, he had looked in their eyes and named them. Reuben was the firstborn. He was tall, arrogant and awaited the death of his father. Simeon, Levi, Judah, Dan, Naphtali, Gad, Asher, Issachar and Zebulun had always fought amongst each other like young dogs. Joseph and Benjamin shared the same mother. They had inherited her beauty and grace and were close to their father's heart.

The old man smiled to himself. Judah poked the embers, sending sparks flying up into the night sky.

'I am so tired,' Reuben groaned, as he yawned, 'I do not believe I will even dream tonight.'

'I always dream,' said Issachar.

'You do?' Benjamin asked his older brother.

'Issachar dreams about having a wife.' Simeon elbowed his brother, who grinned as his family laughed. 'Every night, I hear him talking in his sleep, calling out her name. Shall I tell them whom you wish to marry? Was it Aridah I heard you calling for?'

'Simeon will dream the longest dream when I am finished with him, Father,' Issachar answered, careful not to anger his brother. 'I saw Bonah by the well and she asked for you,' he added, sitting smugly out of reach of Simeon's hand.

'Joseph dreams,' Benjamin said. 'Dreams from the Creator.'

'Not now, Benjamin,' Joseph said quickly to keep his younger brother from talking. 'You weren't supposed to . . .'

'Truly?' Simeon interrupted. 'How do you know these dreams were from the Creator?'

'Joseph told me that God gave him dreams,' Benjamin defended his brother. 'Ask him.'

All eyes turned slowly towards Joseph. 'So, Joseph,' Dan sneered, 'tell us your dream.'

Joseph paused for a moment; he looked at each of his brothers and then at his father. Then he sat up, straightening his coat.

'Well, we were binding sheaves of grain out in the field when suddenly my sheaf rose and stood upright, while your sheaves gathered around mine and bowed down to it.'

'Bowed down?' Reuben asked. 'Bowed down to you?'

Before Joseph could reply, Asher jumped up, fist clenched, towering over his brother. 'So, it's not enough that Father gave you a rich new coat,' he seethed, 'but now you are going to rule over us?'

'Enough, Asher!' Jacob said. 'If I gave Joseph a new coat, what is it to you?'

'I am your son, too, Father,' protested Asher. He gestured to the men sitting around the fire. 'We all are. Yet, you behave as if you love Joseph more than the rest of us!'

They were all silent. Joseph stared at each of them before he spoke.

'Joseph was the first son of Rachel,' tears constricted Jacob's voice. 'She died giving birth to Benjamin. When I honour her sons, I honour her memory.'

Their father's words were not enough for Benjamin.

'God also sent Joseph another dream,' he snapped without thinking. 'This time the sun and moon and eleven stars were bowing down to him. He told me . . . and I know what it means.'

Benjamin heard the gasps from his eleven brothers and knew he had gone too far. It was too late. He looked wide-eyed at his father, who rose slowly to his feet. The old man snorted and kicked the dirt.

'Joseph, what is this that you are telling Benjamin? It is not enough that you will rule over your brothers . . . will their mother and I actually bow down to you as well?'

Joseph held out his hands. 'Father,' he pleaded honestly, 'I did not say this . . . it was in my dream. It wasn't an ordinary dream . . . I just knew it had been whispered to me by the Creator.'

'It had been whispered to me by the Creator,' Levi mocked.

'Who are you that the Creator should speak to you in dreams?' Zebulun demanded.

'Enough!' Jacob's voice echoed angrily across the desert. 'Enough talk. We will not speak of these dreams again. It is time to sleep. Judah, Naphtali, Gad, you three stand watch. The rest of you, go to your tents.' Jacob shuddered as the breeze blew in from the desert. He looked at each of his sons to make sure they understood; then he turned and slowly crossed the camp.

Zebulun glared at Joseph and then stalked off into the night with his brothers following behind. Joseph and Benjamin walked silently to the tent they shared. When they got inside, Benjamin grasped his brother's arm.

'I'm sorry, Joseph,' he whispered. 'I should not have spoken.'

'It's all right, Benjamin,' Joseph said as he removed his coat and laid it carefully across a sack.

'Why do our brothers treat you this way, Joseph?' Benjamin asked as he lay down on his mat. 'You and I had the same mother and they do not treat me that way. It is as if they hate you.'

'I do not know, Benjamin,' Joseph sighed as he lay down.

'I believe in you, Joseph,' Benjamin yawned and closed his eyes. 'The Creator has a great purpose for you; why else would he give you these dreams?'

Joseph sighed as he wondered. 'Goodnight, Benjamin.'

'Goodnight, Joseph.'

In the days that followed, although none of his brothers mentioned the dreams, Joseph could tell they had not forgotten. The brothers would not speak to him; if they did, hate sliced through their words like a knife. It was a relief when their father sent his ten older sons to graze their flocks far to the north. For several weeks, Joseph and Benjamin worked around the camp during the day and spent the evenings urging their father to tell stories of their ancestors and of God.

'Joseph,' Jacob said one morning, 'go and find your brothers. See how they and the flocks are doing and then come and tell me.'

Joseph packed food and water, a blanket and a knife, and left the camp. He walked through the hills and across the sun-parched land. Day followed day and soon became a week. Still he searched for his brothers. They were not in

Shechem, as his father thought. Joseph went on further, looking for them.

One morning by an oak that hung over a parched riverbed, he saw several people tending flocks on the last of the grass. He asked if they had seen Reuben. One man told Joseph he had seen the brothers and had heard them say they were going to move the flocks to Dothan. Joseph followed on. Here the grass was richer, as if there had been rain. Late one afternoon, he saw them in the distance, watching over their grazing sheep.

Joseph cupped his hands to his mouth. 'Reuben! Naphtali!' he called. When his brothers turned, he waved at them.

'Look,' Asher sneered, 'it's the dreamer.'

'I hate him,' Dan said. 'Always carrying bad reports of us to Father.'

'It's too bad a wild animal didn't kill him as he came looking for us,' said Issachar.

'It still can,' said Gad.

'What do you mean?' Simeon asked.

'We can kill him and throw his body . . .' Gad looked around and pointed, '. . . in that dry well. Then we can tell father that an animal killed him.'

'Kill him?' Reuben was shocked. 'I don't like that. He's Father's favourite, but to . . .'

'That's a good idea, Gad,' Zebulun interrupted.

In their rebellion, the other brothers agreed, each adding a morbid suggestion on how to kill Joseph.

'Don't kill him,' Reuben said. 'We would be guilty of murder. Throw him into the dry well, but don't shed his blood.'

His brothers were silent, pondering his advice. Then Gad nodded. 'All right, we won't kill him.' He laughed, 'We'll leave his life in the hands of his *blessed Creator.*'

'Then we'll see what happens to his dreams,' Zebulun added.

Out of breath, Joseph was smiling when he arrived. 'I have been looking for you for over a week,' he said. 'I wasn't sure whether I would find you.'

'Let me take your bag,' Gad smiled warmly. 'You look hot.'

'And thirsty,' Zebulun added, holding out a hand.

'I am,' Joseph admitted. 'My water bag is nearly empty and I would only allow myself sips until I found you.'

Levi put an arm around Joseph's shoulders. 'This well is almost empty,' he said as he guided him towards the yawning, dark hole in the ground. 'But this well has what you need. You can even smell the water; isn't that right, Dan?'

'Levi's right,' said Dan. 'Look, lean over – I'll hold on to your coat – smell the water. It is cold and fresh.'

Joseph closed his eyes and leaned over. He took a deep breath. 'I don't smell anything,' he said.

'You aren't leaning far enough,' Levi said.

'If I lean any further, I'll fall in,' said Joseph.

'You know,' said Dan, 'I think you're . . . right.'

Suddenly, Levi shoved Joseph into the mouth of the well. The edge of his coat caught on an old tree root and kept Joseph from falling to the bottom.

'Help!' he cried, flailing his arms trying to grasp hold of the edge. 'Dan, Levi, someone! Help me!'

'Oh, Joseph, you've fallen,' Asher laughed.

'Asher, help me.'

Issachar knelt next to the well. 'Careful, Joseph. Here, let me help you.' He pulled a knife from the sheath at his waist and, inserting the blade inside the coat, began sawing at the fabric.

'Issachar,' Joseph yelled, 'what are you doing?'

'Why, I'm trying to keep you from ripping the coat,' Issachar grinned. 'How else will Father believe you have died – if we don't show him the coat.'

The fabric ripped from Joseph's weight and he fell, screaming, to the bottom of the well.

Issachar stood, holding up the coat. The fabric was shredded in several places.

'We couldn't have planned this better,' said Dan as he hugged Levi. 'His coat looks as if it were torn by a wild animal.'

'Reuben!' Joseph cried. 'Naphtali! Why are you doing this? Please help me! Brothers!'

'Come,' Reuben said angrily, his heart torn like the coat. 'Let's move away from here. I don't want to have to listen to him.'

'Good idea,' Gad answered. 'I think I have some wine left. We can celebrate . . . the dreamer is out of our lives forever!'

'You eat,' Reuben said, throwing his bag over his shoulder. 'It is my turn to watch the flocks. I shall spend the night in the hills and keep the wolves from the sheep.'

When Reuben was gone, Asher built a fire, while the rest opened their packs and brought out bread, cheese, olives and dates.

The sound of harnesses and snorting caused them to look up. Two men riding camels approached their fire.

One of the men called out, 'May strangers enjoy the comfort of your fire?'

'You are welcome to warm yourselves,' said Judah, 'and to share in our humble meal.'

The brothers looked at the men and wondered who they were. This was far from the trail that went to Egypt.

'You are most kind,' said the other man as his camel knelt so he could climb down. 'I am Reka,' he said, and then pointed to his companion, 'and this is Kallah.'

'Be welcome to our fire,' said Judah.

'You are most kind. Please let us return your hospitality,' answered Reka and, reaching into a pack, he brought out a cloth. When he unwrapped it, a sweet scent filled the air. 'Perhaps some cinnamon would add to the flavour of the food?'

'Cinnamon!' Asher exclaimed. 'Where did you get this?'

'We are merchants from Gilead,' he answered. 'We are carrying spices, balm and myrrh to sell in Egypt.'

'Are spices all you sell?' Judah asked.

'A good merchant sells whatever he can,' said Kallah. 'Why do you ask? Do you have something you wish to sell?'

'A . . . slave,' he answered.

Issachar's eyebrows arched in surprise and Asher's mouth dropped open. Judah merely looked at the strangers.

'You have a slave you wish to sell?' Reka asked. 'I must see this slave first.'

Without speaking, Gad and Asher pulled Joseph out of the well. They bound and gagged him and dragged him back to the fire.

Gad pointed to the gag. 'He talks too much.'

'He will soon learn to keep silent,' Reka said. 'He looks well enough – if not a little bruised and arrogant. How much do you want for him?'

After much bartering, thirty coins were counted into Judah's hand. As the sun set and the campfire raged, Joseph, still bound and gagged, was lowered back into the dark well.

The next morning, whilst Reuben was still in the far hills, Joseph was thrown onto the back of a camel.

The brothers watched until the caravan could no longer be seen and then burst out laughing, clapping each other on the back. 'What an amazing idea,' they congratulated Judah.

'We traded the dreamer for silver,' said Zebulun. 'What could be better than that?'

While they were eating, Reuben stumbled wide-eyed into the camp. 'Simeon! Levi! Dan!' he cried. 'The well is empty. Joseph's gone!'

Gad eyed his older brother. 'What were you doing by the well, Reuben? Were you thinking to pull the dreamer out and hide him from us?'

'I . . . I . . .' Reuben stuttered, thinking how he had planned on protecting Joseph from his brothers.

'You can rest easy,' Asher said. 'Joseph is still alive, but he will never bother us again. We sold him to merchants in a camel caravan.'

'What do we tell Father?' Reuben asked.

Issachar grinned as he lifted the shredded robe and pulled his knife from the sheath. 'Bring me a goat.'

* * *

'Father . . .' Reuben stood at the entrance to their father's tent. He was covered in the dust of five long days.

'Ah . . . you're back!' Jacob smiled. 'I asked Joseph to bring news of you, but he brought you instead . . . Good boy!' Jacob noticed the sombre looks on his sons' faces. 'What is it? Joseph did find you, did he not?' Their continued silence frightened him. He began trembling. 'What is it? Please tell me? Where's Joseph?'

Reuben looked at Issachar and nodded. Issachar opened a bag and brought out a cloth, dripping in blood. Jacob began moaning before he heard his son say, 'We found this . . .'

'He's gone . . . God help me . . . Joseph is gone.'

Far away, in the dry, narrow streets of Egypt, a soldier walked ahead of a boy tied to him by a short chain.

'Keep moving – don't stop – you are not a shepherd now,' he shouted above the sound of the market that filled the narrow road between the houses.

'God, please help me,' Joseph whispered through cracked lips, his hands still bound. He still couldn't believe it all; it was like a bad dream. *Dreams . . . Ha!* he thought. *I dreamed I would be ruler over my brothers, over my father. Now I am a slave.*

7

The Prison

In the darkness of the prison cell, Joseph prayed. The words echoed around his mind as if he was waking from a dream.

'Help me, Lord. Why am I here? Potiphar's wife is lying: I didn't attack her. Why am I in Egypt? Is my father still alive? Why did my brothers hate me?'

The words spilled from his lips and echoed around the mud-lined walls of the tomb-like prison.

'Still praying, Joseph?' The warden asked slowly, his tongue flickering like a spitting cobra's as he stared through the bars of Joseph's cell. 'Do you think anyone is listening?'

Joseph looked up at the warden. He could see his dark eyes staring through the rusted bars of the door, looking pityingly at him. Abazi was as large as a mountain and smelled as foul as the sewage that drained in a gulley through the streets of this foreign city. His arms dripped with sweat that clung to the long black hair that covered all of his skin.

Like a glowering bear, the warden would taunt Joseph night and day, waking him from his sleep and giving him the scraps of food left by the others. Abazi had often beaten him. The warden would take the young man to one side and thrash him in front of all the other prisoners.

'Just to exercise my arms, Joseph. Don't take it personally. But anyone who attacks Potiphar's wife should be discouraged from doing such things in future.'

Day in and day out, Abazi would beat him. That was, until the morning when Joseph told him about three prisoners who were stealing food. They had taken it from those who were weak and dying, mocking them as they starved. Their cackling echoed through the jail and, through fear, no one protested. Joseph had warned them to stop, but they had laughed at him.

'Will your God strike us down?' they had taunted like hyenas.

Abazi did not believe in the God of Joseph. When he discovered what the three thieves had done, his vengeance was swift. There was no forgiveness, no grace, no mercy. The crows picked at their lifeless bodies hanging from the prison walls for all to see.

From that time, Abazi stopped beating Joseph and began listening to him. Joseph was lonely and didn't care who he spoke to. He told the warden about his family, being sold into slavery, and the lies that Jamila, the wife of Potiphar, had told about him. Joseph also told Abazi about the Creator.

'I don't know why God allowed all this,' Joseph told him, 'but I know it was for some purpose. Nothing is ever wasted by God.'

'You're still praying to your God?' Abazi asked again as he walked into Joseph's cell, carrying two mugs of beer. The guard sat down and handed a mug to Joseph. 'It's been nearly eleven years since you were sold into slavery and still you pray to him?'

'I can't stop believing, Abazi,' Joseph got up from the floor and sat down. 'If I didn't believe that God has a purpose in all of this, I'd go mad.'

'Well, even if it is because Jamila lied about you, I'm glad you got thrown into prison.' The warden grinned and took a deep drink, wiping his mouth with the back of his hand. 'Perhaps your God knew I needed help and that is why you are here. You know how to organize things, and I've been able to relax and let you run the jail. What Joseph has lost in freedom, Abazi has gained. By the way, I came to tell you that we're getting two famous additions to our prison.'

'Oh?'

'Yes . . . Pharaoh's cupbearer and chief baker. Seems they offended the king.' The man chortled, 'Perhaps we can convince the baker to cook for us . . . The cupbearer could taste our food to see if it is poisoned. If he did it for Pharaoh, he can could do it for us.'

'A cupbearer and a baker?' Joseph asked. 'Attendants of Pharaoh?'

'Here . . . waiting outside.' The man stood and walked towards the prison's main door. 'Two of the most trusted men in Egypt and now they are my prisoners.'

Abazi soon returned, dragging two men bound in chains. He puffed his chest out, stomped and glared at them; his face wrinkled, revealing several broken teeth.

'Any trouble from you and I shall flog you both. Pharaoh will not be bothered what happens to you. He was betrayed. Your former loyalty was for nothing,' Abazi said sharply as he turned to Joseph and gave a sly smile. 'Joseph. You take care of them.'

The two men stared at Joseph. Their eyes were wide and trembling.

'Come,' Joseph said quietly, extending a hand. 'Let me show you to your . . . *rooms.*'

The day passed slowly for the new prisoners. They both wept, and the kohl rimming their eyes trickled down their faces in black rivers. Joseph had stayed with them until he felt it safe to leave.

As he slept, he could hear the cupbearer still weeping and calling out the name of Pharaoh, begging his forgiveness. Early the next morning, Joseph found the two men lying on the floor of the cell, their eyes red.

'We've both had dreams,' the cupbearer said, 'but there is no one to interpret them.'

'Do not interpretations belong to God?' Joseph asked. 'Tell me your dreams.'

The cupbearer looked hesitant.

'In my dream, I saw a vine that had three branches. While I watched, the vine budded and then blossomed and then made clusters of grapes, which ripened. I held Pharaoh's cup and I took the grapes, squeezed them into the cup and put the cup in the king's hand. In all my sadness, I do not know what it means.'

Joseph thought for a moment.

'A vine and branches? Ripe grapes?' he asked.

'That is what I saw,' the man nodded as he wiped the tears from his face.

'Then you should be thankful,' Joseph said, 'this is what your dream means. The three branches are three days. Within three days, Pharaoh will free you from prison and give you back your position as his cupbearer. When you are free, mention me to Pharaoh and get me out of this prison, for I have done nothing to deserve being put here.'

'Thank you, Joseph!' the cupbearer smiled. 'When I am free, I promise I will remember you. I will not forget all you have done.'

'And what of me?' the baker demanded, angrily. 'Tell me the meaning of my dream.'

'What did you dream?' Joseph asked.

'In my dream, I had three baskets of bread on my head. In the top basket were all kinds of baked goods for Pharaoh, but birds kept eating them.'

Joseph's stomach twisted as he listened.

'Three baskets?' Joseph asked.

The baker saw Joseph's face. 'Please tell me what it means. Don't hold anything back; I want to know.'

Joseph put a hand on the man's shoulder.

'This is what it means,' he said. 'The three baskets are three days. Within three days Pharaoh will . . . hang you . . . and the birds will eat away your flesh.'

The baker shook his head, unbelieving. 'You have it wrong,' the baker said. 'He wouldn't kill me . . . not for what I did.'

'You asked me to be honest with you. That is the meaning of your dream.'

The baker did not speak for three days. He waited as if a condemned man. On the third day, Abazi came for them both. Just as Joseph had prophesied, they were taken from the prison and put before Pharaoh.

In the hall of the palace, the king had called a feast. All the powerful men of Egypt were gathered in celebration of Pharaoh's birthday.

As a show of his mercy and power, Pharaoh had the cupbearer and baker brought to the room. In an instant, the cupbearer was forgiven his crimes and restored to his former position; the baker, however, was hanged, as a warning to all who would betray the king.

Later that night, Abazi crept quietly down the steps into the prison and knocked at Joseph's door.

'It happened just as you told them,' Abazi said. 'I heard the baker's body hangs from the gates of the palace.'

'The Creator told me what their dreams meant,' Joseph said. 'Soon, I will be free. The cupbearer will not forget me – he promised me . . .'

'You are a wise man, Joseph, but you do not know the human heart. Make your bed as comfortable as you can.

There will be many more dreams before you leave this place.'

Abazi was right. As the weeks turned into months, it became obvious that the cupbearer had forgotten his promise to Joseph. Two years passed slowly by. Joseph did all Abazi asked and their friendship grew.

Early one morning, Joseph heard footsteps echoing along the corridors, doors slammed and keys turned in the lock.

'Joseph . . . Joseph . . . wake up,' the warden shook Joseph's shoulder.

'What . . . what . . . Abazi?' Joseph asked, rubbing his eyes.

'You have a guest.' Abazi was grinning.

'A guest?' Joseph sighed and rolled over. 'I am not in the mood for your jokes.'

'This is no joke, Joseph.' Abazi grabbed Joseph's arm and pulled him up. 'The king's cupbearer is here to see you.'

'What?' Joseph looked at his friend. 'What do you mean?'

'I am here,' the cupbearer said as he entered Joseph's cell, 'to ask your forgiveness for forgetting you. And to take you to the king.'

'Take me to the king?'

'Pharaoh has had dreams that have haunted him. None of his wise men or magicians can interpret them. He is in fear of what the dreams foretell. Then I remembered you. When I told Pharaoh how you interpreted the baker's dreams, and mine, he sent me to get you. But first,' the cupbearer wrinkled his nose, 'let's clean you up. You smell as bad as . . . Abazi.'

Thirteen years after he was sold into slavery – and had spent years in prison – Joseph found himself in the throne room, kneeling on a marble floor before Pharaoh.

The king of Egypt wore a white, pleated linen kilt and a transparent ankle-length robe. Pharaoh wore the sacred beard and an elaborate head cloth, inlaid with gold and precious gems. His eyes were lined with kohl. Gold bands encircled his upper arms, gold rings glittered on his fingers, and a gold falcon – covered in lapis – hung from chains around the king's neck. Standing around the throne were the king's counsellors, the royal magicians and, in the corner, Potiphar, the captain of the guard.

'I had a dream, and none of my wise men or magicians can interpret it,' Pharaoh said. 'But my cupbearer said that when you hear a dream you can interpret it.'

'It is not me, Your Majesty,' Joseph replied to Pharaoh, 'but God.'

'God? Then hear my dreams . . .' the king said. 'I was standing on the bank of the Nile, when seven cows walked out of the river. They were fat and sleek, and they grazed among the reeds. Then seven more cows came up; they were scrawny and ugly. The lean, ugly cows ate the seven fat cows. But even after they ate them, no one could tell any difference; they looked just as ugly as before. Then I woke up.

'When I lay back down, I had another dream. I saw seven heads of grain, full and good, growing on a single stalk.

Then seven more heads sprouted – withered and thin and scorched by the east wind. The thin heads of grain swallowed up the seven good heads.' Pharaoh paused and then said, 'I told this to the magicians, but none could explain it to me.'

Joseph closed his eyes. *Almighty Creator, You brought me to this place,* he prayed. *Please tell me what the dreams mean.*

The room was silent, except for the sound of Pharaoh tapping his fingers on his throne as he waited. After a moment, Joseph looked at Pharaoh.

'Pharaoh, your dreams mean the same thing,' he told the king. 'In these dreams God has revealed to you what is about to happen. The seven good cows and seven good heads of grain are seven good years. The seven ugly cows and seven worthless heads of grain are seven years of famine.'

'Famine?' asked Pharaoh disbelievingly.

Joseph nodded. 'God has shown you what He is about to do. There will be seven years of great abundance throughout the land, followed by seven years of famine. This famine will be so great that the seven years of abundance will be forgotten. God gave you these dreams so that you will know that it will happen soon.'

'Seven years?' Pharaoh asked, as the magicians sneered at Joseph.

'Let Pharaoh find a wise man and put him in charge of the land of Egypt,' Joseph said. 'Let Pharaoh take a fifth of the harvest of Egypt during the seven years of abundance.

This food should be stored, held in reserve for the country, to be used during the seven years of famine that will come upon Egypt, so that the country may not be ruined by the famine.'

When Joseph finished speaking, he brushed back the ringlets of black hair from his brow and held his breath. Pharaoh studied him for several minutes.

'Thus speaks one who hears the word of God,' Pharaoh said. Joseph let out his breath. Looking around the room, Pharaoh turned and asked his officials, 'Can we find anyone like this man, one in whom is the spirit of God?' Then he looked at Joseph. 'Since God has made all this known to you, you shall be in charge of my palace. All my people are to submit to your orders. Only in matters of the throne will I be greater than you. Rise.'

Joseph stood as Pharaoh stepped down from his throne. The king took his signet ring from his finger and put it on Joseph's finger.

'But Majesty, he is not one of us,' Potiphar argued with Pharaoh.

'Have fine robes of linen be made for Joseph,' the king gave instructions to his steward, 'and put a gold chain around his neck.' Pharaoh turned to Potiphar, 'Give Joseph a chariot to ride in and, wherever he goes, have men assigned to clear the way before him.' Pharaoh turned back to Joseph, 'From this day you will be called Zaphenath-Paneah, for you are a revealer of hidden things and a seer of what is to come. Now, tell me . . . do you have a wife?'

By the end of the day, all Pharaoh had ordered had been done.

Soon, all in Egypt knew that Joseph heard from God. The harvest that year was abundant. Joseph travelled throughout the land, collecting a fifth of all the food and storing it in each city. There was so much food stored that, after a while, Joseph stopped keeping records of the amount. So much was stored in abundance that the people could not believe a famine would strike. But Joseph didn't doubt the word of God. He knew the prophecy would come true.

*   *   *

Seven years later, as he watched the flowing Nile waters one evening, the sky darkened as if a storm would burst. But the clouds withheld their rain and the burning wind of deprivation blew in from the desert. In the whispering of the wind Joseph heard the voice of the Creator and knew the time of starvation had come.

Within three moons, the famine came not only in Egypt, but also in lands beyond. When the people ran out of their supply of food, they went to Pharaoh.

'Go to Joseph and do what he tells you,' Pharaoh said.

Joseph opened the storehouses in the cities and sold the grain to the Egyptians as well as people from the far countries.

In Canaan, Joseph's family was suffering from the famine too. Jacob called his sons to him.

'I have heard that there is grain in Egypt,' he said. 'Reuben, take your brothers and go down there and buy some for us. Benjamin will stay with me. I could not bear it if harm came to him.'

The brothers did as their father had said. They sojourned through Canaan until they reached the town of Memphis in Egypt. The streets were crowded with people – many foreigners like themselves – who had come to buy grain.

As they waited their turn, Reuben and his nine brothers stared at the magnificence they saw around them, pointing out the gold thread in the clothing, the massive statues at the entrance to the pagan temples, and – in the distance – the towering pyramids.

As they moved forward, Gad nudged Reuben. 'Look,' he whispered, 'that must be Zaphenath-Paneah, the king's governor. He is in charge of selling food. Bow, bow, bow . . . we don't want to offend him.'

Throughout the heat of the morning and in the swirling, burning dust, Joseph had stood on the steps of the storehouse, supervising the sale of food. He had seen all manner of people come to Egypt, people from the far north and from deep to the south. He recognized his ten brothers when they drew closer, bowing to him.

'Creator . . . after all these years, it has happened as I dreamed it,' he whispered.

Folding his arms, Joseph scowled at his brothers. He motioned to the interpreter at his side. 'Where do you come from?' he asked in Egyptian. The interpreter repeated the question to the brothers.

'Sir,' Reuben said, 'we come from Canaan to buy food.'

Joseph stared at them. 'Spies!' he spat. 'You have come to our land to see if we are unprotected.'

His brothers gasped.

'No, sir!' Reuben spoke out. 'We are not spies. We are brothers here to buy food for our father and our family.'

'You're brothers?' Joseph sneered.

'Yes, sir,' Reuben said. 'Our father had twelve sons. The youngest is at home with our father and our other brother . . . is no more.'

'I don't believe you. Guards!' he turned to the soldiers standing nearby. 'Put these men in prison! In three days, I will decide what will become of you.'

The brothers were bound and chained, and dragged through the streets to the prison. Abazi was told to do them no harm, but to keep them for three days.

On the morning of the fourth day, Joseph had his brothers brought to the council room. The men were filthy; stumbling as the guards prodded them with the butts of their spears. Trembling, they knelt – faces to the floor – before the gold-inlaid chair where Joseph sat. Several men stood near Joseph.

'Do you still claim to be brothers?' Joseph asked through the interpreter.

'Before the Creator, who is our God, we spoke the truth, sir,' Reuben said. 'We are brothers. Our youngest brother is with our father.'

'Since I also fear God, do what I say and you will live. One of your brothers will be kept in prison, while the rest of you go and take grain back for your family. However, you must return with your youngest brother. Then I will know that you speak the truth.'

Issachar tilted his head slightly towards Reuben. 'God is punishing us because of Joseph,' he whispered.

Reuben hissed, 'Didn't I tell you not to harm him? But you wouldn't listen! Now we are being called to account by the Creator for his blood.'

Joseph's throat constricted as tears welled up in his eyes. *I cannot let them see me weep,* he thought. Then he stood up and walked away, cupping his hand over his brow, so that, to the people in the room, he would appear to be thinking. Joseph subtly moved a finger to wipe tears from his eyes. He swallowed several times before turning back to face the room. Pointing to Simeon, he snapped, 'Guards, take this one.'

While the other nine watched, Simeon – shaking with fear – was bound.

'Reuben, Reuben,' he cried as guards led him away. 'Help me!'

Joseph turned to one of the men at his side. 'Sell them the grain they need. Make sure they have enough provisions for the trip. We wouldn't want them to starve before they come back.'

'Thank you, sir,' Reuben said; his brothers echoed his words. As they turned to leave the room, Joseph stopped his aide.

'Put their silver into their sacks,' he spoke in Egyptian.

The man's eyes widened in surprise. 'What?'

'Put their silver back into their sacks,' he repeated. 'I wish to see just how honest these men are.'

Reuben and his brothers left Memphis as quickly as they could, travelling until the fiery sun was setting over the horizon.

'Let's stop here,' Reuben said. 'Asher, you feed the animals, while the rest of us prepare a meal.'

Asher lifted a bag of grain from the donkey and opened it. 'Ahhhhhh!' he screamed. 'Look!' he cried, turning to his brothers. As he held out the opened bag, silver glinted at the top. 'It's the silver I used to pay for the grain.'

They opened all the bags of grain; their silver was there.

'What has the Creator done to us?' Naphtali asked, trembling.

When the brothers returned to their father, they told him everything that had happened. 'We have to return with Benjamin and the man will give Simeon back to us.'

'No!' Jacob cried. 'Joseph is gone, and now Simeon, and you want to take Benjamin. No!'

'Father,' Reuben said. 'I swear on the life of my sons that I will bring Benjamin back safely to you.'

Jacob looked at his son for a long time. 'No,' he said. 'If anything happened to Benjamin, I would die.'

The famine was relentless and, before long, Jacob and his family had eaten all the grain from Egypt.

'Go back and buy more food,' Jacob told his sons.

'Father,' Judah said, 'the man told us not to come back unless we bring Benjamin.'

'Why did you tell him about Benjamin?' Jacob asked.

'He thought we were spies,' Asher said. 'He questioned us about our family and we answered him. How were we to know he would say, "Bring your brother down here"?'

'Father,' Judah knelt before Jacob. 'Send Benjamin with me. I will take care of him. I promise.'

Jacob stared at his son and then slowly nodded.

'Go. Take Benjamin with you. Also take some gifts to this man – a little balm, some honey, spices, myrrh and some nuts. Take twice as much silver with you, so you can return the silver you found in your bags. May the Creator give you mercy, so that the man will let you bring both Simeon and Benjamin back with you.'

The brothers followed their father's instructions and hurried back to Egypt. Once they arrived in Memphis, they went to Joseph. Kneeling on the floor, they bowed.

'This is our youngest brother, as we told you,' Reuben said.

Joseph was shocked when he saw Benjamin. *He was a child when last I saw him,* he thought. He gestured to his steward.

'Take these men to my house and prepare dinner. They will eat with me at noon today.'

This was not what the brothers had expected, but they were too afraid not to obey. 'Do you think he found out about the silver?' Dan whispered, as they followed Joseph's

steward through the streets of Memphis. 'Maybe he plans
to make us his slaves.'

'I don't know what to think,' Reuben whispered back.
'But we have no choice but to follow.'

Joseph's house was luxurious, made from white stone. In
the centre of the atrium was a pool surrounded by flowers
and trees.

'You will wait here,' the steward said. 'My master will join
you soon.'

'Sir,' Reuben said, 'we need to explain something.' He
told the man about how they found the silver in their bags.
'We don't know how it got there. We have brought it back,
along with extra silver to buy food.'

'Don't be afraid,' the steward said. 'I have the silver you
brought before. Your God must have placed silver in your
sacks. Ah . . . here is your brother.'

Turning, they saw Simeon walk into the courtyard.

'You are alive,' Reuben said.

'And well,' he answered.

'Sirs,' said the steward, 'if you will come this way, I will
provide you with water to wash your feet and see that
someone cares for your donkeys.'

'Get the gifts for the man from our bags,' Reuben whispered to Asher.

When Joseph arrived at noon, the brothers bowed to
him, presenting the gifts from their father.

'How is your aged father?' Joseph asked through the
interpreter.

'It is kind of you to ask,' Judah said, bowing. 'Your servant . . . our father is still alive and well.'

'And this is the brother you told me about?'

Reuben drew Benjamin forward.

'Sir, this is our youngest brother, Benjamin.'

'Master, I am honoured.' Benjamin bowed before Joseph.

'God bless you,' Joseph said. *He looks like Mother,* Joseph's throat constricted with unshed tears. Turning, he ran through the house and to his private room. Shutting the door, he collapsed on a couch and wept. *I never thought to see my family again. Now they are all here, and father still lives.* Joseph took several deep breaths and then went to the washbasin to splash water on his face.

He returned to the atrium. 'We will eat now,' he told them. 'Follow me.'

He led them to a dining room where two tables were set with silver plates and cups. 'Please, be seated,' Joseph said, indicating one table. He crossed the room to sit at the other table. 'Serve the food,' Joseph told his steward.

The meal was rich, with lamb, rice, bread, cucumbers, honey and nuts. Joseph was always served first and then his guests. Instead of serving Reuben first, for the brothers had been seated in the order of their ages, Benjamin was served first and his portion was larger than his brothers. While they ate, Joseph asked about their family and their homeland. When the meal was finished, Joseph stood.

'You have done as I asked and returned with your brother,' he said. 'I believe that you are not spies. Rooms have been prepared for you tonight. I have instructed my men to fill your bags with grain to take back to your family. May your God bless you and your honoured father.'

The brothers bowed. 'Thank you, sir. You honour us.'

The next day, they left at dawn, anxious to return to their father. They had travelled for about an hour when Issachar cried, 'Look! Behind us!'

Turning, they saw soldiers in chariots racing towards them; in the lead chariot was Joseph's steward. They surrounded the brothers, spears levelled at them.

'Why have you repaid good with evil?' the steward said. 'You took the cup my master drinks from and also uses for divination.'

'We would never do anything like that,' Reuben insisted. 'We even brought back the silver we found inside our bags. If you don't believe me, then look through our things. If any of us have it, he will die and the rest will become your master's slaves.'

'Let it be as you say.' The steward turned to the soldiers. 'Search their things.'

The bags were pulled from the donkeys and opened. Beginning with Reuben, the steward shoved his hand into the bag. In each bag, nothing was found.

Coming to Benjamin, the steward thrust his hand down into the bag and cried, 'Ah ha!' Pulling out his hand, there was the cup Joseph had drunk from at the meal. Benjamin shook his head, his eyes wide with fear and confusion.

'Take him!' the steward pointed to the youngest brother.

'No!' Benjamin cried as the soldiers tied his arms and threw him in a chariot. 'I did not do this. Judah! Reuben! Help me!'

'No!' Judah yelled as the Egyptians drove away. He grabbed the neck of his robe and tore it. 'Creator God! This cannot be!'

The brothers loaded the sacks onto the donkeys and returned to Memphis. They found Joseph still in his house. Benjamin was kneeling on the floor. Reuben and his brothers fell before Joseph, weeping.

'What have you done?' Joseph said through the interpreter. 'Didn't you know the gods speak to me?'

'We don't know how this happened, sir,' Judah cried. 'We are in your hands. My brothers and I are now your slaves.'

'No!' Joseph replied. 'Only the man who stole my cup will become my slave. The rest of you can go.'

'We cannot, my lord,' Judah said. 'You have asked about our family and you know that we have an aged father. He did not allow Benjamin to come with us before, for fear harm might come to him. The only reason we brought him this time was because you commanded it. I promised our father that I would take care of Benjamin. Please, sir, let me stay here, as your slave, and let my brother return to our father. I could not bear to see my father's grief.'

Watching his brothers weep was more than Joseph could bear. Turning to his steward he commanded, 'Have everyone leave my presence.'

The steward bowed his head and gestured for the servants and soldiers to leave. Closing the doors, Joseph locked them. Grasping his head, shoulders shaking, he began moaning. Throwing his head back, he cried.

'Sir, sir, what is it?' the guards called out, rattling the doors.

Wiping his eyes, Joseph reassured them, 'I am all right.'

Then he turned to his brothers, who were still kneeling on the floor, uncertain and terrified by this powerful man crying as though crazed.

Joseph crossed the floor and fell on his knees in front of his brothers. 'Do you not recognize me?' he spoke in their language.

Reuben stared at him, his brow furrowed.

'It is I . . . Joseph.'

Reuben gasped, covering his mouth, his eyes wide.

Joseph grabbed Reuben by the shoulder, tears turning to laughter. 'Reuben. Judah. Dan, Gad! I am your brother, Joseph.'

'Joseph?' Reuben whispered.

'Yes.'

The older brother jerked away in fear and dropped his head on the floor.

'Please,' he begged, 'do not kill me. Do not kill us. We have wronged you. Make us your slaves, but please do not kill us.'

'Sit up. Reuben, please, look at me.'

Joseph leaned over and lifted his brother by the shoulders until he was looking at Reuben's face. 'Don't be angry with yourselves,' he said. 'What you did was wrong, but it was not you who sent me here, but the Creator. You intended to harm me, but God intended it for good – to accomplish what is now being done, the saving of many lives.'

'Joseph?' Benjamin took a step towards his brother. 'Is it really you?'

'Yes, Benjamin, it is I.'

Running, Benjamin threw himself on the floor and hugged his brother. Joseph dropped his head on his brother's shoulder and wept. Judah, Levi and all the other brothers crowded around Joseph and Benjamin, reaching over to touch him, crying out praises to God.

'I prayed that the Creator would let me see you again,' Joseph sat back, wiping his eyes. 'Now, one prayer remains. Come, let us make arrangements to bring Father here.'

8

The Boy

It was night when the soldiers walked into the village. They stood, torches burning against the star-clad sky, and surrounded every house. Their faces were set like flint, eyes filled with hatred and loathing.

'Listen,' shouted the captain, beating his sword against his shield. 'I have a message from Pharaoh.'

From every house and shelter, men appeared. In the dark shadows crouched frightened children.

'Pharaoh?' asked an old man, sitting by his door in the light of a fire. 'What have we done that is so important that he should want to send a message to us?'

'You breed like rats,' the captain answered. 'You are so numerous that something has to be done before you inhabit the whole world.'

'Are we not men? Do we not just do what is ordained?' the old man scoffed.

'You do it too well. From now on, Pharaoh demands that every male child that is born be thrown into the Nile.'

'You will murder our children?' the old man asked, not caring if he lived or died.

'Old man,' the captain said, his eyes narrowed, 'it is fortunate your life is near its end or I would have killed you for your words. Pharaoh is god, his word law – and you Hebrew slaves must obey. Any male child who has not lived beyond two harvests is to be taken at dawn tomorrow.'

'This night will be a time of weeping,' the old man said, struggling to his feet.

'There is a time for everything, old man – even for you Hebrews,' the captain replied as his soldiers turned to leave the village in the darkening twilight.

'Did you hear that, Mother?' Miriam asked, stepping into the darkness of the mud-walled house.

'It is to be expected,' Yochaved answered as she sat on the low bed that rested on the dirt floor. 'Our Egyptian masters live in fear of us growing in number and changing their land.'

'But we have done nothing – we work for them, our backs burn in the sun, and now they want to kill us,' the girl lowered her voice. 'And what of . . .'

'The baby?' her mother whispered.

'He has lived only three moons and has never seen a harvest. Will you just give him to the river?'

The woman looked at the baby boy sleeping in the cot by the bed.

'Miriam,' Yochaved said to her daughter, 'help me with this shawl.'

Miriam crossed the room to her mother. One room was all the space within the house and was divided by the curtains that Miriam and her mother had woven. The floor was packed dirt and, to protect against the killing heat, the house had no windows. During the day, light came from the open door.

Miriam reached behind her mother and grabbed the end of the shawl. She brought it to the opposite side and tied it on her mother's shoulder, forming a sling in front. Miriam held the widest part of the sling open, while her mother leaned over the small woven basket daubed in black pitch where the child lay.

Yochaved picked up the baby and put him into the sling. She stood awkwardly, with one hand holding the baby's back. 'Now help me with my robe, Miriam,' she said.

By the dark of night, Yochaved and Miriam left the village. They could hear the crying of neighbours as the women grieved the coming dawn. In her hands Yochaved carried the wicker basket. Wrapped under her cloak, the baby slept on, not knowing its fate.

By morning, they had walked many miles. The arid lands had turned to green fields with palm tree borders. The smell of the great river covered the land. In the dawn, a fine white mist ebbed back to the water. Yochaved stopped by the well and washed her face. Miriam hid in the tall reeds by the river.

'Yochaved?' asked a woman washing clothes. 'It is good to see you again.' She looked up and smiled.

'Della, you too are far from home – and so early in the morning,.' Yochaved answered, hoping the child would not stir.

'I could not be in my village – not this morning.' Della scrubbed a shirt with reddened hands.

'I do not understand why the Creator allows this to happen,' Yochaved said. 'He brought Joseph to Egypt to save both Egyptians and Hebrews from the famine that ravaged the land. Our people settled in Goshen and tended not only their herds, but Pharaoh's herds as well. Now this pharaoh forgets all of that and wants to destroy us.'

'I think he is afraid our men will rise up as a great army and join with Egypt's enemies. We should lie and tell Pharaoh that the Hebrews are only a nation of women.'

'Then we must pray that someone will deliver us from all this.'

'Even threatening to kill an Egyptian would mean death,' Della whispered, looking around to be sure her words were not overheard.

'I will not stand by and watch women and children be harmed,' Yochaved said as a crowd of women began to gather at the well in the first light of morning.

'You must trust the Creator to protect us,' Della replied in a whisper. 'The world will not always be this way. There is a land for us, but not in this place.'

Yochaved's shoulders slumped. 'I know. I do trust the Creator,' she sighed. 'It is just hard knowing there is nothing – *nothing* – I can do to protect you from *vermin* like Pharaoh.'

Della touched her arm. 'Have faith,' she whispered. 'The Lord will send a saviour to free us from slavery.'

Yochaved smiled. 'From your lips to the Creator's ears,' she whispered.

The morning sun grew in the sky, scorching the earth and steaming the dew and puddles of water around the well. Della and Yochaved sat in the shade of a palm and shared a cup from the well. Soon, the sounds of weeping, wailing and the shouting of the soldiers were carried on the wind.

'It is happening,' Della said slowly, tears rolling down her face. 'And the boy you had – what of him?'

Yochaved did not know how to answer.

'He is no longer mine. I will give him to the river – but I will decide when.'

Della looked at her as if she could see the story in her eyes.

'You . . . you have your baby?' she asked.

Yochaved smiled. 'All the captain said was that the children had to be put in the Nile and that is what I will do,' she said. 'I will trust God to keep him safe.'

She moved from the shade of the palm tree into the light of the sun. The torment in the women's screams echoed down the Nile.

'I will not watch them offer the children as sacrifice to Sobek,' Della said as she dug her dirt-stained nails into her palms.

The Egyptians worshipped many gods of the Nile, but the crocodile god, Sobek, was above them all.

'They feed the leather-backed beasts,' Della said. 'They will pay for what they have done. A curse upon Egypt and a curse upon Pharaoh.'

Yochaved smiled at her friend. 'Pray for me and my child,' she said as she turned and walked away.

'Yochaved . . .' Della's words chased the young mother. 'You will be blessed and so will the fruit of your womb.'

Yochaved picked the basket from the dry earth and walked towards the river. Miriam came out from her hiding place and joined her mother.

When the morning wind had calmed and the beasts of Sobek lay on the dry banks on the far side of the river, Yochaved and Miriam made their way to the edge of the water. The bank was thick with tall reeds. Birds sang in the boughs and the water was still.

Yochaved nursed her baby until he fell asleep. She lifted him, kissed his forehead and laid him in the basket.

'Almighty Creator, into Your hands I place my son,' she prayed over the child. 'Protect him and, if it be Your will, return him to me.'

Lifting the basket, she carried the sleeping baby down the path to the edge of the river. She scanned the surface of the water, but could see no signs of hippos or crocodiles.

'The Nile is quiet today,' Yochaved whispered to the sleeping child. 'The Lord silences the river to protect you.'

Slipping into the water, Yochaved guided the basket into the reeds that grew along the edge of the river. She opened the basket again and looked at her sleeping son. 'You have been a blessing to me, little one,' she whispered, her eyes filling with tears. 'Now you are in the hands of the Almighty.' Leaning over she kissed him, and then closed the basket. With a small push, the basket floated away on the water, bumping into the reeds.

Yochaved and Miriam climbed out of the water. 'I must return before I am missed, but you stay here. Follow "the ark", Miriam,' Yochaved told her daughter, 'and see where it goes.'

Miriam slipped back into the water as the ark floated down the Nile. The reeds hid her and prevented the basket from moving into the middle of the river.

The sun had climbed in the sky when the ark bumped into a block of stone. Miriam took a step towards the basket, when she heard voices floating over the water. She quietly pushed the small ark between a stand of reeds and sank down in the water, until only her nose and eyes were clear.

The block of stone where the ark rested was the edge of a path that led from the river to a platform.

Ornate columns rose many feet from the platform, supporting a linen roof that glistened white in the sunlight. On the platform was a table laden with fruit and bread and cheese. Goblets made from silver stood next to pitchers glistening with condensation. In the background, hidden behind massive ferns, a group of musicians played on flutes and lyres. Tall palm trees shaded the structure and the three women who were bathing in the water.

'It is so hot!' complained one of the women.

'It is Egypt, Akila,' another woman said, 'it is always hot.'

'We could go back to the palace, Nabirye, where it is cooler,' Akila said. 'What do you think, Bithiah?' she asked.

Bithiah? Miriam knew that name. *That is the princess, the Pharaoh's daughter.*

'I want to stay here a little longer,' the princess replied, wading away from her companions, to the edge of the stone pathway. A gentle wave knocked the ark against the stone, drawing the princess's attention. 'What have we here?'

'What is it, Bithiah?' Nabirye called. 'What have you found?'

'It's a basket floating on the Nile,' the princess replied. 'Akila, go bring it to me.'

Akila waded to the other side of the pathway to guide the ark back to the princess.

'Sobek has sent you a gift,' Akila said.

'Open it,' said Nabirye.

Holding the basket still, Bithiah lifted the lid. Inside, the baby lay, still asleep from the lulling touch of the water.

'It is a baby!' cried Nabirye.

'The river gods brought you a son,' Akila said.

The voices woke the infant and he opened his eyes. After staring at the strangers for a moment, he furrowed his brow and began to cry.

'Poor little thing,' Nabirye said.

'Look at this cloth in the bottom of the basket,' Akila said, 'I do not recognize the pattern of the weave.'

'It is Hebrew,' Bithiah said.

'Someone must have placed him in the ark to save him from your father's edict,' said Akila.

'And the Nile gods brought him to me.'

Bithiah reached into the basket and lifted the infant to her shoulder. He turned his head and nuzzled her neck. His cries increased.

'I think he's hungry,' Nabirye said.

'I cannot feed him,' said Bithiah. She looked at her companions, who shook their heads.

'We can't either,' said Akila.

Miriam stepped out of the river and approached the women. She knelt down.

'Who are you?' Bithiah asked.

'One of Pharaoh's Hebrew servants, my Lady,' she said, 'I saw the basket in the river and followed it. Shall I go and get one of the Hebrew women to nurse the baby for you?'

'Go and fetch one,' the princess said. 'Tell her to nurse this baby for me, and I will pay her.'

As Miriam turned to run home, she heard the princess say, 'This baby will become my son and I will raise him as a prince.'

'What shall you name him?' Nabirye asked.

'Because I drew him from the waters, I shall name him . . . Moses – one who is drawn forth.'

9

The Sea

Above the far horizon, a burning cloud touched the pinnacle of the sky, hiding the sun. A burning mist rose from the earth as if it was spewed from the mouth of a volcano. The swirling embers twisted in smoke and brimstone like the trunk of a gigantic tree many miles high. It had been that way for several days. Each day it was a pillar of cloud and each night, a rod of fire. It never moved on the horizon and now it began to blot out the sky.

'So,' said the man to his two companions. 'Moses said that *the Creator* has told him to take us through the canyon that leads to the sea.'

'I think Moses is lost and wandering in confusion,' the younger man replied, fearfully looking at the sky.

'And we follow him, Korah,' the first man said as he leaned against a rock wall, his cloak wrapped tightly around him.

'Where else would you go, Dathan?' Korah asked. 'And you Abriam – who would you follow?'

The third man reached out a long arm and pulled Korah close. 'You speak too loudly for your own good,' he whispered in a deep voice. 'You will get us killed. If Moses ever found out that we were spies and worked for Pharaoh, we would be dead.'

Korah smiled nervously. He looked up at the high mountains. 'There must be hundreds of thousands of people hemmed in on the beach,' he said. 'If Pharaoh were to strike now, they would have no way of escape.'

It was true, the two mountains – with the small dividing ravine – created a place large enough to hold Moses and all the Hebrews whom Pharaoh had freed. Before them was the Great Sea and behind them a range of towering cliffs.

Korah looked at the full moon as it rose beyond the sea.

'I want to go back,' Korah said. 'Even life as a slave was better than this.'

'Only because we spied on our brothers and sisters and reported back to Pharaoh,' Dathan answered.

It was by accident that Korah had discovered that Dathan and his brother Abriam had sided with their Egyptian masters. The three men became friends long before the plagues destroyed the land and turned the Nile to blood.

They had left Egypt when Pharaoh sent the Hebrews away; it was the night when the son of Pharaoh had been found dead. There was not a mark on his body, nor any sickness. It was as if the life had been snatched from him by an angel of death.

As the three men had spied on the Hebrews whilst in the land of Pharaoh, so now they conspired to do the same as they travelled through the desert.

After leaving Egypt, Moses had led the Hebrews through the desert and then turned to follow the long and winding canyon that led them to the edge of the sea. For several days, the whole nation of Hebrews had camped by the sea. They could not go back through the canyon and could not go on through the sea.

'What should we do, Dathan?' Korah asked.

'Send word to Pharaoh,' Dathan replied. 'Moses thinks these two mountains makes this beach a secure camp. However, as the only way out is through the canyon . . .'

'Or through the sea,' Abriam sniggered.

'Yes, Moses *could* lead the people through that deep sea with no boats,' Korah laughed.

'This beach could cage people in, with no escape,' Dathan added.

'How do we get word to Pharaoh?' Abriam asked.

'You two go among the people. All you need to do is . . . *suggest* . . . that Moses didn't really hear from the Creator and that it would be better for us to return to Egypt. I can hear the grumbling of empty stomachs. Starving people are always in need of rebellion.'

Abriam clapped his brother's shoulder. 'Dathan, you have thought of everything.'

'A word here and a groan there . . . soon people will not trust in Moses. Who would believe a man who says he speaks to God?'

'But what if it is true?' Korah asked.

'You are young . . . and stupid,' Dathan answered. 'Stories such as that are not real. The only god I know is gold and lines my pockets.'

'So we tell them that we should go back and you will take word to Pharaoh?' Abriam asked.

'At dawn, just before it is light, I will go back through the mountains. I will send word to Pharaoh where we are encamped.'

The next morning, before it was light, Dathan slipped away through the mountains while Abriam and Korah wandered through the camp.

It was easy for them to become just another face in the crowd. Soon, Abriam found a group of women at the water's edge, washing clothes.

'Ah, it is so nice to be sitting,' one woman laughed, rubbing a wet robe against a large rock. 'I am weary from walking.'

'And the breeze blowing off of the sea is cool,' added another. 'Much better than the heat of Egypt.'

'Ah, but the heat of Egypt is not the breath of death,' Abriam stepped closer to the women.

'What do you mean?' the first woman asked.

'Being a woman, you would not realize that we are entangled in the land,' he smiled. 'We are shut in by the mountains.'

'But Moses told my husband this place would be safe for us,' another woman said.

'Of course he did,' Abriam replied. 'Would he want to admit he is lost and that he led us to an area where we could be trapped?' He spread his hands out with an innocent look on his face. 'I'm not saying that Moses did not hear from the Creator, but . . .' He wandered away without finishing his statement. *Let those women make what they would of that,* he smiled to himself.

By a circle of stones, Korah found a wizened old woman talking to a group of children.

'Name the plagues that YHWH sent on the Egyptians,' the woman said.

'Blood!' one little boy cried. 'YHWH made the waters of the Nile and in all of Egypt turn into blood. But not our water in Goshen.'

'Good, good,' encouraged the old woman. 'What else?'

'Frogs,' another boy said, crouching and hopping around, making the girls squeal. 'And lice!'

'Flies biting all over the Egyptians,' one girl answered, waving her arms and buzzing.

'A plague that killed all the Egyptians' cattle, but not ours,' said the girl sitting next to her.

'Painful boils all over the Egyptians' bodies,' laughed an older boy.

One little boy grabbed a handful of dust and threw it in the air. 'Hail that killed the Egyptians' animals and destroyed their crops.'

'Locusts,' called out another boy.

'Darkness in all of Egypt that lasted three days,' said an older girl, 'but not in Goshen.'

'Yes, yes,' said the old woman, 'you're all right. But what was the last plague?'

The children looked at each other, shifting uncomfortably.

'YHWH killed the firstborn in all of Egypt,' the old woman whispered. 'From the animals to the firstborn of the prisoners in the dungeon all the way to the firstborn of Pharaoh.'

The children stilled, listening in wide-eyed fear.

'Yes, it was sad, but after that, Pharaoh summoned Moses and his brother Aaron and said, "Up! Leave my people, you and the Israelites! Go, worship your God as you have requested. Take your flocks and herds and go. And also bless me,"'

For a moment the old woman was lost in thought, remembering the miraculous story of how the Lord had appeared to Moses in a burning bush and told him to rescue the Israelites from Egypt. If anyone asked who had sent him, Moses was to say, 'YHWH, I AM WHO I AM. Tell them that I AM has sent you.'

'Now, where was I?' The old woman looked around at the children and said, 'Remember this, for one day you will tell your children how YHWH sent these plagues and freed us from slavery.'

'Or you will tell them how Moses led them to the desert to die,' Korah said.

'What do you mean?' the old woman demanded.

'Only that we have no place to go but into the sea or back to Egypt,' he said. 'Do you know how to swim? Would you want to swim across that sea?' He bent down to put his face near the littlest girl. 'Who knows what creatures live in those waters . . . monsters larger than hippos and crocodiles . . . with large, snapping teeth that will bite you in two!'

The little girl screamed and jumped up.

'Why are you scaring the children?' the old woman demanded, waving her walking stick at him.

'They need to hear the truth.' Korah shrugged and walked off before the old woman could hit him.

With every passing hour, Abriam and Korah talked to more people. Their dissent was spread in whispers. Their sedition passed on in half-truths spoken quickly.

'Our plans are proceeding well,' Abriam said as he met Korah near the water carrier. 'By now, Dathan should have met with Pharaoh.'

'We spread . . . *suggestions* . . . throughout the camp,' Korah said. 'You know how women gossip.'

'And how children tend to *enlarge* stories,' Abriam grinned. 'By now, they will have told anyone who would listen that Moses is planning to kill them and feed their bodies to the sea monsters.'

'Look,' Abriam said, pointing to the tent where Moses rested. 'They gather outside like rats around a midden heap.'

Korah turned to see a gathering of men before Moses' tent. From where he stood, he could hear their grumbling and arguing.

'See,' Abriam said. 'Dathan was right. It is by rumour – and not war – that empires fall.'

Korah and Abriam watched the men from a distance.

'Moses . . . Moses . . .' shouted one man. 'We would speak with you . . .'

The crowd fell silent as they waited.

The flap of the tent opened. Moses walked out and leaned on his wooden staff. He greeted the two men standing before him and nodded to the rest.

'What do you require?' Moses asked.

'We want to talk to you, Moses.' The man paused and took a deep breath. 'We've heard . . . stories . . . that we might be . . . in danger.'

'Danger?' Moses frowned. 'What do you mean?'

'My youngest daughter was very upset. She said someone told her that you led us here to die in the Sea of Reeds.'

'Isn't your daughter only four years old?' Moses asked.

'What about my wife?' another man asked. 'She heard that we are lost and that we could be trapped in this place.'

'Look at the opening between the mountains,' the first man pointed. 'That pass is the only way out. If someone tried to get to us, we have nowhere to run.'

'Who would try to get to us?' Moses asked.

'Bandits,' someone in the crowd called.

'Or an army,' yelled another.

'An army?' Moses was incredulous. 'The only army in this area would be from Egypt. Do you believe that Pharaoh is going to send his army after us? Especially after the ten plagues?'

'Yes, the plagues,' a man said. 'Some of the people don't . . .'

'Don't what?' Moses asked.

'Don't really . . . believe the plagues.'

'Don't believe the plagues?' Moses opened his eyes, shocked. 'How could you not believe the plagues?'

'We didn't see them,' the man answered. 'You and Aaron told us about all the plagues that YHWH *supposedly* sent to Egypt.' He gestured to the men behind him. 'We were all in Goshen . . . nothing happened to us.'

'Are you doubting Moses?' Aaron walked up. Taller than his brother – taller than many Hebrews – his eyes were narrowed in anger. 'Are you saying that Moses lied to you? Why would he do that?'

None of the men in the crowd spoke.

'Moses could have stayed in Midian, tending his father-in-law's herds.' Aaron folded his arms. 'He came back to Egypt because the Creator told him to, in order to free YOU people from slavery. Would you prefer to be back in Goshen, building Pharaoh's store cities?' His glare made the men drop their heads and shuffle their feet. 'Well, would you?'

'No, Aaron,' one man answered. 'But, our wives and children are frightened. We had to ask.'

'No!' Aaron spat. 'You should have trusted YHWH. Now go, before you make Moses angry.'

The men in the crowd looked at each other. One shrugged his shoulders and gestured with his head at the others.

'Moses, you understand, don't you?'

'We had to ask.'

'I understand,' Moses said. 'But, *you* need to understand, when you doubt me, you doubt YHWH.'

The crowd moved back and fell away like sand through fingers. Aaron watched until they were gone. 'I cannot believe they would dare doubt the plagues.'

'Well, they really didn't see the plagues,' Moses said. 'It takes faith to believe in something you do not see.'

As Moses and Aaron walked through the camp, people watched them. Some nodded and smiled; others stared.

'It is as though they expect . . . something . . . to happen,' Aaron said.

'Something will always happen,' Moses answered. 'We may not like what it is, but as with Joseph and his brothers, YHWH can take what appears to be bad and make it good.'

Throughout the night, Moses walked amongst his people.

The dawn streaked the clouds pink and blue. The wind blew the waves over the shore, etching deep gouges in the sand. Moses stood at the entrance to his tent, breathing in the moist air. He looked over the vast sea.

'YHWH, You created all this,' he prayed. Then he looked over the sea of tents. 'You created these people. Give me the wisdom to lead them.'

Beyond the tents, the mountains rose up to the sky. The wind moaned against the heights and echoed back, growing in volume. Moses frowned, sensing that something was wrong. From the mountain heights, a shofar – a horn – pierced the sky.

From one tent and then another, people emerged, shielding their eyes against the sunlight and staring towards the mountains. A figure was running from the mountain pass. As it drew near, Moses could make out Korah, panting.

'Soldiers!' he yelled. 'Hundreds of chariots! Egyptians! Pharaoh's army is coming.'

'Run!' a woman screamed.

'Where are you going to run?' Abriam stood next to Korah. 'We are surrounded by mountains on one side and the sea on the other.'

'We're going to die!' Korah pointed towards Moses. 'It's all Moses' fault. He led us here.'

Someone in the crowd echoed the words.

'It's Moses' fault!'

'Was it because there were no graves in Egypt that you brought us to the desert to die?' Abriam asked.

'It's better to be alive and serving the Egyptians,' Korah yelled, 'than to die here.'

The people surged towards the tent where Moses stood, Aaron at his side. Moses held his walking staff in one hand and looked at the frightened people, whose voices rose above the sound of the wind and the approaching army. Lifting his staff, he slammed it into the ground; the earth shook, the sound echoed through the camp, silencing the voices.

'Do not be afraid,' he said. All around them, the ground trembled under the weight of the advancing Egyptian army. 'Today you will see the mighty hand of God. YHWH will fight for you.'

Turning, Moses pushed his way through the crowd and walked to the edge of the sea. The waves broke on the shingle beach. Grasping his staff with both hands, he pointed it over the water. 'Stand still and see the deliverance of the Creator!' he proclaimed and spread his arms wide.

The clouds over the mountains gathered together – boiling and whirling, lightning striking like fire, screaming in its fury – and settled into the pass, blocking the army of Pharaoh from entering.

From the west, the wind howled, convulsing the waves. Suddenly the sea began to ripple as if it was being pulled apart. As the Hebrews watched, the waters before them divided. On each side, they piled up like giant cliffs, the waves pushing back the sea.

On the shore, the Hebrews fell to their knees, their cries silenced at the hand of YHWH.

'Aaron,' Moses called urgently, 'lead the people through the sea.'

'Gather your things,' Aaron yelled. 'Quickly – the Egyptians are near.'

Women ran to stuff bags while the men pulled up the tent pegs. Small children helped their mothers.

As soon as Aaron's wife and their sons, Eleazar and Ithamar, joined him, he led them to the edge of the shore. He glanced over his shoulder at Moses, then stepped onto the sea floor.

Without another backward look, Aaron and his family began walking between the massive walls of water. They towered above them to the height of a citadel. The sea boiled and churned, and the spray from the waves filled the air.

Moses stood with his staff pointed over the waters and watched as first one family and then another followed Aaron. Hours passed and still the people walked across the sea floor. When the last man stepped between the waters, Moses walked to where Zipporah and their sons waited on the shore, their belongings on the ground near them.

'It is time for us,' he told them.

His wife nodded and bent to pick up a bag. Their sons followed and started walking down the shore and between the water.

As the ground sloped down to the lowest point of the sea, the waters rose on either side, waves rolling as if fighting against an unseen hand. Here and there, fish of all sizes could be seen through the waves.

At last, the sea floor began to slope up, towards the distant shore where Aaron stood waiting with the Hebrews. Moses gestured for his wife and sons to stand with Aaron and he turned back to face the sea, holding the walking staff over the waters.

Across the divided waters, the Hebrews could still see the roiling clouds of fire. While they watched, the lightning ceased and the clouds lifted. From between the mountains the chariots of Pharaoh poured, crossing the beach and following the Hebrews. Within moments, the entire Egyptian army rode between the walls of water. Their war cries drowned out the roiling sea as the soldiers screamed for the blood of Moses.

The first chariot shuddered, as if stuck in marshy ground, and then fell as its wheels broke. The horses lunged against the reins. Another chariot lost its wheels, and then another, as chariots ran into each other. The soldiers tried to free the frightened horses and recover the wheels. Soon the entire army was trapped. It could not go forward another inch.

'Watch,' Moses' voice echoed above the sound of the waves. 'Today you will see the armies of Egypt no more,' he said and brought both arms together.

The sea shimmered as if something flew over the water. It was as if the wings of a gigantic creature hovered over the sea. The wind blew and twisted the peaks of the waves until they stood completely still – as if frozen. All the time, the Israelites watched in fear as the soldiers got closer and closer.

Suddenly, the sea gave way. The walls of water collapsed, surging across the dry seabed. The Egyptians tried to out-run the water, but the sea flooded. The waters crashed, waves as tall as mountains throwing bodies of soldiers and horses into the air to land with a splash on the surface.

Moses turned from the sea to face the people, his staff still raised. One by one, the people fell to their knees, stunned.

'OUR GOD . . .' Moses' voice – carried on the wind – was heard by every man, woman and child. 'IS GOD!'

10

The Spies

It was still dark when a procession carrying burning torches crossed the barren earth towards the mountains. The moon hung in the sky like a curved knife cutting the black of space. A gentle breeze blew through the camp; this would be the day's only coolness. Soon the sun would climb in the molten sky.

The gathering drew closer to a tent that was barely visible against the rocks and trees that formed a small oasis.

Each man carried a torch; in the half-light, they looked like ghosts. Daubed with the dirt of the road, their faces glistened in the flickering light. One man broke from the circle and stepped forward. 'Caleb,' he called.

The tent flap lifted and a man stepped outside. 'You want me?' he asked.

'Moses has asked for you.'

Caleb knew not to keep the Hebrew leader waiting. 'Then let's go.'

The group walked through the rough settlement of several thousand tents that stretched across the land as far as the eye could see. Swirling smoke wafted high into the sky, and goats and children scurried back and forth like a living sea. When they reached Moses' tent, Caleb lifted the flap and entered.

In the flickering light of a lantern, Caleb could see men seated on cushions. Their faces were lined from many years of travelling through the desert. All were leaders of the people – he recognized Joshua, Nahbi and Ammiel. Nodding to the others, he walked to Joshua.

'Greetings, Joshua,' Caleb said, sitting next to him.

'Caleb.' Joshua grinned at his old friend.

Joshua had been Caleb's friend since boyhood, when they used to carry sun-baked bricks to the builders and dream of being free from Egyptian slavery. They remained friends into manhood, when they became leaders of their tribes and began laying the bricks to build a storehouse for grain. It was then they heard that Pharaoh *was* freeing the Hebrew slaves. Caleb and Joshua led their tribes to follow Moses out of Egypt, across the dry seabed and to Kadesh, in the desert of Paran.

'Do you know what Moses wants?' Caleb whispered.

Joshua shrugged. Moses had chosen him to be one of his aides and he met frequently with Moses and Aaron. 'I'm not certain, but I think –'

The tent flap lifted and Moses stepped inside, followed by Aaron. Everyone fell silent; they were in the presence of the man who talked with God.

Moses was old. His hair and beard were white as sheep's wool but his gaze was still penetrating.

'We are encamped on the edge of Canaan,' Moses said slowly. 'This is the land YHWH promised to us: a land of great bounty with rivers full of fish and where the earth will never be barren.

'Last night, the Creator instructed me to send one leader from each tribe to explore the land.' Moses looked at his brother, 'Aaron, read the names of these men. When you hear your name, lift your hand to let all know you are willing to go.'

Aaron stepped forward, holding up a parchment. 'Shammua . . .'

A man across from Caleb lifted his hand.

'Shaphat; Caleb,' Caleb lifted his hand.

'Igal; Joshua; Palti; Gaddiel; Gaddi; Ammiel; Sethur; Nahbi and Geuel.' Each man in turn lifted his hand. Aaron finished reading and stepped back beside Moses.

'In the morning, go up through the Negev and into the hill country,' Moses said. 'See whether the people who live there are strong or weak, few or many. Are the towns unprotected or fortified? Is the soil fertile or poor? Do trees grow on it or not? It is the season for the first ripe grapes. Do your best to bring back some of the fruit.' Moses looked at each man. 'Take your time, make a complete report, but try to come back within two months.' He lifted a hand in blessing. 'May YHWH protect you and guide you.'

Moses nodded at the men and left the tent.

Aaron looked at the gathering, his lips tight, as if trying to judge the hearts of each man. 'Take writing tools to make

maps and write down the information Moses requested . . .
YHWH be with you all,' he added before following his
brother.

'We are going to spy on the Canaanites,' Caleb said.

Joshua nodded. 'And if we are caught, they will kill us,'
he said.

The next morning, the men gathered on the edge of the
camp. The sun was peeking over the distant mountains,
promising another day of scorching heat. The wind blew
from the Great Sea and swirled the sand high into the air.

'It would be best for us to get as far as we can before the
evening,' Joshua said.

'Who are you to tell us what to do?' Palti sneered. A
short man, Palti made up for his lack of height with a sharp
tongue and critical spirit. 'Did Moses make you a leader
over us?'

'No, he did not,' Joshua said. 'But someone has to lead.
Do you wish to, Palti?'

Palti looked at the other men; none appeared to stand
with him. He hunched his shoulders.

'No,' he spat, 'I would not assume to take something that
was not given to me.'

'Neither would I,' Joshua answered, 'but neither am I
adverse to good advice. It will take us most of the morning to reach the summit of those mountains.' He pointed
to a range of mountains in the distance. 'If we do not
begin soon, we will find ourselves still in the desert by
midday.'

'Joshua speaks wisdom,' Caleb said. 'Let us get started; we can discuss plans later.'

'Good idea,' Igal laughed and started walking away from the camp.

The twelve men did not talk in the morning heat. Having grown up in the Egyptian desert, they knew the sun could sap a man's strength.

By midday, they had found a path through a gorge with red sandstone walls that towered above them. The whistling wind sounded as if it were the voices of the dead.

This was the wilderness of Zin. The only difference between it and the desert of Paran was that the wind blew away dirt and sand, leaving gravel.

The men were surprised to find caves in the side of the mountains. After inspecting several, they chose the largest one to make camp. They broke off branches from a small acacia tree for a fire; then they sat down to eat flatbread.

'I do not know what we are going to eat,' Palti complained. 'Moses said nothing about bringing more manna.'

'What should we do?' Shammua asked, shrugging his shoulders. 'YHWH sends only enough manna for each day.'

'Except on the day before the Sabbath,' Gaddiel added.

'Except then,' Shammua agreed. 'Then we gather twice as much.'

When the Hebrews first left Egypt, each morning, they would find a substance on the ground in the morning; manna – 'the bread of heaven' – Moses called it. It looked like coriander seed. The Hebrews gathered the manna, ground it and made bread that tasted like it was sweetened with honey. Moses instructed them to gather just enough for each day; whenever anyone tried to store extra, by morning it was rotten.

YHWH had commanded the Hebrews to rest on the Sabbath and, on the day before, they were to gather twice as much manna. Any manna gathered on that day did not rot when kept until morning.

'I brought the manna I gathered this morning,' Shaphat said, combing his beard with his fingers. 'I don't know what we will eat tomorrow.'

'I think that, while we are spying out the land, YHWH wants us to taste the food of Canaan,' Joshua said. 'So we can tell Moses if the food is good.'

'After eating manna for so long,' Caleb grinned, 'I'm not sure I'll know whether something tastes good or not.'

Everyone laughed, agreeing with him. After passing a water bag around, the men pulled out their blankets and laid down to rest.

When the sun rose, the men followed the edge of the mountain to a waterfall that fed into a small spring. The water was too brackish to drink, but felt cool for bathing. Near the spring, several pomegranate trees grew, covered with fat, heavy fruit. Breaking one open, the men sucked on the sweet, red seeds.

'If manna is the bread of heaven,' Gaddi laughed, his mouth stained from the fruit, 'then pomegranates must be the nectar of heaven.'

For several days, the spies walked across the Negev. One evening they entered a small village and stopped by the well. A young girl was drawing water to pour into a large pitcher.

'Greetings, child,' Joshua said.

'Greetings, sirs,' she replied.

'We are travellers from the land of Egypt. What is the name of this place?'

The child's eyes grew wide. 'This is Hebron . . . Are you truly from Egypt? Are there truly pyramids taller than mountains? Is Pharaoh as mighty as the Anakites?'

'Who are these . . . Anakites?'

The little girl looked around to make sure no one was nearby.

'The Anakites are giants!' she whispered. 'Taller than two men with one standing on the other's shoulders. They are fierce and will eat little children who do not do their work,' she said with a shiver. 'That is what my mother tells me. And my father said that Ahiman, Sheshai and Talmai, who are the sons of Anak, live nearby.

All the Hebrew men – except Palti – hid smiles behind their hands as Joshua listened intently to the little girl.

'They do sound fierce,' he said, 'much more fierce than Pharaoh. Is that not so, Caleb?'

'Oh . . . uh . . . yes,' Caleb said, and he frowned, furrowing his brow. 'Pharaoh is fierce, but he is not as tall as two men.'

'We will be sure to watch for these sons of Anak,' Joshua said.

After that the little girl balanced the pitcher on her shoulder, waved goodbye and left.

'This land is filled with giants!' Palti gasped. 'What are we going to do?'

'The land is not filled with giants,' Caleb answered.

'That girl's parents told her,' the little man insisted.

'She also said that these *giants* eat children who do not do their work,' Caleb replied. 'Just like our parents told us that the Nile gods would eat children who did not go to sleep.'

The other men laughed; but Palti folded his arms, frowning. 'You don't know that,' he was adamant. 'I will report these giants to Moses and the people.'

For many days, the spies journeyed across Canaan. Wherever they went, they would pretend to be from Egypt – 'Which we are,' Joshua pointed out – and discussed crops with the farmers, and animals with the shepherds.

In fortified cities, they counted their footsteps as they walked through the city gates, to determine the width of the walls.

In the crowded marketplaces, they split up into groups of two. They haggled with merchants over the price of melons or dates. As they handed over the coins for the fruit, the Hebrews commented that they should call the city guards to arrest the merchant for outrageous prices. Generally one of the merchants would shrug and comment that the guards were of no use in protecting the city.

After a month, the spies had reached Rehob in the north of the country and here they turned back. The full moon was rising when they reached the Valley of Eshcol and made camp for the evening.

Nahbi dropped his bag and sunk down into thick grass. 'This grass is as soft as Eden.'

'Mmmmm.' Ammiel sniffed the air. 'That smells like grapes.'

'Well, it's too late to look for them tonight,' Sethur yawned. 'We will look tomorrow.'

'What was that?' Palti said.

'What was what?' Shammua asked.

'Shhh . . .' Palti said. 'Listen!'

The men fell silent, listening. Over the night sky, Caleb heard . . .

'Footsteps,' Caleb said. 'You heard someone walking.'

'Large footsteps,' Palti said.

'Palti, don't mention giants again,' Joshua said, 'I'm going to sleep now.'

As the sunlight pinked the morning sky, the men woke up to find that their camp was in a lush valley. On three sides were hills; on the fourth side was a thick wood of acacia trees.

'I'm hungry! Ammiel, let's go and find those grapes you smelled last night,' Shammua shouted.

The men each grabbed a knife and an empty bag. They walked into the woods, while the other men began gathering their belongings and dousing the fire.

Suddenly a crashing sound came from the woods. As the sound grew louder, Joshua drew his knife; the other men did the same.

'Joshua! Caleb!'

Shammua and Ammiel stumbled from the wood, carrying a long pole from which dangled a gigantic cluster of . . .

'Grapes!' Gemalli cried, dropping his knife. 'Have you ever seen grapes as big as these?'

The other men gathered around the two men, plucking grapes the size of quail's eggs and popping them into their mouths.

'Where did you find these?' Igal asked, spitting grape juice.

Ammiel pointed. 'Beyond those woods,' he said. 'The vineyard is massive, stretching for miles.'

'And you should see the pomegranates and figs,' Shammua grinned.

'Figs?' Igal asked. 'I love figs! Show me where it is.'

'Come!' Ammiel gestured. 'Moses asked us to bring back some of the fruit of the land.'

Caleb and the other men followed Ammiel and Shammua, pushing through the brush growing under the trees. Stepping out of the woods, Caleb stumbled to a stop.

Gigantic grapevines surrounded them. Around the vineyard grew pomegranate and fig trees.

Joshua stared. 'These vines must be over twenty feet tall,' he said.

'Find the largest cluster of grapes and let's take it back to show Moses,' Caleb said excitedly.

The men walked through the vines. Igal and Shammua cut a cluster of grapes, while Caleb plucked several pomegranates and figs that were twice the size of any he had ever seen.

There was a sudden, fearful shout. Caleb turned to see Palti staring down between two grapevines. He ran over to where the small man stood, the blood draining from his face.

'What is it?' Caleb demanded.

Palti lifted a trembling hand to point at the ground. 'Look . . .' he stuttered.

Caleb looked down and saw . . .

'It's a footprint,' Palti shivered.

'It can't be,' Caleb said. 'It's too big. It would have to be the footprint of . . .'

'. . . a giant,' Nahbi whispered.

Gemalli's gasp echoed through the men.

'That little girl was telling the truth,' Palti said. 'The Anakites are real. I heard them last night.' He swept his hand out, indicating the vineyard. 'This must be their vineyard.'

'Palti is right!' Nahbi said.

'Let's go before they come and find us,' said Gaddiel.

He jumped up and ran through the woods, the rest of the Hebrews following. They grabbed their bags and started running.

'Don't forget the fruit!' Caleb said.

'Are you crazy?' Palti said. 'It'll just slow us down.'

'Moses asked us to bring back fruit,' Joshua said. 'We're going to take some back.'

'You can carry it,' said Palti, 'but don't expect me to help.'

The Hebrew spies raced through the land, stopping only when it was too dark to see where to place their feet.

Crossing the desert and mountains, it still took them almost a week to make it back to the Hebrew encampment.

The men's appearance – as well as the colossal fruit – drew the attention of many, who followed them to the tent where Moses and Aaron waited.

'Look at the grapes . . .' someone cried.

'The wine from one alone would fill an entire wineskin,' laughed another.

Moses studied the men's expressions. He lifted his hand, silencing the crowd's laughter.

'You have come back safely, YHWH be praised,' he said. 'Joshua, tell us what you saw.'

Joshua looked at Palti and the nine terrified men, and then looked at Caleb, who nodded.

'Canaan is everything the Creator promised,' he said. 'The land is bountiful, as you can see.'

'But there are giants,' Palti interrupted. 'Real giants. Anakites as big as two men and they eat children. We heard them walking and saw their footprints, didn't we?' he turned to the men standing near him. Igal and Shammua nodded in agreement. Palti continued, 'The people are powerful, and the cities are fortified and very large.'

A gasp ran through the crowd, a woman screamed.

Caleb waved his arms, yelling, 'Please, please listen! YHWH promised us that land. We should go up and take it, for we can certainly do it.'

'We can't attack those people,' Igal cried. 'They are stronger.'

'The land devours strangers,' Palti yelled. 'All the people we saw there are of great size. We seemed like grasshoppers compared to them.'

'Even the girl by the well, Palti?' Caleb asked.

Palti stopped, his mouth opened. He gulped, blushing.

'The land is cursed!' a woman yelled. 'If only we had died in Egypt.'

'Moses brought us here to kill us,' a man cried. 'Our children will be taken as plunder! Why did YHWH bring us to this land to die?'

'We should choose a leader and go back to Egypt,' a man cried.

'Palti!' Igal cried. 'It was he who warned us about the Anakites. He should be our leader . . . not Moses.'

In the midst of the crowd's accusations, Moses and Aaron had dropped to their knees, their faces to the ground.

Seeing the man chosen by YHWH with his face in the dirt was more than Caleb could stand. Grabbing the neck of his robe with both hands, he ripped it. He turned to see Joshua tearing at his clothes as well.

'The land we explored is amazing,' Caleb said. 'If YHWH is pleased with us, he will lead us into that land and will give it to us. Do not rebel against him.'

'Don't be afraid of the people of the land,' Joshua added. 'We will swallow them up. Their protection is gone, but the Creator is with us.'

For a moment, silence reigned over the crowd.

'Stone them!' someone yelled. The cry was echoed across the camp. 'Stone them! Stone them!'

Suddenly, the earth shuddered and groaned. A wall of mist encircled the camp as, over the Tent of Meeting, a light appeared that made the sun look dark. Its radiance burnt down as if it could see into the hearts of those gathered below.

Moses and Aaron knelt in prayer as a voice filled the land.

'How long will these people treat me with contempt?' The crowd fell stunned to the ground, dropping their heads to their knees. *'How long will they refuse to believe in me, in spite of all the miracles I have performed among them? I will strike them down with a plague and destroy them, but I will make you into a nation greater and stronger than they.'*

'O great Lord,' Moses rose to his knees, hands raised to the blinding light. 'If you destroy them, the Egyptians will find out. They will tell all the inhabitants of the land about it. If you kill these people, the nations who have heard about you will say, "Their God was not able to bring these people into the land He promised them; so He slaughtered them in the desert."'

The voice was silent, yet the earth still shook.

'YHWH is slow to anger, abounding in love and forgiving sin and rebellion. In accordance with Your great love, forgive the sins of these people, just as You have forgiven them from the time they left Egypt until now.'

'I have forgiven them, as you asked,' the voice echoed. *'Nevertheless, as surely as I live and as surely as My glory fills the whole earth, not one of the men who saw My glory and the miraculous signs I performed in Egypt and in the desert – not one of them will ever see the land I promised. No one who has treated Me with contempt will ever see it.*

'I will do to you the very things I heard you say. In this desert, you will die – every one of you twenty years old or more and who grumbled against Me. None of you will enter the land I promised you, except Caleb and Joshua. As for your children that you said would be taken as plunder, I will bring them in to enjoy the land you have rejected.

'For forty years – one year for each of the forty days the men explored the Promised Land – you will suffer for your sins and know what it is like to have Me against you. I have spoken, and I will surely do these things to this whole wicked community which has banded together against Me. They will meet their end in this desert; here they will die.'

All was then silent. The radiance from above had gone. The swirling dust of the desert beat against their faces and cut their skin. No one dare move, expecting to be cut down by the living God.

Moses lifted his head as the fog began to fade and the sun broke through the darkness.

'You have heard the Creator speak. Your lies and wickedness have been a curse to us. You doubted and for that will die in the desert and never inherit what was promised. Only Caleb and Joshua believed. They had faith.'

11

The Wall

'And YHWH kept His promise; not one of the people who did not believe Him lived,' the soothsayer said to the children who were listening wide-eyed at her feet.

'No one lived?' asked a frightened girl.

'No . . . Joshua and Caleb lived, for they believed,' the old woman said. 'But the rest of the people did not think that the Creator could do what He said. Even after seeing the many miracles, the waters of the Great Sea parting, the quail and manna that YHWH had sent every day and so many others . . . still they did not believe.'

A shadow crossed the campfire, silencing the crowd. Three men walked into the camp. The tallest carried a long staff that beat the ground as he walked.

'Joshua!' the children cried, running to him.

'Joshua, did you really see giants in the Promised Land?' a young girl asked.

Joshua stretched his hand over his head. 'They were so big that they blotted out the sun.'

A boy tugged on Joshua's sleeve. 'Joshua, did the waters of the Great Sea kill all the Egyptian army?'

'Every one of them drowned . . .' Joshua swept his hand from right to left. '. . .When the waters returned.'

'Joshua did not come here to teach your lessons.' The soothsayer wrapped a long tattered shawl around her shoulders.

Joshua watched the children for a moment, smiling.

'They are good children,' he turned to the old woman, 'and you have done well raising them to believe YHWH.'

She smiled.

'Listening to the stories of all the Almighty has done makes it easy for them to believe.'

Joshua's smile faded as he stared into the distance.

'I wish all people trusted the Almighty like children. It would have made entering the Promised Land easier.' He shook his head and focused again on the woman. 'Where is Eleazar, your husband?'

She pointed towards the hills and a gathering of tents.

'He is with the other priests at the Tent of Meeting.'

Joshua and his two companions walked towards the Tent of Meeting. He listened to the snatches of conversation from clusters of dust-covered people huddled around fires.

'They don't want to fight,' the older man with Joshua said.

'It is as if they expected God to hand them the land,' Joshua answered.

They were soon in the courtyard of the Tent of Meeting. Inside was a gathering of men, the tribal leaders. Some rested in the shade of the linen curtains that surrounded the courtyard. Others rocked back and forth on their knees as they spoke their prayers. They all stood when Joshua and his two companions arrived.

Joshua found the priests offering the morning sacrifice so he waited quietly until the priests had finished.

'Eleazar, I asked leaders from each tribe to come here so I could explain to you and to them what YHWH wants us to do next,' Joshua said.

'May His name be praised,' Eleazar lifted his hands.

'Amen,' the other priests chanted as if one.

'Amen,' Joshua repeated as he and the priests walked towards the group of men.

'Five days ago, I sent Mikal and Salmon to look over the Promised Land, especially Jericho. Jericho is a fortified city that controls the entrance to the hill country and a spring supplies it with fresh water. Mikal and Salmon returned this morning. I brought them here to tell you what happened.' Joshua gestured to two men standing with the tribal leaders to come forward. 'Tell the priests and leaders what you found.'

Mikal looked at those around him. His eyes met the stare of each man before he spoke. 'Salmon and I entered the city and went to the house of . . .' he paused, embarrassed.

'They went to the house of . . . a prostitute,' Joshua explained. 'They believed no one would question two strangers visiting there.'

'That was a wise decision,' Eleazar the priest said.

Mikal sighed in relief. 'The prostitute's name was Rahab,' he continued. 'She told us that the people of Jericho heard how the Creator had dried up the waters of the sea when Moses led the people out of Egypt. They know YHWH has given this land to us and she said everyone in the country is melting away because of us. Rahab hid us when the king of Jericho sent soldiers to find us; she sent them another way. We promised we would spare her life and her family.'

'How will we know which is the house of a prostitute?' one man asked.

'Rahab dropped a thick red cord from her window and we climbed down on that,' Salmon explained. 'We told her to mark her house by leaving the red cord in the window. When YHWH gives us the city of Jericho, we will spare all who are in her house.'

'This morning, I went out to a hill,' Joshua said. 'While I was looking over the city of Jericho, I turned around and there was a man standing near me; he was holding a sword.

'I drew my sword and asked him, "Are you for us or for our enemies?"'

'He replied, "Neither, but as commander of the army of YHWH I have come."'

The men listening to Joshua gasped.

'He was an angel?' a man asked.

Joshua nodded. 'I fell to the ground and asked him what message he had for me.'

'The commander of YHWH's army told me to take off my sandals, because I was standing on holy ground. I obeyed. He told me that YHWH had given Jericho – and her king and soldiers – into our hands.'

A wild cheer rose from the men listening to Joshua. Priests and leaders danced and clapped their hands.

'Then, the angel told me what we are to do.' Joshua said.

The men gaped as they listened to Joshua. When he finished, Eleazar said, 'Our fathers did not obey YHWH and they died in the desert. This time, we will obey.'

Each man took Joshua's instructions back to his tribe.

The next morning, all the fighting men gathered at the courtyard of the Tent of Meeting. Eleazar and the priests were there, with the Ark of the Covenant in front of them. The ark was a box made of acacia wood, overlaid with gold. On the lid were two angels facing each other, their wings touching. It shimmered in power and its presence touched the heart of any man; it was as if the power of YHWH rested within the ark. The ark was the throne of the Creator on earth. Within it were the two stone tablets inscribed with the Law YHWH gave to Moses. There was also Aaron's staff and a golden pot of manna. The ark was kept in the Most Holy Place in the Tent of Meeting and, whenever it was moved, priests carried it by means of two poles. Many would not stand near the ark – or touch it – for fear it would strike them dead.

Eleazar addressed the fighting men. 'Joshua has received YHWH's instructions for taking the city of Jericho. Listening to him is listening to YHWH. Obeying him is obeying YHWH.' He gestured for Joshua to come forward.

Joshua walked to the front of the men. 'YHWH told me to lead you to Jericho,' he said. 'An armed guard will go first. Seven priests with the trumpets made from rams' horns will come next. Behind them will come the priests carrying the Ark of the Covenant. The rest of the fighting men will follow the priests. We will march around the city of Jericho once. While we are marching, the priests will blow the trumpets, but no one is to speak a word.

'We will march around the city once a day for six days. On the seventh day, we will march around the city seven times. After the seventh time, the priests will blow a long blast on the trumpet; then you will give a loud shout. At that moment, YHWH will make the city walls collapse. We will climb the hill, go into Jericho, and take the city.'

As the crowd gasped, Eleazar stepped forward and lifted his hands. 'We will obey the word of YHWH!' he said. After a moment, they all nodded.

Joshua led the priests and fighting men across the plain to Jericho. The city stood before them behind high, stone walls on the top of a hill. Two walls surrounded the city; the outer wall was six feet thick and the inner wall was twelve feet thick. Guards stood atop the outer wall, their weapons glinting in the sunlight.

Joshua faced the Hebrews, lifted a finger to his mouth. He then turned and began to march around Jericho.

At first, there was no sound from the city. As they marched, Joshua glanced up at the city walls; more guards had gathered, he could see them pointing. Some appeared to be laughing.

It doesn't matter if they laugh at us, Joshua thought. *YHWH has promised Jericho to us.*

It took less than an hour to march around the city. Then Joshua led the Hebrews back to their camp at Gilgal.

The next day, Joshua reminded the Hebrews to be silent and then led them back to Jericho. There were twice as many guards on the city walls as there had been the day before. As the Hebrews marched around the city, the guards began laughing, calling down curses and taunting them.

'Are you lost or too crazy to know where you are going?'

'Is this the army we were frightened of?'

'Do you think to scare us away with horns and a fancy box?'

'We heard that your god destroyed the army of Egypt. That must have been a lie . . . or is your god a lie?'

The taunts continued as the Hebrews marched around the city and lingered on the breeze as they marched away.

Again, the army of Joshua marched on the third and fourth day. The guards' laughter and taunts increased. On the fifth day, the guards on the city walls began calling down threats.

'Go away, you fools! You're wasting our time!'

'If you don't leave, you'll regret it.'

On the sixth day, they marched again. All were silent, as Joshua had commanded.

On the seventh morning, Joshua faced the men.

'For the last six days, you have obeyed YHWH and marched around the city without saying a word, no matter what the guards on the city walls said. Today we walk around Jericho seven times,' Joshua said. 'After the seventh time, the priests will blow their trumpets. Then all of you – everyone – shout as loud as you can . . . call upon YHWH. The walls of the city will fall. Kill everything that breathes, except Rahab the prostitute and everyone in her house. Everything is dedicated to the Almighty; destroy it all – except the silver, gold, and anything made from bronze or iron; they are sacred to the Almighty.'

A shudder of excitement surged through the men. The walls of Jericho were tall and strong; no one doubted they would fall. Their feet beat in time as they marched around the city time after time after time.

More guards had gathered on the walls, screaming, taunting, throwing rocks, bricks and debris. By the seventh time, the tops of the ramparts were packed with soldiers. The army of Joshua marched on. Like a low rumble of thunder, the ground shuddered beneath their feet.

As the Hebrews marched around to the city gates, Joshua lifted his sword to the sky.

'SHOUT . . . For YHWH has given you the city!'

The Hebrews shouted as the priests blew a long, low blast on the trumpets. Louder and louder . . . stronger and stronger. . . the trumpets blared as the shouting increased. After the last shout died away, a silence settled over Jericho. The city was unmoved.

'Hey!' cried a guard on the wall, laughing. 'Is that it? You've walked all this time for . . . what?'

Joshua pointed his sword at the laughing man. He felt something. Looking down, he noticed gravel shifting near his feet. He shifted as he felt a tremor. Rocks began rolling; the ground in front of him – at the base of the walls – began pitching, shifting. While he watched, a chasm split the earth in front of the city gates and began running around the base of the walls. Joshua braced himself as the walls swayed as if shaken by a violent hand.

With a roar, the inner and outer walls of Jericho crumbled, guards screaming as they were thrown from its heights; dust billowed out from the city in waves. Stones, rocks and timber crashed to the ground. Men screamed as the deluge of rock consumed them.

The Hebrews shouted, waving swords and spears, as they ran up the hill, over the fallen walls, killing any guard that had survived. They searched the city as they fought street by street. The people ran. Some tried to hide. The Hebrews obeyed YHWH, killing everything that breathed: all the people and all the animals.

The two spies found Rahab's house with the red cord hanging from the window. Everyone in the house was spared.

The Hebrews ransacked the city. They carried off all the items of gold, silver, bronze and iron – everything that was sacred to the Almighty – and burnt everything else.

As the city of Jericho burnt, Joshua spoke: 'YHWH will curse anyone who tries to rebuild Jericho. At the cost of his firstborn son will he lay its foundations; at the cost of his youngest will he set up its gates.'

Turning to the Hebrews, Joshua cried, 'Today, you obeyed the Almighty. Our forefathers did not obey Him and died in the wilderness. You obeyed the Almighty and He fought for you! Our God is God! Praise be to the Creator'

As the Hebrews raised their swords and spears, shouting, 'Our God is God!' Joshua turned back to look at the burning city and wondered at all that he had seen that day.

12

The Fleece

It had been seven long years since the plague of the Midianite invaders had descended on the once bountiful Valley of Jezreel. Just as the sun set on another hard day, Gideon looked out over the valley and watched the dust of the invaders' horses as they rode west. The young man stood up straight and brushed back his long, black hair from his weather-beaten face. Gideon could not understand how his home had been conquered so swiftly. The town of Ophrah in Jezreel was swept away just the same as every dwelling place in the whole of Israel.

Like wolves that prowled on the slopes of Mount Moreh, the enemy soldiers didn't fight in battle like other invaders. They waited until the growing season – when the Israelites were planting and growing their crops – and then descended like locusts destroying the harvest. They broke down barns and storehouses, destroyed crops ready for harvest and burnt the seed. The hordes of soldiers laid waste to the countryside and the towns, and left starving people in their wake.

They mocked the people of the Valley of Jezreel.

'You have no seed – your god has abandoned you – how will you eat?' they sneered as they pillaged the towns. When the invaders departed, they took all the oxen, sheep and beasts of burden back to the land of Midian.

Year in and year out it was always the same. But the people of Ophrah in Jezreel would not give up. By the town well, inside the city gates, from house to house and door to door, they talked and schemed of how to overcome the Midianites.

'Why is this happening to us?

'Someone should do something.'

'But who? Ophrah is just a tiny town belonging to one of the smallest tribes in all of Israel. Even if we convinced the other tribes to join us, Israel doesn't have a king like the nations around us.'

'I heard a prophet say that God sent the Midianites to punish Israel for building altars and idols to Baal and Asherah.'

'If God is against us, we're doomed.'

'Which god? The God of our fathers or the gods of the Midianites?

'None of the gods are protecting us; we must do something.'

'What can we do? We're farmers, not soldiers.'

'How can we be farmers without seed to plant?'

'Does anyone have seed left?'

'The Midianites can't have destroyed *all* the seed.'

The talking went on late into the night. Even as the sun rose, the people still did not have an answer.

'All is lost – let us just give in to them and die a broken people,' one man shouted in his hunger.

Yet, despite their brokenness, the people of Ophrah carried on. They shared what they had. Every time a farmer had a bag of hidden seed, they divided it equally and everyone went home to plant. And to hope – until the Midianites descended again.

Gideon and his father, Joash, planted the last of their wheat. As the weeks went by, they cared for the crop, pulling weeds and carrying pots of water when the rain didn't come. They prayed every day that God would protect the grain He had given them from pestilence, disease and the Midianites.

The grain grew tall and golden.

'Soon,' his father told his family, 'we'll be able to harvest the grain.'

Two days later, Joash left their home at dawn to check the crop. 'Hurry with your meal, Gideon,' Joash laughed, 'we might be able to harvest the wheat today.'

Gideon could feel his father's excitement; the Midianites weren't going to get this harvest. Stuffing the piece of flatbread into his mouth, Gideon grabbed the sickles used to harvest grain. As he left the house, movement stopped him.

'Midianites!' his mother hissed.

The enemy soldiers swept through the fields on camels. They were like a wall of destruction, hacking the wheat with their swords, watching it scatter on the wind, and laughing as the beasts trampled the golden grain into the dry earth.

Gideon saw his father in the midst of the field, trying to stop the Midianites, unmindful of the massive animals. Without a thought, he dropped the sickles and ran towards the field. He saw Joash grab at one beast and then another, begging the soldiers to stop.

'Please leave us alone. Have you not destroyed enough of our crops? What more do you want?' his father cried.

A brawny soldier pulled harshly on his reins, stopping the camel in front of the elderly man.

'I'll tell you what we want, old man . . .' The Midianite leaned over and slapped Joash's head with the broad side of the sword. 'We want all your kind to die!'

'Father . . .' Gideon screamed, running to him through the wheat as the old man crumpled. Blood oozed from Joash's ear, covering Gideon as he lifted his father and held him close. Joash moaned, lifting a trembling hand to his head.

The soldier was unmoved at the sight of the elderly man bleeding in the arms of his son.

'Hey, you dog of Jezreel,' he laughed. 'Give everyone a message from Midian . . . Keep planting and we'll keep coming back.' Cutting down the last standing stalk of wheat, he and the other soldiers rode off.

Gideon carried his father home. His mother bandaged Joash's wound. The next day, while his father rested, Gideon crawled through the ravaged wheatfield, gleaning through the mud to find any grains that had escaped the camels' broad flat feet. As the sun burnt down, Gideon harvested several bagfuls from the dirt. It was not enough to feed the family through the winter but, if something didn't happen soon, the Midianites would see that they didn't live until spring.

After a week, his father felt strong enough to leave the house. He and Joash carried the wheat Gideon had found to the old winepress, a series of vats carved into the side of a hill, behind a massive oak tree.

'Here we are shielded from view,' Joash told Gideon. 'We can thresh our wheat without anyone seeing us.'

They threw the wheat into the lowest press and picking up flails – long jointed sticks – began beating the wheat. Threshing time was supposed to be joyful; the harvest was in, and there would be laughter and celebration. Today, there was no laughter or celebration. Joash and Gideon toiled like slaves with fettered feet and broken hearts.

The winepress was much smaller than the threshing floor and the men didn't need oxen to thresh the small amount of wheat.

Even if we did need oxen, Gideon thought, *the Midianites have stolen them and our donkey.* He beat the wheat harder. *We'll have to till the ground without our farm animals.* He beat harder. *They destroyed our food.* Harder. *And beat my father.* 'You Midianite dogs!' Gideon growled, beating the wheat with his stick. 'Touch my father again and I'll . . .'

'Shhhh . . .' Joash warned, putting a finger to his lips. 'Do you want to lose this wheat, too?'

'I'm sorry, Father,' Gideon sighed. 'I still get mad when I think of those dogs destroying our grain, stealing our animals and beating you. That fat oaf could have killed you.'

'But he didn't. God protected me.'

'God?' Gideon threw down his flail. 'God didn't protect you from being beaten. God didn't protect our wheat and our animals. Why is He allowing those soldiers to starve us? Why, Father?'

Joash put a hand on Gideon's shoulder. 'I don't know, Gideon. Maybe the prophet is right; maybe we have done evil and God is punishing us. But I don't believe we are doomed. YHWH will deliver us from our enemies. Come, let us take the grain to your mother. Perhaps we can persuade her to make honey cakes in celebration of the harvest.'

His father climbed out of the winepress, carrying the bag of kernels as if they were gold. Joash walked on, leaving Gideon alone.

Some harvest, Gideon thought. *A single bag of grain.* The young man sat down on the edge of the winepress and dropped his head into his hands. He felt as beaten as the wheat.

'The Lord is with you, mighty warrior.'

Gideon jumped up, his heart pounding. A man sat on the other side of the winepress. He was taller than anyone Gideon knew, with curly hair and beard, and dark, penetrating eyes. He was not a Midianite or from Jezreel. Gideon didn't want to take chances; he might be the prophet spoken of in the town.

'If the Creator is with us, why are we having so many troubles?' Gideon asked. 'We have all heard the stories about the miracles He did for our ancestors. But He has abandoned us to the Midianites.'

'You have the strength to save the people of Jezreel from the Midianite soldiers,' the man said. *'Go . . . I am the one who is sending you.'*

'You sound like a prophet,' Gideon said, 'but you don't know me. How can I save Jezreel or Israel? My family is the smallest in the whole tribe of Manasseh and I am the least important person in my family. I am not much older than a boy.'

The stranger's stare was uncomfortable, as if he could see through Gideon to what he was really thinking.

'I will be with you.' The stranger's voice softened.

'If you are pleased with me,' said Gideon, 'give me proof. Please wait and let me bring an offering.'

The stranger smiled. *'I will wait.'*

Gideon bowed. 'Soon I will return.'

He could feel the stranger's gaze as he began running. When he got back to his home, it was empty. *Good,* he thought, *I don't know how I would explain this stranger to Mother and Father.* Looking around he thought out loud. 'What do you offer to the Lord? The only thing of value we have is our food.' The meat was boiling in a pot over the fire outside. Covering the fire was the flat stone with some freshly baked bread. Gideon wrapped the warm bread in a cloth, grabbed the pot with the meat and carried it back to the winepress.

The stranger was still there and smiled as Gideon walked towards him and bowed. 'I have brought a meal for you. It was all we had.'

The stranger pointed to a flat rock near the winepress. *'Put the meat and bread on the rock.'*

Gideon carried the pot over and put it down next to the rock. He placed the cloth on top of the rock and unwrapped the bread. His mouth watered from the smell of the food as he lifted the meat from the pot and put it next to the bread.

As Gideon turned towards him, the stranger pointed to the pot. *'Pour the broth over the meat and bread.'*

Gideon hesitated, staring at the stranger, who continued to smile. *Is he mad? That would ruin the food.* . . Picking the pot up, he poured out the broth. The cloth was soaked and the bread bloated; even the meat no longer looked appetizing.

When Gideon turned around, he jumped back in surprise, stumbled over the pot and fell down. The stranger was standing next to him, holding a long stick. Reaching over Gideon, the stranger touched the sodden food with the staff.

The food exploded. In the twinkling of an eye, the meat and bread had become an inferno. Thick acrid flames shot up from the rock. Gideon fell back, his mouth open in shock. He stared as the fire consumed the wet food and cloth. Turning his face away from the scorching heat, he saw the stranger standing with his eyes closed, breathing deeply of the smoke. The stranger opened his eyes, looked at Gideon, and then . . . vanished.

Terrified, Gideon lost his balance and collapsed. He rolled in the dust. 'I'm done for!' he shouted, scrambling onto his knees and bowed, his head touching the ground. 'YHWH! Have mercy on me. I have seen your face.'

A voice came from the crackling fire. *'Calm down.'* It was the stranger's – *YHWH's* – voice. *'You will not die.'*

Gideon stayed on his knees until the flames died down. Struggling to his feet, he picked up more rocks and laid them on top of the scorched rock. *I must build an altar,* he thought. *When a man meets the Creator face to face, it has to be done.* He didn't know how he was going to explain what he had seen.

That night Gideon was tormented by dreams and questions. *Was it real? Maybe I fell asleep and dreamed everything. Maybe I'm going . . . Maybe I'm . . .*

'Gideon.'

The young man shot up in bed. 'Who's there?'

'Gideon.' The room pulsed with the Creator's voice. *'Pull down your father's altar to Baal and the idol to Asherah that is next to it. Build an altar to YHWH and use the wood from the idol to sacrifice two bulls on the altar.'*

The echoes were still reverberating as Gideon threw back the bedcovers and felt around for his sandals. He put on his cloak and secretly went out into the darkness . . .

The next morning, just as Gideon was explaining to his parents what he had done, the door shook as fists pounded against it.

Gideon's mother screamed, 'The Midianites have come back!' She ran to hide behind her husband, pulling her shawl over her face.

'Would Midianites knock?' Joash crossed to the door and opened it.

A crowd of screaming villagers stood before the house, some were shaking their fists, others waving sickles.

'What is the meaning of this?' Joash demanded.

'Your son Gideon was seen pulling down the altar to Baal and Asherah's idol,' cried one man. 'He must die.' The crowd yelled their agreement.

Joash waved his hands to get their attention. 'Gideon told me YHWH commanded him to destroy the altar and idols,' he said. 'If Baal is a god, let him fight for himself. If nothing happens, we'll know which god is stronger.'

The crowd looked at each other. One man shrugged his shoulders. 'Joash is right, why do we fight for a foreign god?' he said.

'If Baal is real, let him strike Gideon,' said another. 'I don't want to fight against a god.'

'Who knows,' laughed the first, 'maybe YHWH will use Gideon to strike down our enemies.'

Three days later, Gideon's father woke him. He sat up, rubbing his eyes. 'Why do you wake me at such an early hour?' he asked.

'The men from the village are here.'

Gideon threw on his outer robe and went to the door.

The men from Ophrah in Jezreel were gathered outside. When they saw Gideon they said, 'Gideon! We heard that the Midianites are joining with the Amalekites – and other tribes from the east – to attack us. What can we do?'

Gideon didn't hesitate. 'We'll fight them.'

'Who will lead?'

'I will lead. This is what YHWH called me to do. I do not fear the Midianite gods; why should I fear the Midianites?'

'That's right. Gideon stood against Baal and Baal did nothing.'

'Gideon can lead us.'

'Assemble all the men of the tribe,' Gideon said. 'We prepare for war.'

It was as if the Spirit of the Creator moved amongst the Hebrews. Broken men stood tall and strong, fear ebbing away. 'With the Almighty and Gideon,' they shouted, 'we will defeat the Midianite dogs and drive them from our land.'

As Gideon watched them leave, the thought of what he'd said washed over him. 'I'm going to lead men into battle? How, Lord?' Gideon grabbed the fleece his mother kept by the door, threw it around his shoulders and left the house. 'What did I just agree to? YHWH, you called me a mighty warrior and said I would save my people, but you didn't tell me how.'

When Gideon looked up, he was near the threshing floor. Rocks encircled the flat surface; someone had left an old bowl near the edge of the threshing floor. *Threshing . . . the last time God talked to me, I had been threshing . . .* As Gideon dropped to his knees, the morning dew standing on the rock-hard surface soaked the hem of his robe. 'Lord God,' he cried out. 'You told me I was to save my people, but is this the time?'

There was silence.

'How do I know, Lord? Please tell me. Give me a sign.'

All Gideon could hear was the wind howling eerily through the rocks. It grew louder and louder until, without warning, the strong wind blew over Gideon, knocking the fleece from his shoulders. Gideon watched as the wool soaked up the morning dew on the ground.

'Lord God,' Gideon lifted the fleece to the sky. 'You said you would help me save Israel. I will put this fleece on the threshing floor tonight. In the morning, if there is dew only on the wool and not on the ground, then I will know what you told me is true.'

Gideon spread out the fleece in the middle of the threshing floor and placed rocks on the corners to hold it in place.

The sun was a sliver over the horizon when Gideon arrived at the threshing floor the next morning. He took off his sandals and stepped past the rock circle . . . onto dry ground. There was not one drop of dew anywhere on the ground. Walking to the centre of the circle, he reached out with a trembling hand to grasp the fleece.

It was wet. Soaking wet. Gideon was certain. He ran, grabbed the abandoned bowl and carried it back to the centre of the floor. Kneeling down, Gideon picked up the fleece and twisted it over the bowl, squeezing out the water. He kept twisting and wringing, filling the bowl, until no more water dripped from the wool.

Gideon dropped his head. 'YHWH, don't be angry with me. Let me make one more test. I will leave the fleece on the threshing floor again. If you want me to lead my people against the Midianites, let the fleece be dry while the ground is wet.'

He placed the fleece back on the ground and went home.

The next morning, Gideon left the house even earlier. He slowed down as he neared the threshing floor.

Taking a deep breath, he lifted a foot, stepped over the rock wall . . . and sank into mud. Laughing, he tugged on his knee to free his foot from the sucking ooze and stumbled towards the fleece. He knew what he would find.

Within a matter of days, all the fighting men from Jezreel to Megiddo had gathered. When the count was finished, there were thirty-two thousand men. They set up their camp on the slopes of Mount Gilead, near the spring of Harod. The tents were garlanded with flags, and fires burnt brightly well into the night.

To the north, the Midianites were encamped in the valley at the bottom of Mount Moreh. Their spies looked down from the mountain, ready to give warning should Gideon's army attack.

It was before sunrise that Gideon climbed Mount Gilead with Ja-ar, one of his captains, to look over the camp. The sight of so many men was amazing. From horizon to horizon, the camp stretched out as if it filled the whole land.

'Look at them, Gideon,' Ja-ar said as he swept his hand to indicate the vastness of their camp. 'With such a company of men, we will wipe out the Midianites.'

'It's too many,' a still, small voice whispered across the mountaintop.

Gideon didn't need to look at Ja-ar to know he alone had heard the voice. 'YHWH, what do you mean?' he prayed.

'You have too many men to defeat the Midianites. I don't want the Israelites to brag that they saved themselves. Tell the men that any man who is afraid may leave.'

Gideon didn't hesitate. 'Ja-ar, tell the men, "Whoever is afraid may leave."'

Ja-ar stared. 'What?'

'You heard me. Go and tell them.' Gideon smiled as Ja-ar left, still shaking his head.

Two hours later, Ja-ar climbed back up the mountain, 'I did as you commanded. Thousands of men were fearful and went home; we have ten thousand left.'

Gideon smiled, 'It's still a good number.' He looked at Ja-ar for a moment and then said, 'Tell the men to meet me by the spring.'

Ja-ar again went down the mountainside, while Gideon followed at a slower pace. By the time Gideon reached the path that led to the spring, the men were gathered, some carried spears and swords; others carried bows and had quivers of arrows laced to their backs. Ja-ar walked over to stand by Gideon.

'Do we fight now, Gideon?' one called out.

'Let us fight before we die of old age,' laughed another.

Gideon looked over the men. 'Ja-ar, tell the men to drink of water from the spring.'

Ja-ar stared at Gideon, but didn't question him in front of the men.

'Men,' he called, 'get a drink of water from the spring.'

The men looked at each other. One man shrugged and shifted his spear from his right hand to his left and reached down to the spring. He scooped up a handful of spring water and drank, lapping the water like a dog. Looking around, he nodded to the others.

It took time for all the ten thousand men to get a drink. Some knelt like the first man, while more dropped to their stomach and stuck their mouth in the cool spring to drink.

'Ja-ar.'

'Yes, Gideon?'

'Separate the men. Tell the ones who lapped the water like dogs to stand on one side and the ones who knelt to drink on the other. Then count them.'

Ja-ar stared at him for a moment and then shrugged. 'If that is what you want . . .' he answered.

A while later, Ja-ar returned to tell Gideon, 'Three hundred men lapped the water like a dog; all the rest knelt down to drink.'

'Tell the second group to go home.'

'What?' Ja-ar gasped. 'Send over nine thousand men home? How will we overcome the Midianites?'

Gideon looked at his captain. 'Ja-ar, YHWH told me that with these three hundred men, he would allow us to destroy the Midianites.'

Ja-ar looked at the men near the stream. 'Gideon, I don't doubt that you've heard from YHWH,' he whispered. 'I just don't know how you're going to convince the men that are left after today.'

It took hours for the nine thousand men to leave. Gideon stood at the opening of his tent watching them pack their weapons, stop to speak to comrades, nod good-bye to Ja-ar. None of them looked at Gideon; not the ones who were leaving, or the ones staying.

'They are afraid, YHWH,' Gideon whispered. 'Maybe I am too.'

A sudden wind blew around Gideon's tent. If anyone had looked at him at that moment, they would have seen him cock his head as if listening. He nodded his head and called for his personal servant, Purah.

Gideon waited until every man was asleep before he and his servant slipped out of the camp. Within an hour, Purah and Gideon came running back, elated.

'Get up!' Gideon's cry woke the camp. 'YHWH has defeated the army of Midian for you!'

The men gathered around him.

'What do you mean?' Ja-ar asked, rubbing sleep from his eyes while strapping the buckle on his chest plate.

'We are all afraid of facing the Midianites with just three hundred men,' Gideon said. 'So YHWH told me to take Purah and go to the edge of the Midianite camp. He said what we heard would convince us to not be afraid.

'When Purah and I got to the camp, we could see it was a huge fighting force. It looked like a swarm of locusts.

'Two guards walked our way. We heard one man say, "I had a dream about a giant barley loaf. It rolled into the Midian camp and hit the tents, flattening them."

'Then the other man said, "Your dream is about the sword of Gideon the son of Joash." And then Purah said, "God will let Gideon defeat Midian and the whole army."

'You wanted to know when we were going to attack the Midianites?' Gideon asked. 'Now. Each man, get a trumpet and a jar with a burning torch inside. Here's what we are going to do.'

Covered by the still, dark night, three groups of soldiers surrounded the Midianites' camp on all sides. When Ja-ar brought Gideon word that the men were ready, Gideon whispered, 'Remember, do what I do.'

Standing up, he blew his trumpet, broke the jar and shouted, 'A sword for YHWH and for Gideon!'

From all sides of the Midian camp, hundreds of trumpets sounded. The warriors smashed their jars against the rocks and shouted, 'A sword for YHWH and for Gideon!'

In the light of the torch flames, it looked as if winged creatures swept over the encampment lashing out at the invaders.

Confusion, shock and horror reigned inside the Midian camp. The warriors looked up to the sky and fell to their knees, screaming in fear.

'The army of Gideon!'

'We're damned.'

'We cannot fight against their god.'

'What creatures come upon us?'

In the dark, no one could tell friend from foe. Drawing their swords, many Midianites began fighting each other; others fled on camel or on foot.

'Ja-ar,' Gideon shouted. 'Send messengers on horseback to the nine thousand men who were sent home. Tell them to take control of the Jordan River before the Midianites can get there. We will drive the enemy towards them and crush these Midianite dogs between us.'

Gideon lifted his sword, the blade glinting in the torchlight. He looked to the heavens and the full moon that broke through the clouds over the mountains.

'Remember this day,' he shouted to his men, 'and follow me. For YHWH!'

'For YHWH,' the warriors echoed, drawing their swords, 'and for Gideon!'

13

The Strongman

As he walked through the narrow avenues of market stalls in the city square, the mob parted as if he were a gigantic ship bearing through the sea. The man lumbered like a behemoth across the ground. He was taller than everyone who looked at him. His arms rippled with muscles that appeared to be carved in the skin and hewn from stone. Everything about him was god-like. Thick black ringlets brushed his chiselled jaw and fell well below broad shoulders.

'Is there anything I can tempt you with, Samson?' a merchant called.

'I have seen it all before,' the man replied, his voice deep and harsh.

'I heard you killed a lion with your bare hands,' the man said.

'Ripped it in two,' Samson answered, holding out his hands, 'and then killed thirty dirty Philistines just for the shirts on their backs.'

The man looked around and then whispered, 'Then I will toast you with wine. Tell me – is it too strong for you to drink?'

'I am a Nazarite. One of our vows is no drink,' Samson answered as he walked away. 'Even if I did drink, the smell of Philistines makes me want to be sick.'

Samson ignored the people glaring at him, some with disdain and others in fear. They had all heard the story of how an angel had foretold his birth. That an Israelite child would grow to be the curse of the world and bring fear to the hearts of the Philistines. With every passing year, the legend of Samson grew, spoken in whispers. He had killed a thousand soldiers, beating them to death with the jawbone of a donkey. Many had tried to kill him, but no way could be found. It was as if he had no weakness, no brokenness and no vice. Yet, as this man-monster walked through the marketplace, mischievous eyes followed his every step.

Without warning, a woman who had been watching him stepped out from behind a stone roof pillar. Samson saw her across the marketplace. Her face was the hue of peaches, with emerald-coloured, almond-shaped eyes, and the long curls that escaped her headcloth were the blueblack of a raven's wing. If her face was beautiful, her curvaceous figure – clad in a cream robe that suggested more than it revealed – was enough to make his heart pound. She was laughing with the merchant who was trying to sell her a gold necklace; her voice was low-pitched and hypnotic.

Samson looked at her quite beguiled. It was as if she had charmed him with a spell – he had to meet her.

Striding over to the merchant's booth, Samson reached into the pouch at his waist, pulled out a heavy bag of coins, and dropped it on top of the jewellery.

'The lady will take it,' he said.

She turned to look at him, arching a delicate eyebrow.

'Sir, I do not know you,' her smile was slow and intimate. 'It would be wrong for me to accept a gift from you.'

Samson picked up the necklace. 'It would be wrong for anyone else to wear it. Only you could do it justice.'

'It is fit for a princess,' the merchant jumped in. 'It is made from beaten gold and inlaid with moonstones.'

Samson looked at the woman. 'Not a princess,' he said, 'but a goddess . . . a goddess of the night.'

The woman threw her head back and laughed, drawing the eyes of many in the marketplace. 'You, sir,' she smiled, 'have the tongue of a serpent . . . smooth and quick. I will accept the necklace, then.'

The merchant snatched up the bag of coins, wrapped up the necklace in a cloth and handed it to Samson with a bow.

Samson extended the necklace to the woman but when she reached for it, he pulled it away. 'First, I must know your name,' he said.

She smiled as she looked at him, her eyes following his muscular contours.

'Not here,' she said in a low voice, 'follow me to the brook of Sorek.'

'Why such a place? It is barren – there are no people,' Samson asked as the woman walked away.

'If you want to know me then I will see you there.'

In an instant, she was lost in the crowd of people. He looked all around, but could not see her.

'Beautiful lady, where are you?' Samson shouted.

A man stepped from the shadows. He was wrapped in a tight shawl, his face covered against the dust of the desert.

'I saw her leave the market and take the path to Sorek – perhaps you will find her there,' he said, his hand extended for a coin.

Samson sneered at him as he pushed him from his path.

'Sorek, the place of fruitless trees,' he whispered. 'The woman plays games with me.'

Within the hour, Samson sat by a small stream that fell over stones to the pool below. All around him was the orchard of trees that never gave fruit. Hanging in the branches of the fig tree was an old serpent slowly shedding its skin.

'You followed me,' the woman touched his shoulder.

'As you commanded me,' Samson answered without turning. 'If I came here, you would give me your name.'

'If you know my name, you have power over me,' the woman said, tracing his jaw with her fingernails.

'A promise is a promise,' he answered.

She studied him for a moment and then smiled. 'Delilah.'

Samson handed her the necklace and asked, 'Do you live here, Delilah?'

Delilah put the wrapped necklace in the basket she carried. 'I have always lived here in the Valley of Sorek.'

'Are you engaged or married?' he asked.

She laughed. 'Should you not have asked that before offering me such an expensive gift?' she asked. 'My husband might have been jealous enough to kill you.'

Samson laughed too, flexing a massive bicep. 'No man is strong enough to kill me.'

She smiled. 'Ahhh, as modest as he is strong . . . but although you have not told me your name, I know you are Samson. What man has such confidence in his strength . . . or such long hair?'

'You are right,' he responded. 'I am Samson.' When she turned away, he grabbed her hand. 'Delilah, I would see you again.'

She looked down at his hand, her eyebrow arching, and then up at him, frowning. 'Do you believe that because you gave me a necklace, you have the right to request such a thing from me?'

'Not because I gave you the necklace,' he said, 'but because I gave you my heart.'

His comment obviously surprised her; she stepped back, her eyes widening. She stared at him; he felt as if her eyes plumbed the depths of his soul. *A man could drown in those eyes*, he thought. Finally, she nodded. 'You are as bold as you are strong, Samson,' she said. 'I like both in a man. You may call at my house.'

'Today,' he insisted.

'Tomorrow,' she replied, 'for the evening meal.' She gave him directions to her home and then left.

'Tomorrow,' Samson whispered, placing his hands on his head. 'How shall I fill the hours until then?'

He walked the few miles from Sorek to his home. Walking through the door, he called for a servant to prepare a bath.

'A bath, my son?' Samson's mother entered from a back room. Even though the wife of a wealthy man, his mother dressed simply and often worked alongside their servants to ensure their home was clean and the food prepared the way her husband and son liked. 'Although a mother is not going to complain when her son wishes to bathe,' she smiled as she embraced him, 'I would like to know what causes you to desire a bath today? Sabbath is not for several days.'

'I met a woman today,' Samson replied.

'Ahhh . . .' she smiled, 'that does not surprise me. When your father first met me, he bathed so often, he said his skin wrinkled. Who is she? Is it Merada, the daughter of Lamech and Tabitha?'

'No, Mother,' he replied. 'Her name is Delilah.'

His mother's brow furrowed. 'Delilah, Delilah . . . I do not remember her.' She smiled, 'I must be growing old.'

'You are not growing old,' Samson kissed his mother's forehead. 'You do not remember her, because you do not know her. I met her today in the marketplace. She lives in the Valley of Sorek.'

His mother's smile disappeared. 'Samson, she is not one of our people.'

Samson frowned. 'My wife was not one of our people.'

'Your father and I were wrong to agree to that marriage,' his mother said. 'Moses' law states that we must marry one of our own.'

'You must have been relieved then, when she died.'

'Samson!' Tears glistened his mother's eyes. 'How can you say that? I wept when she died. I was hoping that, after marrying a foreigner, you would marry a Hebrew girl.'

Samson wiped his mother's eyes with the edge of her head cloth. 'Forgive me. I did not mean to make you cry. You and Father have never denied me anything, even when it hurt you. But do not worry about me this time,' Samson grinned. 'No one said anything about marriage.'

The sun was shimmering over the edge of the horizon, the night stars peeking in the darkening sky when Samson arrived at Delilah's house the next evening. He dusted his robe, smoothed his hair; satisfied, he knocked on the door.

A servant answered and showed him to an inner court-yard.

'Wait here,' she bowed. 'My mistress will join you soon.'

While he waited, Samson looked around. Delilah's home was arranged on four sides of the courtyard where a garden of lush plants grew. Lamps flickered here and there, illuminating the water in a fountain.

'Do you approve of my garden?'

Samson turned to see Delilah standing in the doorway. She was clad in a simple robe, a thick braid of hair pulled forward over her shoulder was brushing the golden neck-lace he had given her.

'It is beautiful,' he walked to her and took her hand, 'but it cannot match the beauty standing in front of me.'

She smiled. 'That serpent's tongue. I must watch out, lest I am bitten.'

'I would never hurt you.'

'Never say, "Never."' She removed her hand to lead Samson to a table in the centre of the garden. 'I like to dine here in the evenings,' she explained. 'The night air is cool.'

The table was laden with bread, cheeses, fruits, olives and almonds. Delilah lifted a narrow amphora from a bowl filled with cool water. 'Do you drink Egyptian wine?' she asked.

'My family does not drink wine,' Samson replied. 'But tonight is a night for . . . enjoying new tastes.'

Delilah smiled and poured dark wine into two goblets. Handing one to Samson, she took a sip from her own. 'Then try it and tell me what you think . . . of my wine.'

Samson tilted the cup and emptied it in one swallow. He gasped and sputtered as the wine burnt its way to his stomach. 'It tastes like fire!'

Delilah laughed. 'You do not drink wine as you would water, Samson.' She refilled his cup. 'Like love, you savour it, sip by sip.'

The next morning, Samson kissed Delilah before returning home.

Walking towards the city gates, he saw three Philistine guards. They nudged each other, pointing at him. One of the guards – a large, fat man with a bulging nose and a wicked smile – stepped up to block his way.

'Who have we here?' the fat man sneered. 'Up early – no wares to trade, no bag for travel. It appears that you have had . . . other things to occupy you last night.'

'You are not a Philistine,' another guard with a scar down the side of his face commented. 'Are there not enough loose women where you come from that you must visit ours?'

'Maybe if we came to where you live, you could share your women with us,' the fat man laughed.

Rage surged through Samson's veins. Faster than a striking serpent, he hit the guard in the face, knocking him down and breaking his nose.

The other guards circled Samson, swords drawn, ready to strike. Samson planted his feet wide, crouching like a lion, turning this way and that, watching the two men.

'Gath him . . .' The fat man staggered to his feet, spitting blood from between broken teeth. 'Kill him . . .'

Scarface lunged. Samson waited until the last moment and then jumped to the side, catching the guard's wrist. Swinging him around, Samson slammed Scarface into the fat man. The two guards went down in a heap and lay there, motionless.

The other guard looked at his companions lying unconscious and then took off running. Samson laughed.

'I have killed Philistines before,' he cupped his hands to yell at the guard. 'Tell your friends I don't mind killing more.'

A week later Samson met Delilah in the marketplace.

'I heard you had a brawl,' Delilah smiled.

'I wouldn't call it a brawl,' Samson laughed. 'It was like playing with children.'

Samson's voice carried. Several soldiers standing at a merchant's booth, turned to stare at the Hebrew.

'Samson,' Delilah saw and lowered her voice. 'I think those soldiers overheard you.'

Samson shrugged. 'These Philistines think they are men, but I will teach them never to insult you again.'

Delilah stopped. 'You were defending my honour? No one has ever done that.'

He touched her cheek. 'No one has ever loved you as I do.'

Samson spent most of his days with Delilah. He brought her gifts of jewellery, fine cloth, baskets of fruit.

'Samson,' Delilah was seated before a dressing table a month later, brushing her hair. Samson was sitting on her bed to put on a sandal. 'Tell me about your family.'

He shrugged. 'My family is from the tribe of Dan. My father has a large farm that has done quite well.'

'Do you have any brothers or sisters?'

'No. My parents could not have children.' He laughed. 'My mother told me that our God, YHWH, sent an angel to tell her he had heard her prayers and she would have a son.'

Delilah put the brush down and began braiding her hair. 'I look forward to meeting your parents.'

'No.'

She looked in the polished bronze mirror. Samson was staring at her.

'What do you mean?'

'Why would you meet my family?'

'As your betrothed,' she hesitated, 'it would be natural –'

'My betrothed?' he interrupted her. 'I am not going to marry you.'

Now she stared at him. 'You're . . . not . . . going to . . . marry me?'

'No, I'm not,' Samson replied. 'You're a . . . well, an *experienced* woman. I am a judge among my people. If I marry, it would have to be to a girl who has never been with a man.'

'Yes, I've been with a man.' Delilah stood, folded her arms and turned away from him. *'I've been with you!'* she seethed. 'And though I can *be with you*, am I not good enough to *marry you?'*

Samson knew his words had struck like a knife. He crossed to Delilah and wrapped his arms around her, pulling her against his chest.

'Delilah,' he whispered, 'you don't understand.'

She wrenched away from his grasp and turned to face him. Her eyes burnt emerald fire.

'Oh, I understand. You are no better than the others. You're no better than the Philistines.'

The force of his hand slapping her cheek nearly broke her neck. Her eyes stung and her ears rang from the weight of it.

'Never say that again!' Samson's whisper was cold as winter. He gathered his cloak and walked to the door. 'Never.'

A minute later, the door slamming shook the house.

Delilah walked leadenly to the dressing table. The mirror reflected the red imprint of Samson's hand on her cheek. She had been struck by men before, but they had never hurt her heart . . . until now.

He told me he loved me, she thought. *He was so handsome and said such . . . things to me. Things I had never heard before.* Her hand crept across the table's surface to the box that held her jewellery. The gold necklace with the moonstones rested on top. *I thought this was a gift of affection, but he was just buying me. Just like all the others.* Her face hardened. *Never again. I will show Samson what it takes to buy Delilah; and then I will be free from the power of men.*

She rang the small gong on her table; a moment later a servant appeared at the door.

'Go to the house of Hazaroth, the governor of the city,' Delilah ordered. 'Tell him that Delilah requests his presence, to discuss . . . business.'

After the servant had bowed her way out, Delilah finished braiding her hair and then moved to select her most beautiful robe. For what she was about to do, appearance was everything.

Hazaroth arrived within the hour and Delilah explained her offer.

The governor was surprised.

'Let me see whether I understand this,' he said, as he sat next to Delilah, leaning against the pillows of her bed. 'You are going to convince Samson to tell you the secret of his great strength and how we can overpower him, so we may capture him. In return I, and each of the leaders of the other Philistine towns, will give you eleven hundred shekels of silver.'

'Yes.'

'Why?'

'What?'

Hazaroth lifted one of Delilah's curls and twisted it around his finger.

'Delilah, it has been a secret to no one that you have been with Samson. Some even thought that you were . . . in love . . . with the Hebrew?'

Her response was icy. 'I love no man.'

The governor smiled. 'You hide it well.' He looked at the woman's profile, noting the faint imprint on her cheek. He dropped the curl. 'I agree with your terms, Delilah. I'm certain I can convince the other governors. When can you begin?'

'Tomorrow.'

He raised his eyebrows. 'Are you certain he will return so soon?'

Delilah's faced hardened. 'He will return.'

The following afternoon, she was reclining on a couch in the courtyard, allowing the cool of the garden to soothe her anger, when she heard a knock at the door. A moment later, footsteps approached.

'Samson is here to see you, mistress,' the servant said.

Delilah's smile was grim. 'Show him in.' She arranged the drape of her robe, fluffed her curls and smoothed the edge of her lip rouge. She looked up when Samson walked through the door. He looked at her, shifting from foot to foot, hesitant. *He's uncertain of his reception,* she thought.

She extended a hand. 'Samson.'

With a relieved smile, he strode across the courtyard and took her in his arms. His embrace left her gasping for breath.

'I was afraid you would refuse me,' he whispered into her hair.

'None would condemn me if I did,' she pouted. 'You hurt me.'

He turned his head to look at her cheek. 'If I had marred your beauty, I would have killed myself.'

That would be too easy, Samson, she thought. *I want you to suffer.* Aloud she said, 'I should not have aroused your anger.' She ran her fingertips along his massive biceps. 'You are so strong. I've never seen a stronger man than you.' She struggled to suppress a sneer when she saw him preen under her words. She leaned over to whisper in his ear, 'You are almost a god. I doubt there is a way to overcome your strength.'

'I am but a man,' Samson said. 'And my strength can be undone.'

She laid her head on his shoulder, running her hand across his chest. 'Tell me how . . . please?'

'If anyone ties me with seven fresh leather straps that have not been dried, I'll be as weak as any man.'

After Samson fell asleep on the couch, Delilah sent her message to Hazaroth. Soon a group of armed guards arrived. One of the men handed her seven new leather straps. Delilah told the guards to stay in the garden while she took the leather straps and carefully bound them around Samson's wrists and ankles. Then she stepped back, smiling. *At last, you will suffer humiliation.*

'Samson,' she screamed, 'the Philistines are upon you.'

Samson's eyes flew open and he jumped up, snapping the straps as easily as a piece of string snaps when it comes close to a flame. 'Where?' he cried, looking around. 'Where are the Philistines, Delilah?'

She quenched the anger boiling in her. She threw herself in his arms. 'I'm sorry, Samson,' she said. 'I thought I heard them at the door. But I was wrong. Please forgive me.'

He stroked her hair. 'Do not be frightened, my love,' he said. 'I will protect you.'

Delilah curled her hand into a fist, digging her nails into her palm.

'Samson, you were teasing me when you said the fresh straps would hold you,' she pouted. 'You do not trust me any more.'

'That is not true, Delilah,' he insisted.

'Then tell me how you can be overcome.'

Samson sighed. 'If anyone ties me securely with new ropes that have never been used, I'll become as weak as any other man.'

'Have some more wine, Samson,' she said, 'and then sleep.'

After several cups of wine, Samson was snoring on the couch.

Again, Delilah went to the front of her house, where the Philistine guards still waited. 'I need some new rope,' she told them.

An hour later, she had tied the sleeping Hebrew to the couch with several lengths of new rope. Moving to the edge of the courtyard, she screamed, 'Samson, the Philistines are upon you!'

Samson jumped up, carrying the couch as if it weighed nothing. Extending his arms, he snapped off the ropes. When he saw there were no Philistines, he turned to Delilah.

'What game is this, Delilah?'

She crossed to him, sulking.

'After you left me yesterday,' she said, 'I believed I had lost your love. I thought if you could trust me with the secret of your strength, then you really loved me. Apparently, you don't love me any more.'

Samson grasped her hand. 'That's not true, Delilah,' he insisted. 'I love you.'

'Then why won't you tell me the secret of your strength?'

'Why does it matter?' he asked.

'Because it does,' she said. 'If you love me, you will tell me. It is the only way.'

Samson ran his hands through his hair and sighed. 'It's my hair. No razor has ever been used on my head, because I am a Nazirite, dedicated to God from my birth. If my head were shaved, my strength would leave me, and I would become as weak as any other man.'

Wrapping her arms around his neck, Delilah kissed Samson.

This time I know you've told me everything, Samson, she thought. Taking his hand, she led him towards her bed-chamber. 'Come,' she said, 'we must . . . sleep.'

The stars were fading in the early morning light when Delilah sent a servant to Hazaroth. 'Tell him to send the silver. Samson has told me everything.'

She walked back to the bedchamber and slipped onto the bed next to Samson. He stirred when he felt her weight. 'Shhh . . .' she said, pulling his head onto her lap. 'It is nothing.' When his breath slowed into sleep, she gestured for the manservant standing in the hall.

He came into the room, carrying a razor. With light strokes, the man shaved Samson's head.

When the servant left, the guards entered and surrounded the bed.

Nudging his shoulder, Delilah said, 'Samson . . . Samson, wake up.' After a moment, she leaned over and screamed into his ear, 'Samson, the Philistines are here!'

Samson's eyes widened and he sat up on the bed. 'Have you come back for another beating?' he asked, seeing the guards around him. Standing up, he spread his arms wide and gestured, flexing his fingers towards his palms. 'Come then, I will take you one at a time or all at once. It's your choice.'

A guard rushed Samson, slashing his sword along the Hebrew's forearm. Samson gasped in shock as blood gushed from the wound; he screamed when Scarface ran up from behind and stabbed him in the shoulder. All the guards moved in; soon, Samson was bound and struggling.

'YHWH,' he cried. 'What has happened? Why have You turned Your back on me?'

'I do not think your God turned His back on you, Samson,' Delilah said. She held up something long in front of his eyes; it was a lock his hair. 'You abandoned Him.'

'Take him,' the fat guard ordered as he handed Delilah several heavy bags. 'This is the agreed payment.'

'Wait,' she stopped the guard. 'I want to see Samson punished.'

He smiled, 'I have never met a woman with a strong stomach like yours.'

'What do you mean?' she asked. 'I've seen men beaten before.'

'Oh, the Philistine governors have different plans for Samson,' he said, laying a thumb on his prisoner's closed eyelid. 'Beginning with gouging out his eyes.'

The screams of Delilah could be heard several streets away.

The guards dragged the blinded Hebrew to the prison in Gaza. They put bronze shackles on his ankles and on his wrists and attached the shackles to the pole of a large grist stone.

'The donkeys are tired of the millstone,' Scarface told him. 'So you are taking their place.' Samson cried out as a whip stung his back. 'Get started.'

Grabbing the pole, Samson pushed; after a moment, he felt the massive stone move.

'Good,' Scarface told him, 'you are good for something.'

Hour after hour, Samson pushed the grist stone around. He stopped twice each day to eat. Without sight, the only way he knew it was night was when the guards moved him to the wall and tied his shackles to a bar on the floor.

'YHWH,' Samson cried. 'Let me die. I have betrayed my family and you.' When the Creator did not answer his prayers, Samson fell into an exhausted sleep filled with nightmares.

A guard's boot kicking his ribs woke him. 'Get up, Samson. Time to work.'

Days passed and then weeks; Samson pushed the wheel around and around. His wounds healed, but not his heart. Every night before he fell asleep, he pleaded with God, 'Please let me die. I have betrayed my family and you.'

He had no comfort in his dark world. Even the memory of the beauty of Delilah brought anguish to his heart.

One morning, after Samson had been kicked awake, the guard told him, 'You're going to do something else today, Samson.'

'What?'

'You'll see —' the guard laughed, 'Sorry . . . I mean, you'll find out.'

Samson was dragged from his cell, jerked up several flights of steps and through a door. He felt the heat of the sun on his skin and turned his face upwards. Gravel crunched under his feet as he was led down what he thought was a road. He could hear voices – many voices – that grew louder as he walked. He felt a threshold against his foot and, when he stepped over it, the voices erupted.

'It's Samson!'

'Look at him! He's nothing to be frightened of!'

'Praise to our god, Dagon, who delivered our enemy into our hands.'

Samson turned to the guard at his side. 'What is this place?'

'This is the temple of the Philistine god, Dagon. The governors have come to offer a great sacrifice to Dagon for delivering you into their hands. Over three thousand people are in the temple.'

'Hey, Samson,' a voice called, 'look out, the Philistines are coming for you!'

He flinched as a whip stung his back.

'Look out, Samson,' called another. 'The Philistines are here!'

Samson tripped and fell as a pole beat his legs. He thrashed on the ground as he was beaten with whips and poles.

'Bind him to the great columns,' someone cried, 'so Dagon can see him as the sacrifices are offered.'

Someone grabbed Samson's shackles and pulled him across the temple floor. When his toe hit a stone step, he lifted his foot, to walk up several steps. 'I am tired,' he said. 'Please let me rest against the pillars that support the temple.'

'Whatever you want, Samson,' the voice laughed.

He leaned against the pillar that supported the roof. It was cold against his skin and as smooth as ice.

If I had my strength, he thought as he reached out, *I could pull this temple down. I would die, but I would take all these Philistines with me. Better to die fighting YHWH's enemies than to live as a blind slave.*

'YHWH,' he prayed, 'please remember me. Almighty God, strengthen me just once more, and let me, with one blow, get revenge on the Philistines.'

Then Samson reached towards the other pillar on which the temple roof stood and braced himself against the two columns, his right hand on the one and his left hand on the other. 'Let me die with the Philistines,' he screamed.

'What is the madman doing?' a voice cried as the temple began to shake.

'May it fall on you all!' Samson screamed as he pushed against the stones.

The stone roof caved in. Death came quickly as the walls collapsed, stone upon stone, silencing the screams of the Philistines.

'YHWH,' Samson whispered as the weight of the roof crushed him. 'Take my spirit to be with You.'

14

The Giant

There had never been such a dark day in the land of the Valley of Elah. The ground was burnt dry. The rains had failed and all was barren. The throat of every creature that lived in the once lush land felt like parchment. Thirst swelled the tongues of the animals and gripped the voice of men like the hand of an unseen demon. The sun had risen and set each day but could never be seen. Dark clouds covered the sky, but still no rain came. It was as if the land of Elah in Judah was cursed; even the branches of the terebinth trees that once shaded and covered the ground as far as the eye could see had all begun to wither and die.

It had been that way since the Philistines had brought their vagabond army to attack the town of Socoh that stood on a small hill on the far side of the valley.

In the dark of night, their dirty feet had tramped the sacred earth as they approached. The clattering of shields had shaken men from their sleep. Their screams and shouts had terrified the children who huddled in the dark corners of the houses. Their approach sounded like an earthquake.

It rumbled through the night and no one dared look from their window to see what terror was out in the far darkness, on the other side of the valley, beyond the small stream littered with gleaming white stones.

Near the town of Socoh, the Philistines set up their camp. Billowing tents with red cords were aligned in precise rows. Their fires burnt long into the dry nights and the echoes of hammers striking against anvils suggested mountains of weapons being crafted and sharpened. They were so great in number that, during the day, it looked like a swarming plague of locusts ready for war.

King Saul received news of the invaders. It took many days for Saul and the Israelite army to get to the town and the campsite. Then, nothing happened. Neither army moved, each waiting for the other to advance.

Every morning, King Saul stood looking down from the hill across the stream to the Philistine camp. His hands trembled as he stroked his beard. Those surrounding him were fearful to speak, knowing that Saul was often blinded by an uncontrollable rage that left the king mumbling to himself, his eyes glistening with madness. In fear and suspicion, Saul would lash out at those standing near; what was worse was when he lashed out at a person – or thing – that no one else could see.

Early one morning whilst the king pondered how to fight the Philistines, he saw a solitary figure. At first, King Saul could not believe his eyes. Lumbering from the Philistine camp was the biggest, tallest, most frightening man Saul had ever seen. By the giant's side was a soldier carrying a shield so massive that it dragged on the ground. The two men approached the steep banks of the Elah brook and looked up at the Israelite camp.

'Who is it?' King Saul croaked in fear. 'What is it?' he demanded, his eyes glowing with rage. There was silence from those around him; none of his advisors knew what to say. After a moment, an aide stepped to Saul's side.

'It is the Philistine's hero,' he whispered. 'His name is Goliath of Gath. He is nine feet tall and has four brothers who are just like him.'

The king whirled, pushing the man away. 'Why didn't anyone tell me about him?' he screeched. 'Look at him! What do you think the sight of such a monster will do to my army? And you say he has *four* brothers?'

Those around Saul gaped anxiously, hoping the king, in his madness and rage, would not notice them. All turned to look at the giant.

Goliath wore a bronze helmet and had bronze armour. In an enormous hand he carried a bronze sword and had, strapped on his back, a spear that was longer than two men; the iron spearhead alone weighed more than the corner-stone of a house. Goliath threw his head back and laughed mockingly; then he took three paces forward and screamed to the army of Israel:

'Why are you lining up for battle?' His voice was like the roar of a lion, echoing down the valley and through the empty streets of the town. 'I'm the most glorious fighter in our army, and you, feeble remnant, are in the control of a mad coward. Choose your finest warrior – if you have one – to come out and fight me! If he kills me, our people will be your slaves. But if I kill him, you will become our slaves.'

The eyes of Goliath burnt blood red as he beat his bronze chest plate with his fist and, waving his sword at the Israelites, he spat on the ground.

King Saul trembled as he listened. 'Who do we have who could kill such a monster?' the king rasped.

The aides shuffled their feet, looking at each other. Before anyone replied, the giant shouted again.

'Well? Tell me, Saul, which of your warriors will fight? You are the anointed one of your god – surely he does not want a coward for a king?' Goliath turned and walked away.

For the next forty days, at dawn and at sunset, Goliath came to the same place. His gnarled, sandalled feet wore a wide path from the Philistine camp to the banks of the stream. He screamed his challenge, but Saul never answered, his attendants were silent and no warrior dared fight the giant.

With each passing day, Goliath's scorn increased. He insulted the God of Israel and taunted the Israelites to defend the name of their Creator.

The people in the land beyond Elah learnt of Goliath's challenge. Shepherds muttered around campfires on distant hills.

'My sons, Eliab, Abinadab and Shammah, are with King Saul,' said Jesse. The old man lay on a rolled fleece before the flickering firelight.

'You should have tied them in sacks and kept them at home, Jesse,' scoffed a man with a weathered face, sitting on a stone across from Jesse. 'I have heard this Goliath is a giant. Even though he mocks YHWH, King Saul does nothing. The giant swears by his gods that we shall all become the slaves of the Philistines; *by the prophets,* I pray that day will not come.'

'Why don't the soldiers fight the giant and stop his lies?' asked a Samaritan woman, ladling a thick stew from a blackened pot dangling over the campfire.

'He is too fearful – a monster – some say he is a demon dressed as a man,' Jesse replied, nodding his thanks for the bowl the woman handed him. The old man wondered if any of his three sons would challenge the giant. He looked through the flames of the fire to David, his youngest son, who sat quietly mending his sling. 'David, you carry food to your brothers; what have you heard of Goliath?'

'Whenever I go to the camp, Shammah won't let me go near enough to see,' the boy protested. 'They think I am only fit for looking after the sheep.' The boy thumped his chest. 'If I were a soldier, I would kill Goliath of Gath.'

David was tall for his age and feared nothing. Once, he had killed a mountain lion with his bare hands. It had tried to kill a sheep that had strayed from the flock. David had followed the sheep's terrified bleating; it was stuck in a ravine. The lion was about to pounce, when David jumped from the rock, grabbed the lion's neck and twisted it, killing the beast.

'Why don't you send David?' the other man laughed, chewing loudly.

'Let me go, Father. I have my sling and my staff,' the boy asked.

'Goliath of Gath is not a lion or a wolf,' his father snapped. 'He is a monster from hell.'

'So . . . you are all frightened of this Philistine?' the woman asked. 'Didn't you tell me that your God created the whole world and promised He would deliver you from evil and wickedness?'

Everyone around the campfire fell silent. The wind rustled the dust, sending spirals of dead leaves scurrying to and fro. David looked at the sling in his hand and then to the burning flames of the fire. Leaning against his fleece bundle, he closed his eyes and thought of his brothers. His father's voice woke him.

'David, tomorrow take a sack of roasted grain and ten loaves of bread to your brothers, who are with Saul,' Jesse said. 'Take ten large chunks of cheese to their commanding officer. Find out how they are doing.'

That night, David could not sleep. Whenever he closed his eyes, a voice in the night whispered on the breeze. Its words echoed through the cedar groves and to the tops of the hills.

Take the five stones, David, white, smooth and flat. You will know what to do . . .'

The voice haunted him in his half-sleep; its whisperings would not be silent.

In the morning, David did as his father had asked. Before anyone else in the shepherds' camp was awake, David loaded the bread, grain and cheese on the back of a donkey and walked towards the dawning light.

Three hours later, he reached the Israelite encampment. David had dragged the reluctant donkey the last mile; it stopped whenever it could and tried to turn back. As the young boy entered the camp of King Saul, he saw a line of a thousand soldiers stretched across the hillside. The warriors shouted and screamed at the Philistine encampment.

David's gaze followed where the soldiers were pointing. Across the valley, Goliath swaggered down the well-trodden path to the edge of the stream.

'Another morning and all you do is shout at me?' the giant laughed, slipping his helmet onto his head. 'Will none of you dare take up my challenge? Come out and fight me!'

David searched the ranks of Israelites for his brothers. The giant continued to shout. The soldiers of Israel trembled.

David found the adjutant in charge of the army's food. The soldier took the food from him and placed it in a tent away from the line of warriors.

'Why doesn't someone fight Goliath?' David asked. 'Listen to what he is saying. He is insulting YHWH.'

'Can't you see how frightened they all are?' the adjutant asked, pointing to the silent troops. 'Every day Goliath of Gath keeps coming out to insult us, yet no one dare fight him. The king has offered a great reward to whoever kills

Goliath. That man will marry the king's daughter and no one in his family will ever have to pay taxes again.'

'Then why does no one fight him?' David demanded. 'Who does that heap of camel dung think he is? He mocks the army of the living God!'

'And you are the man to do it?' a soldier laughed. 'I know you. You are David, the shepherd brother of Eliab. If your brothers won't fight the giant, why should you? Where is your sword and armour? Where is your horse for battle?'

Eliab, David's older brother, stomped over and grabbed David by his coat, shaking him.

'What are you doing here?' Eliab asked. 'Who's taking care of our sheep out in the desert? You spoiled brat, David . . .' Eliab threw David to the ground. 'You came here just to watch the fighting, didn't you?'

David got up, dusting off his clothes. 'What have I done?' he asked. 'Can't I even ask a question?'

'This is not a lion or a bear, this is Goliath the giant,' Eliab sneered.

David turned to another soldier and asked the same question. 'Who will fight this man?'

Eliab grabbed David and tried to drag him away from the crowd of soldiers.

'What is this?' King Saul stepped up. 'I heard raised voices and thought that while Goliath distracted us, we had been attacked from the side.' He looked at David. 'Who are you?'

Eliab let go of his brother and bowed his head. David

bowed also and then folded his arms and straightened his back so he would look taller and stronger.

'Your Majesty,' he said, 'Goliath the Philistine shouldn't turn us into snivelling cowards. I'll fight him.'

'You? You don't have a chance against him,' Saul mocked. 'You're only a boy, and Goliath's been a soldier all his life.'

'I take care of my father's sheep,' David said. 'When one of them is dragged away by a lion or a bear, I pursue it and beat the wild animal until it lets the sheep go. If the lion or bear turns and attacks me, I grab it by the throat and kill it.'

The king looked at the boy and laughed; the soldiers joined him. Only Eliab was silent. 'You kill wild beasts?' Saul asked. 'I have a gnat in my tent that could be dispatched – would you do it with a spear or a sword?'

'Majesty, David speaks the truth.' Eliab put his arm around David's shoulders. 'My brother is a good shepherd.'

'Shepherd? Israel does not need a shepherd; it needs a warrior,' the king turned away.

'I have killed lions and bears; I can kill this worthless piece of dung.' David grabbed the king by the sleeve of his garment. 'He shouldn't insult the army of the living God. The Almighty has rescued me from the claws of lions and bears, and He will keep me safe from the hands of this Philistine.'

The soldiers waited for the command to drag David away and kill him for touching the king. But the king stood in silence, looking at the boy. A trickle of sweat rolled down David's cheek.

'So you say that you can kill a bear and a lion?' Saul asked.

'With my sling,' David answered.

'All right,' Saul said, 'go . . . fight Goliath of Gath. And I hope YHWH – God Almighty – will help you.'

'We can't send him dressed like that,' the adjutant insisted as thunderous, black clouds rolled closer and closer. 'What will the Philistines think if we send out a shepherd against the giant?'

The king laughed. 'Give him my own armour to wear. Dress him as a king and let him take my sword.'

David was soon strapped into the king's armour. He stood stiffly, unable to move or breathe, for the heavy breastplate reached down to his knees.

'I can't move with all this,' David protested. 'I can't fight.'

'You can't stand against Goliath without armour,' Saul said.

'I can't fight him with it,' he stated.

David quickly removed the armour and picked up his shepherd's staff.

'So you'll fight him with a stick and a sling?' the king asked.

David nodded. He left the tent and walked towards the stream.

On the far side of the rock-strewn bank, Goliath taunted the army of Israel. 'Send someone. I have stood forty days and forty nights and still no one comes –' Just then, he saw David walking down the hill, carrying his staff and sling. 'Do you think I'm a dog?' Goliath growled. 'Is that why you've come after me with a stick?'

David did not speak as he stepped into the stream. As his foot touched the waters, he heard the voice again, *'Take the five stones, David,'* it whispered, *'white, smooth and flat. You will know what to do . . .'* The boy bent down, and picked up five smooth rocks. He looked at each stone before slipping them into the pouch that hung from his belt.

The giant screamed at him, rattling the branches of the terebinth trees. He pointed his sword at the boy. 'By Moloch, when I'm finished with you, I'll feed you to the birds and wild animals. I will rip you limb from limb and hang the pieces of your flesh in the branches of the trees. Your father will weep because he will have nothing to bury. Only the stones will be a witness to your death.'

David waded through the stream to the far side. He scrambled up the shale bank and saw Goliath standing in a clearing of trees. To the giant's left were the bone-picked carcasses of several goats.

The giant was taller than David had imagined, his arms thick as the branches of the trees. In one hand, Goliath held his vast spear and in the other a long sword of solid bronze that was taller than David.

'Leave and I will let you live,' David said, inching closer. 'You've come out to fight me with a sword and a spear. But I've come out to fight you in the name of the All-Powerful. He is the God of Israel's army, and you have insulted Him.'

Goliath looked down at the boy and smiled. 'Go home,' he said. 'I will let you live. You are the bravest Israelite I have seen – but you are a child.'

'Goliath of Gath, today YHWH will help me defeat you. I'll knock you down and cut off your head, and I'll feed the bodies of the Philistine soldiers to the birds and wild animals. Then the whole world will know that Israel has a real god. Everybody here will see that the Lord doesn't need swords or spears to save His people. The Almighty always wins the battle and He will help me defeat you.'

'Your god does not care about you,' Goliath sneered, stepping towards David. 'Now I will kill you.'

The giant began running down the hill towards the stream, his feet pounding the dirt like an earthquake. Goliath screamed as he raised his spear.

David stood his ground as the voice whispered, *Wait, David; take the whitest stone.*'

David picked a stone from his pouch. It shone bright and white. It was smooth, the edges washed by the waters of the river.

'*Get ready.*'

David put the rock in his sling and began swinging it round by its straps. The giant came closer and closer, his spear lifted above his head. All was silent; it was as if the world had stood still. David could hear nothing but the whispering voice telling him not to fear.

Round and round, David swung the sling. It beat against the wind and cracked the air.

'*Wait.*'

Goliath was just feet away when he drew the spear back by his ear. 'Die!' the giant screamed.

'NOW, David!'

David let go of the strap; the rock flew. It shot through the air and hit Goliath with a dull thud, sinking into his forehead. The giant stumbled forwards, his face oozing blood. The stone had cracked his skull. Goliath groaned in agony, dropping his spear and then his sword. The giant swayed like a mighty oak tree about to fall. He stumbled back and forth, holding out his hands like a blind man. Then, without warning, he crashed face down, the dust of the Valley of Elah erupting around him and settling over him.

David looked at the massive body that lay at his feet. He lifted the bronze sword and, with one swing, cut off Goliath's head.

For a moment, all was silent. Then the heavens opened and poured out rain. It beat the ground, drowning out the screams of the Israelites as they ran down the hill towards the enemies' camp.

When the Philistines saw what had happened to Goliath, they turned and ran. The soldiers of Israel and Judah let out a battle cry and gave chase. They showed no mercy, littering the road from Shaarim to Gath with the bodies of their enemies. When the Israelite army returned, they ransacked the enemy camp. The tents of the Philistine army were left in place as a sign of YHWH's victory. The tattered flags snapped in the wind as the rain beat against them.

David took Goliath's head to King Saul but kept the giant's sword.

As the celebration continued, the rain nourished the earth. From the dry branches of the terebinth trees, fresh shoots came forth and the Valley of Elah was no longer barren.

15

The King

On the highest building of the city, a cauldron gushed with acrid, black smoke. It spiralled into the still, evening air, the sunlight casting a shadow of the pall across the doors of the palace. In an upper room overlooking the flat, stone roofs of the houses below, a man stood at the window. He was naked to the waist; a torn and discarded garment lay at his feet. Around his head was a tight linen cloth tied with strands of rope. His eyes were reddened with tears.

The prophet drew a shuddering breath as he glanced at the lifeless body that lay on the bed. Then, wiping the tears from his face, he shouted the proclamation from the window:

'David, the King of Israel, is dead.' Nathan's words echoed across the city. *'DAVID . . . IS DEAD . . .'*

In the room garlanded with purple cloth, Solomon and his mother Bathsheba knelt by the bed. Solomon turned to embrace her; she collapsed against his shoulder, sobbing.

'I cannot believe he is dead,' Solomon whispered, tears flowing into his beard.

'May the Creator bless King Solomon with long life,' Nathan proclaimed as he stepped towards Solomon.

'Long live the king!' the people in the room echoed Nathan's blessing.

Solomon stood, lifting his mother with him and set her in a chair. Then he turned to face the people.

'The king, my father, chose me – although I am still young – to be king after him. I ask that you pray for me, that I may be a king as my father was, one who followed YHWH with all his heart, and that I may rule this land under the Law of the Great Book.' He lifted his hands over the people. 'May YHWH bless you all and may He bless all Israel.'

'May YHWH bless Israel,' the people in the room cried, 'and bless King Solomon.'

'Go . . .' Nathan said to the people. 'Leave them with their grief.'

Each person bowed to Solomon and left the room.

'I didn't know death would make me feel this way, Nathan,' Solomon said, holding out his hand to the prophet.

'It is to be endured,' Nathan replied. 'Nothing will ever be the same. David would want you to be like him.'

'How can any man do what he has done? I am not one who can slay a giant or write songs to YHWH,' Solomon said.

'Your father taught you well. Be the man he wants you to be.'

Solomon walked to the window. Bathsheba moved to sit on the edge of the bed. She lifted the hand of her dead husband to kiss it. 'The kingdom belongs to you now, my son.'

'I have inherited more than a kingdom,' he whispered. 'I have inherited a legend.'

The days passed quickly. Solomon had little time for grief. Many foreign rulers came to offer their condolences and renew their vows of peace with Israel. He met with his father's advisors to determine who would retain their positions and who would retire.

'You must decide what to do about your brothers, my King,' Zabud, Solomon's personal advisor, said. 'You were one of your father's youngest sons. There are reports of jealousy and discontent among your brothers.'

Solomon was bone weary and wanted only to eat and then sleep. But he remembered his father's teaching, *A king who does not put his kingdom ahead of his own desires will soon be king over nothing.*

Solomon sighed. 'How would you advise me?' he asked.

'Strike them before they strike you.'

Solomon shot up from his throne.

'I will not strike one of my brothers – or any man – without provocation,' he seethed. 'That would go against all the teachings of my father and YHWH's law.'

'But, Your Majesty –'

'Enough!' The king's voice was cold as ice. 'Do not speak to me of this again.'

Zabud bowed his head. 'Yes, Your Majesty.'

Solomon closed his eyes and rubbed them with his fingers.

'I spoke harshly, Zabud. I know you are concerned for my life and my kingdom and I am grateful for that . . . I am weary.' He opened his eyes, and stood. 'Please have some bread and cheese and wine sent to the gardens,' he told Zabud. 'And call for the High Priest.'

Solomon was sitting under an arbour in the garden, the remains of a meal on a nearby table, when Azariah arrived. The king greeted him.

'I will go to Gibeon, to offer sacrifices to YHWH and to pray for Israel,' Solomon told the high priest. 'Go ahead of me and prepare the sacrifices.'

'Gibeon?' Azariah asked. 'David would be proud of you.'

'One day, I will build a temple here in the city,' Solomon commented.

'And the world will bow before the throne of God,' Azariah said.

'May God grant me wisdom. I fear I will not be a king like my father,' Solomon said. 'Go before me to the place of offering.'

The next day, King Solomon followed the priest to Gibeon. He drove past a valley at the base of a hill where shepherds watched over a thousand head of cattle that were to be used for the sacrifices.

Soon, he arrived at the high place, where he found Azariah, with Zadok and Abiathar, two other priests. They were waiting by the altar next to a pit with raging fire. The king stepped down from his chariot and walked over to greet the high priest. The flames leaped high into the sky as the trunks of a hundred acacia trees charred in the flames.

Bull after bull was brought up the hill to the altar to be sacrificed. They screamed and bellowed as they were dragged toward the flames. Their throats were cut, blood drained and carcasses thrown to the inferno. The sound and smell was sickening; yet Solomon knew that, since the time of Marah and Havva, YHWH had required the shedding of blood to pay the debt of sin.

As each animal was slaughtered, Solomon asked forgiveness. With each drop of blood, he repented of his wrongdoing and that of his people. Death followed death as Solomon prayed. It was dark by the time the final sacrifice was offered. As the last bull was dragged towards the altar, Solomon stared at the beast eye to eye. It snorted as the priest took its life, never taking its glare from the king. The carcass was thrown into the fire and Solomon watched the beast burn in the flames.

'I would be alone,' Solomon told Azariah and Benaiah, the commander of his armies.

They bowed and gestured to the others to leave the high place. Benaiah stationed a guard at a distance that allowed the king privacy and protection.

The king sat down next to a tree. He looked up at the stars, scattered like diamonds across the darkening sky.

'YHWH,' he prayed, 'please accept these sacrifices. Let not one death be wasted.' His jaws cracked as he yawned.

'Please help me.' Closing his eyes, his breath slowed and evened as he fell asleep . . . and dreamed.

He was standing before a throne he had never seen before. This throne was massive and brilliant white. On the throne sat one whose body radiated the sun; Solomon looked down to keep from being blinded.

'Solomon,' spoke the one on the throne, his voice echoing through the heavens. *'I am the God of your father and your father's fathers.'* Solomon fell to his knees, trembling before the Almighty. *'Ask whatever you want Me to give you.'*

Ask YHWH for whatever I want? he thought. *What do you ask of the Almighty? Power? No . . . too selfish. Wealth? No . . . as king, I have what I need.*

'Almighty YHWH,' Solomon prayed. 'You have shown great kindness to Your servant, my father, David, because he was faithful to You and righteous. You have given him a son to sit on his throne this very day.'

Solomon stirred in his sleep as the dream shuddered through his mind.

'You may ask of Me whatever you desire, Solomon.' The voice of YHWH was as gentle as a lamb.

'Almighty YHWH, You have made Your servant king in place of my father, David. But I am only a young man and do not know how to carry out my duties. Your servant is king over the people You have chosen, who are too numerous to count or number. Please give Your servant wisdom to distinguish between right and wrong. For who is able to govern this great people of Yours?'

'I am pleased,' YHWH said. *'Since you have asked for this and not for long life or wealth for yourself or for the death of your enemies but for wisdom in giving justice, I will do what you have asked. I will give you a wise and discerning heart, so that there will never have been anyone like you, nor will there ever be. I will also give you what you have not asked for – both riches and honour – so that in your lifetime you will have no equal among kings. If . . . you walk in MY ways and obey MY statutes and commands as David your father did, I will give you a long life.'*

Solomon stretched out his hands towards the throne and began to worship. He awoke with his arms reaching towards the sky. The vision had gone like a wisp of the night. Solomon arose and returned to Jerusalem, ready to govern Israel.

In the following days, he appointed governors throughout the kingdom. They not only made decisions of government, they also listened to grievances brought by the people and would administer justice in the king's name. Whenever there was a difficult case, they would send the people to the king in Jerusalem.

One morning, Solomon was in the throne room, listening to the petitions that his governors had sent to him, when the cries of a newborn baby interrupted the petitioners.

Looking up, he saw two women. Their clothing clung to their figures and on their eyes were the kohl lines of courtesans. Both wore jewellery and headdresses made of gold. Solomon did not need to hear his advisor, Zabud – who stood next to his throne – whisper, 'Prostitutes,' to know what these women were. They appeared to be fighting – over who held the whimpering infant.

Solomon gestured to them to approach. Even as they walked to the foot of the throne, they continued to try to snatch the baby back and forth between them.

'Stop making the child cry,' he shouted. The women stood still, blushing with embarrassment, and looked up at the king. 'What is your grievance?' he asked.

The woman holding the baby said, 'My Lord, my name is Tirzah and this is Dophkah. We are . . .' she paused, as if seeking the right word.

'I know what you are,' Solomon said. 'Continue.'

Tirzah blushed again but nodded her head. 'Dophkah and I live in the same house. I gave birth to a son a week ago and three days later, she also gave birth to a son.

'I woke up the morning after her baby was born to nurse my own son,' she began to cry, 'only the child was dead. I held him to warm his body and tried to breath into his mouth, but there was nothing I could do. He was dead. Dophkah came over, holding her son, to comfort me. "It appears that you rolled over on him in the night," she said, "and smothered him."

'As I began to wash his body to prepare it for burial, I noticed a large birthmark on his back. That's when I realized that it wasn't my son.' She pointed to the other woman, 'During the night, Dophkah had rolled over on *her* son and smothered him. While I was asleep, she got up and took my son from my side and laid her dead son by me.'

'NO!' Dophkah screamed. 'Tirzah killed her son.' She snatched the baby from the other woman; the infant began wailing. 'This is *my* son!'

'No . . .' Tirzah took the baby from Dophkah, making the infant's wails change to screams. 'The *dead* child is yours; the *living* one is mine.'

Dophkah reached for the hysterical infant.

'Stop! Move away from the child,' Solomon said.

Dophkah looked at the baby and – her eyes flashing defiance – she took one step away.

'Comfort the –' Solomon began, but Tirzah had already lifted the crying infant to her shoulder, gently swaying and murmuring softly to it. After a moment, the baby's screams settled to a whimper and then faded away.

'Now,' Solomon whispered, so as not to wake the baby, 'hand the child to Dophkah.'

The other woman sneered and walked over to jerk the child from Tirzah's arms. The baby's screams echoed throughout the throne room.

'Comfort the child,' Solomon said.

Dophkah lifted the baby to her shoulder and began to jiggle it, whispering. The baby cried louder. She tried rocking, swaying, pacing in front of the throne; nothing made the baby stop crying.

Solomon looked at Tirzah, tears streaming from her eyes as she watched Dophkah and the baby.

'Please hand the baby back to Tirzah,' he instructed Dophkah.

The woman turned to move away, but found a soldier standing next to her. Moaning indignantly, she turned and thrust the screaming infant into Tirzah's arms. In a moment, the baby's cries had subsided as he drifted off to sleep.

'So,' the king said, 'Tirzah claims the boy is hers and the dead child is Dophkah's, yet Dophkah claims the living child is hers and the dead child is Tirzah's.'

He studied the two women for a moment; Tirzah holding the infant and swaying gently and Dophkah, her arms folded in front of her, her mouth grim and eyes narrowed.

Solomon looked at the soldier standing near Dophkah. 'Draw your sword,' he said.

The sword rasped as the soldier unsheathed it and held it ready.

'Cut the living child in two,' he ordered. Gasps rippled throughout the throne room. He raised his voice. 'Cut this child in two and give half to Tirzah and the other half to Dophkah.'

'NO!' Tirzah screamed, hunching over the baby to shield him from the soldier's raised sword. The baby woke again, screaming. She extended a hand to the king, 'Please, my lord, give Dophkah the baby! Don't kill him!' She walked over to lay the baby into the other woman's arms.

'Cut him in two!' Dophkah raised her voice over the infant's screams. She turned to hold the baby out to the soldier. 'Neither I nor you shall have him.' Dophkah's eyes widened; she lifted one hand to cover her mouth, as if to retract her words.

Solomon smiled grimly. 'Put your sword away,' he ordered the soldier. 'Do not kill the child. Give the living baby to Tirzah; she is his mother.'

The king stood and stepped down from the throne to stand in front of the two women. Looking at Dophkah he said, 'You didn't care whether the child lived or died. Only a mother would be willing to give her child to another rather than see him die.'

He turned to Tirzah; he reached out a finger to touch the baby in her arms. 'Take your son,' he said, 'and raise him to love and honour YHWH.'

16

The Troublemaker

A cold wind blew through the corridors of the palace, whistling through the doorways. It burnt skin and the sand it carried cut flesh. The prophet felt none of this as he walked the corridors, thrusting his staff against the stone floor. The guards at every doorway stepped back, fearful to stop him. The old man walked on, face set like flint, his furrowed brow gnarled and lined. As he turned the last corner of the passageway, his eyes steeled as he lifted his staff and banged it against the doors.

'Majesties,' Obadiah, the royal steward, bowed before King Ahab and Queen Jezebel. 'The prophet Elijah is here.'

Jezebel's dark eyes could stare down any man. Like her heart, they were cold and lifeless and had beguiled Ahab from the moment he had met her.

'Show Elijah in,' Ahab commanded nervously.

Obadiah bowed and crossed to the doors.

'Which god is Elijah prophet of?' Jezebel asked.

'He is a prophet of YHWH,' Ahab told her, 'the God of the Hebrews.'

Jezebel waved a hand dismissively. 'How boring to worship only one god,' she drawled. Born a Phoenician princess, she refused to change when she married King Ahab, preferring to remind everyone she came from a wealthy, powerful – and foreign – land. Green malachite, kohl, and red ochre tinted her face. Her dress was dyed purple from the murex, a shellfish found on the Phoenician coast. Her jewellery was of beaten gold, as was the queen's ugal, which adorned her intricate black braids.

'The prophet Elijah . . .' Obadiah said as he bowed to the prophet and then backed away.

'To worship only one god would offend the other gods,' Jezebel said before Elijah could speak. 'I am not only a priestess of Baal, the god of rain, lightning, thunder – even the dew – I am also the priestess of Asherah.'

'It is this worship that led the people of Israel astray!' the prophet said, staring at the queen.

'Elijah . . . you wanted to see me?' the king asked, hoping his wife would be silent.

The man standing – not bowing – before Ahab and Jezebel, was white haired and weathered as stone. His long tunic, made from goat's hair, was belted in leather. The staff he carried was gnarled and bent, but thick enough to use for walking, or beating someone foolish enough to cross him. He pointed it at King Ahab.

'You allowed Jezebel to bring pagan gods into Israel,' Elijah said. 'YHWH told the Israelites not to worship other gods, yet you built a temple to Baal.'

King Ahab was speechless at the prophet's attack, but not Jezebel. The queen shot to her feet.

'You dare condemn me?' she demanded. 'Beware, *old man*, I am a priestess of the god Baal. I can petition him to strike you with lightning!'

'Baal controls lightning?' Elijah sneered. 'Bah! He has no more power than the stone his idols are made from.' Glaring at Ahab, he pronounced, 'As YHWH – *whom I serve* – lives, there will be neither dew nor rain in the next few years except at *my* word.'

Turning, the old prophet left the room.

Elijah stomped down the corridors, his staff echoing as it hit the marble floors. Everywhere he looked were items made from ivory. The palace had been started by Ahab's father, King Omri, and finished when Ahab ascended the throne; but it didn't receive its name – the Ivory Palace – until Jezebel decorated it in the Phoenician style.

'Jezebel marks everything she touches,' Elijah murmured, 'including her husband, who is too weak to stand up to her.'

'Elijah . . . my lord Elijah.'

The old prophet turned to see Obadiah hurrying down the corridors. Elijah waited for the king's steward, who bowed when he reached him.

'Obadiah, do you bring a message from Ahab?'

'No, my lord, I do not,' Obadiah said. 'I came to warn you. After you left, Queen Jezebel continued to rage. She screamed at King Ahab, demanding why he allowed you to speak in such a manner and why he did not defend her gods.'

'Did Ahab reply?' Elijah asked.

'He told her that he was neither priest nor prophet and would not speak for any god.'

'Ahab does not truly believe in YHWH or any pagan god,' Elijah frowned.

'The queen announced that she would see you dead.' Obadiah stepped closer. 'She is a powerful and evil woman,' he whispered. 'If she arranged to have you killed, the king would turn his eyes elsewhere. You must hide.'

Elijah put a hand on the other man's shoulder. 'You are a godly man, Obadiah. I know you have hidden one hundred priests of YHWH from Jezebel. You will be blessed for that. I will ask the Creator for protection.'

The steward nodded. 'I will also pray for you.' With another bow, he walked away.

Elijah left the palace, walked down the hill and paused at the edge of the town.

'Creator of heaven and earth,' he prayed, 'I gave Your message to Ahab. Where would You have me go from here?'

In the rustling of the wind, he heard the voice of YHWH.

'Go and hide in the Kerith ravine, east of the Jordan. You will drink from the brook that is there and I will send ravens to bring you food.'

Elijah knew the place. The Kerith ravine was in the middle of the wilderness, hard and desolate; it was called 'the place that cuts'.

The prophet knew the Creator did unexpected things; telling Noah to build a boat on dry land or Abraham to sacrifice his son. Asking him to accept food from an unclean raven was part of the mysterious ways of the Almighty.

The prophet Elijah walked through the night. He arrived at the Kerith ravine and found a cave that was dry, and deep enough to block the winds. After gathering wood for a fire and grass for a bed, he took a deep drink of water from the brook. Then he lay down, covered himself with his robe and fell asleep.

He woke to the sound of scratching. Silhouetted against the sunlight streaming through the opening of the cave were two large ravens. One bird carried a piece of meat and the other a piece of bread. The ravens hopped to within arms-reach of the prophet and dropped the food on a flat stone. Uttering deep croaks, they turned, flapped their wings and flew away.

Elijah sat up, poked the coals and added wood to the fire. He skewered the meat on a thin stick and set it over the fire to cook. Lifting the bread, he prayed, 'Thank you, YHWH, for your provision,' and took a bite. It had a slightly sweet taste, rather like honey.

After eating, the prophet drank from the brook. He frowned as he thought of the people who would die in the coming drought. 'May Israel soon repent, Almighty God,' he prayed.

That evening, just as in the morning, two more ravens brought bread and meat. The next morning, food arrived in the same way. Day after day, week after week, the Creator provided for the prophet.

* * *

Months passed. Elijah noticed the brook running dry. The sky had held back its rain since the day Elijah had cursed Jezebel. The lands were now parched and wizened like the face of a bitter hag.

'YHWH, tell me where to go,' he prayed. The night the brook dried completely, YHWH spoke in Elijah's dream.

'Go at once to Zarephath of Sidon. You will meet a widow who will give you food.'

The next morning, Elijah left the ravine and walked north-west towards the coastal town of Zarephath. It took several days to travel the distance and he entered the town at sunset. Pausing to rest by the city gates, he saw a woman, robed in the garments of a widow, gathering sticks.

'Greetings,' he said. 'I'm thirsty. Would you bring me a little water?'

She smiled sadly. 'I will,' she said, turning with her load of sticks.

'Wait,' Elijah said, 'I'm hungry. Please bring me a piece of bread.'

The woman paused and turned back to him. Her eyes were stricken and her chest shuddered with each breath. 'I can draw water from the city well,' she said, 'but I don't have any . . . bread. I have only a small amount of flour in the jar and a little oil.' Her eyes filled with tears. 'I am . . . gathering a few sticks to take home and . . . make a meal for myself and my son. After we eat it, we will . . . starve and die.'

Elijah looked at the widow, realizing many were suffering as she.

'Go home and make the bread,' he said. 'But make a small piece of bread for me first and then some for you and your son. For the Creator says, "The flour will not be used up and the jug of oil will not run dry until the day He sends rain."'

The widow stopped crying and returned home. She made bread and brought it to Elijah. When she returned home, she looked in the jars and discovered there was enough flour and oil to make bread for her son and herself.

She returned and invited Elijah to stay in the upper room of her house. From that day, just as YHWH promised, there was always flour and oil until the drought ended.

Several months later, the widow's son grew ill. No matter what she did, he got worse: until he died.

Elijah found her holding the body of her son, weeping.

'He's dead!' she wailed. 'What did I do wrong that God took my son?'

'Give me your son,' Elijah said. He carried the boy to the upper room and laid him on the bed. He knelt.

'Almighty God,' he prayed, 'you sent this widow to care for me; have You brought tragedy by causing her son to die?' Grasping the boy's hands, he prayed, 'Almighty God, let this boy's life return to him!' Elijah felt a stirring and looked down.

The boy's chest was rising and falling; his eyelids fluttered and then opened.

The prophet lifted his arms towards heaven. 'Praise be to YHWH!' he cried. He picked the boy up and carried him to his mother. 'Your son lives!'

'Oh my son, my son!' she cried, rocking him. 'I had lost you. But YHWH sent a prophet to speak words of life.'

* * *

The drought lasted three years. One day, Elijah received a word from YHWH.

'Go to Ahab, and I will send rain on the land.'

He bid farewell to the widow and her son and left for Samaria. As he approached the city, he saw Obadiah driving a chariot.

'Greetings, Obadiah,' Elijah called.

The king's steward stopped the chariot and ran to Elijah.

'Is it really you, my lord?' he bowed.

'It is. Why are you here?'

'King Ahab sent me to look for grass to feed his animals.'

Elijah put a hand on Obadiah's shoulder. 'Go, tell Ahab I am here.'

'What have I done to deserve this treatment?' Obadiah asked. 'The king looks everywhere for you. If I tell him that you are here, and YHWH picks you up and carries you away, the king will kill me.'

The prophet smiled. 'As the Almighty lives, whom I serve, I will present myself to Ahab today.'

By the time Elijah arrived at the Ivory Palace, Obadiah had instructed the guards to send the prophet directly into the throne room. Ahab was there, speaking with Obadiah; however, the queen's throne was empty. When the king saw Elijah, he said, 'Is that you, Elijah, you troublemaker?'

'I am not the one who made trouble for Israel,' Elijah said. 'You disobeyed the Creator to follow other gods. Now the time has come to prove who serves the true God. Send the people of Israel to Mount Carmel. Bring the four hundred and fifty priests of Baal and Asherah that Jezebel feeds. I will meet you there.'

Ahab turned to his steward. 'Obadiah,' he said, 'send word to the people and then gather whatever items Elijah tells you. I will tell the queen to speak to the prophets of Baal and Asherah.'

Obadiah bowed and left the throne room.

Elijah stared at the king and said, 'YHWH will meet us there.'

Sunlight blazed on the people filling the valley between two foothills of Mount Carmel. On one side, King Ahab sat under the shade of a tamarisk tree, surrounded by four hundred and fifty prophets of Baal and Asherah.

Obadiah was nearby, watching over two bulls and dozens of massive jars filled with water drawn from the Great Sea.

On the other foothill, stood Elijah and his servant. The prophet raised his arms to silence the people. 'How long will you waver?' he shouted. 'If YHWH is God, then follow Him; but if Baal is god, then follow him.'

The people's silence angered Elijah. He pointed to the prophets of Baal. 'I am the last of YHWH's prophets, but there are four hundred and fifty prophets of Baal. Get two bulls for us. Choose one of the bulls for yourselves, sacrifice it, and put it on the wood; but do not set fire to it. I will prepare the other bull and put it on the wood and will not set fire to it.

'After the altars are prepared, you call on the name of your god and I will call on the name of YHWH. The god who answers *by fire* – he is God.'

The prophets of Baal gathered large rocks and stacked them to build an altar. After sacrificing the bull, they laid it on top. Then they began calling on Baal to send his lightning to consume the sacrifice. They danced and shouted, screamed and cursed. Some pointed to the sky, others cut themselves with knives and rolled in the dirt. Nothing happened.

All morning, the prophets of Baal called on their god, but nothing happened.

Elijah cupped his hands around his mouth. 'Shout louder,' he called. 'Maybe Baal is busy. Maybe he's asleep and you need to wake him. Baal could be on the toilet . . . Shout louder . . . he could be drunk.'

The taunts infuriated the prophets of Baal. They screamed and begged. They cut themselves with swords and spears. They kept pleading with Baal until the evening. Nothing happened.

Then Elijah stood and lifted his rod over the people. 'Come to me,' he called.

The people moved to the other side of the valley. They watched as Elijah rebuilt the altar of YHWH where it had been scattered. Elijah took a shovel and dug a trench around the altar. Then he stacked the wood on the altar, sacrificed the bull, and laid it on top of the wood. Turning, he called to four men.

'Fill four large jars with water and pour it over the bull and the wood,' he told them. The men walked to Obadiah, who gave each of them a massive jar. They filled the jars, and carried them up the foothill to pour it over the altar.

'Do it again,' Elijah told them.

The men walked down the hill for more water.

'Do it a third time,' Elijah said.

The men poured so much water that it ran off the altar and filled up the trench.

Elijah turned to the people and raised his arms. 'YHWH, God of Abraham, Isaac and Jacob,' he prayed aloud, 'let it be known today that You are God, and that I am Your servant and have done all these things at Your command. Answer me, YHWH, so these people will know that You are God, and that You are turning their hearts back again.'

There was silence. No one dare speak as the fading words of Elijah echoed from the hilltop.

Suddenly, above the mountains, a deep rumbling echoed from one end of the sky to the other. The sound grew as if thousands of drums were being beaten. The sky above grew dark.

A bolt of fire erupted in the clouds and shot down to hit the altar of YHWH. It exploded. The wood burst into flame, burning the sacrifice. The stones of the altar began to melt with the heat as the water boiled in the trench until it was no more.

The people fell to their knees in fear. 'YHWH – He is God!' they cried. 'YHWH – He is God!'

Elijah pointed toward the other altar. 'Seize the priests of Baal,' he cried. 'Don't let them get away!'

The terrified priests tried to run. Their screams echoed into the valley and faded as the mob fell upon them.

'Take the prophets of Baal to Kishon,' Elijah told the people, 'and kill them.'

The prophets screamed, pleading for their lives, begging King Ahab to rescue them.

Ahab stood by his chair; dumbfounded by all he had seen.

'Ahab,' Elijah called to him. 'Go and eat, for there is the sound of a heavy rain.'

Ahab stumbled towards his chariot. After he had climbed in, the driver turned the chariot and began driving towards Jezreel.

Elijah climbed to the top of Mount Carmel and knelt to pray. After a few minutes, he called to his servant.

'Go to the other side of the mountain and look towards the sea,' he said.

The man walked away. When he returned, he told Elijah, 'There is nothing there.'

'Go back again,' the prophet told him.

Seven times Elijah sent him to look and, on the seventh time, the man said, 'A cloud as small as a man's hand is rising from the sea.'

Elijah stood. In the distance, he saw Ahab's chariot driving away as if chased by a demon.

A drop of rain hit Elijah's face. Then another. And another. A rain as heavy as the rain of Noah's flood poured from the sky.

Elijah breathed deeply, his chest swelling. Reaching down, he grabbed the hem of his robe and tucked it into his belt. Turning, he ran down the hill and across the valley. The power of YHWH came upon the old prophet and he outran Ahab's chariot. As he passed the chariot, he cried, 'YHWH *is* God!'

Not long after that day, YHWH spoke to Elijah, *'Anoint Elisha, son of Shaphat to succeed you as prophet.'*

Without hesitation, Elijah set off and found Elisha. He was ploughing a field with twelve yoke of oxen. Elijah went up to him, took off his cloak and threw it around the young man. He left the field and continued walking down to the road.

Elisha recognized the old man and was stunned by the prophet's action. Leaving the oxen, he ran after Elijah.

'Let me say goodbye to my parents,' he said, 'and then I will come with you.'

'Do what you must,' Elijah replied. 'I only obeyed what YHWH told me to do.'

Elisha ran back to the field. He slaughtered two oxen and burnt the plough to cook the meat. He gave the meat to his family and neighbours. 'I am not coming back,' he said and set out to become Elijah's follower.

Elisha spent many months with Elijah. The older man taught him what it was to be a prophet of YHWH, how to listen to the voice of God, how to speak YHWH's message to the people; but most of all, how to obey, no matter what might happen.

One day, he and Elisha were travelling from Gilgal and he told the young man, 'Elisha, you have been a good pupil. You have studied diligently and served YHWH faithfully. I must tell you that today YHWH will call me to Him.'

'What?' Elisha was incredulous. 'How can YHWH take you today? Israel needs you . . . I need you.'

'I am just a man, like you,' Elijah said. 'There is only One Israel needs; He will redeem the people. I have helped to prepare His way; you will too. Now, stay here; the Lord has sent me to Bethel.'

Elisha grabbed Elijah's hand. 'As surely as YHWH lives and as you live,' he said, 'I will not leave you.'

As they continued on their journey, Elisha asked, 'Who is this One you speak of, who will redeem Israel?'

Elijah shrugged. 'I do not know. YHWH has told me that this One will heal the broken-hearted and reconcile families.'

As the two entered Bethel, a group of men – who were also prophets – met them. Several of the men took Elisha aside.

'Do you know that YHWH is going to take Elijah from you today?' they asked.

Elisha nodded, his face grim. 'Yes, but do not speak of it.'

'Elisha,' Elijah called, 'stay here, for YHWH has sent me to Jericho.'

Elisha shook his head. 'I told you; as surely as YHWH lives and as you live, I will not leave you.'

They said goodbye to the other prophets and continued their journey.

'What will I do when you are gone?' Elisha asked.

'You will do as you have done,' Elijah said. 'Seek YHWH and obey Him. As I have prepared for the One who is to come, so now must you.'

When they went through the gates of Jericho, another group of prophets met them. Again, several took Elisha aside, 'Do you know that YHWH is going to take your teacher from you today?'

'Yes,' he replied, 'but do not speak of it.'

'Elisha,' the older prophet called. 'Stay here; the Lord has sent me to the Jordan.'

Elisha clenched his fists. 'As surely as the Lord lives and as you live, I will not leave you.'

Elijah looked at him and nodded. They walked on together to the River Jordan. Elijah walked up to the raging river, which was nearly overflowing its banks. He removed his cloak and rolled it up. Lifting one end over his head, he swung it down, striking the water.

The waters began roiling back and forth, as if shifted by an unknown hand, and as the waves peaked, the water divided, as it had for Moses.

Elijah stepped onto the riverbed – which was dry and firm – and walked across, with Elisha at his side. After they had stepped onto the opposite bank of the Jordan, Elijah turned to Elisha. 'What can I do for you before I am taken?'

Without hesitating, Elisha answered, 'Let me inherit a double portion of your spirit.'

The old prophet closed his eyes for a moment, as if listening intently. Then he looked at the young man. 'What you ask is a difficult thing,' he said, 'however, if you see me when I am taken, it will be yours.'

The two continued walking, enjoying the bright sunlight and gentle breeze. They shared thoughts and memories as of those who know that they will not see each other for a long time.

'Elijah, you have been more than a teacher to me,' Elisha said, his voice thick with unshed tears. 'You have been like a father.'

Elijah smiled, his eyes glistening. 'You are the son I never had,' he said.

The wind began picking up, blowing first one way and then another, forming a whirlwind. The sky above grew brighter, drawing the eyes of both men. The clouds were dancing like flames, reflecting golden, crimson and orange. From the midst of the clouds appeared a fiery chariot drawn by horses of fire. It swooped down between the two men and back up again with Elijah inside, riding the whirlwind.

'My father!' Elisha cried, waving his hands over his head. 'My father! The chariot and horsemen of Israel!'

From the fiery chariot, Elijah turned. He removed his cloak and dropped it over the chariot's side. Then he lifted a hand in farewell.

The chariot, bearing the prophet of YHWH, rode through the clouds. Elisha watched as it grew smaller and smaller and then . . . was no more.

'Ahhhhh . . .' Elisha screamed and, grabbing the neck of his robe, tore it apart. He picked up Elijah's cloak where it had fallen. 'YHWH, I will follow You as Elijah taught me,' he prayed. 'I will take up where he left off and will help prepare the people for the One who is to come.' He raised his hands to the heavens. 'Come, Almighty One . . . Your people are waiting.'

17

The Fish

The desert sun blazed down on the back of the old man. He sat in the dust on a mound of broken pots on the outskirts of the city and looked at the high walls that rose up from the ground. Around him were the fragments of what was once a tall bush. It had grown up overnight, shaded the old man from the sun and then, without warning, had withered and died. With a long, gnarled finger, the old man wrote in the dust at his feet inscribing his name: JONAH.

As Jonah pulled his long coat over his head to provide shade from the heat, he moaned to himself, spitting out the words and looking to the sky.

'You never keep Your word . . .' he shouted, shaking a fist at a solitary cloud above him. 'You said You would destroy this city and yet it still stands . . . You make me look a fool. I did what You commanded. Told them of their wickedness – and You promised to destroy them . . . am I not a prophet?' the old man raged as he got to his feet.

The desert wind blew the dust around his feet. Shards of broken pot rattled across the ground. Jonah closed his eyes as the sun burnt even brighter. He shielded his face from the light as he slumped to the ground.

Jonah . . . Jonah . . .' the still, small voice spoke from the wind. *'Think of what I have done for you. Teshuvah is not just for you but also for this city . . .'*

'Repentance . . . forgiveness . . . it is all You say,' Jonah screamed. 'You are the Creator of the Universe, the Almighty, and yet You let them live. What is wrong with smiting them? Why don't You send down lightning from the sky and destroy their houses?'

'Look back Jonah – look back and see . . .'

It was as if Jonah were taken back in time. The world grew dark. No longer could he see the city. There before him was the cluster of houses that made up his village. The vision was so real he could even taste the dry, brittle dust on his lips.

The news that Assyrians had attacked a caravan in the nearby hills swept through the marketplace. Jonah was by the fruit stall near to his house. Everyone was gathered around, listening to the news.

'They took everything, including the donkeys, and killed all but one man,' said an old woman wrapped in a torn cloak as she stacked fruit on the market stall. 'Killed everyone and what for? Nothing . . . there was not a thing to take.'

'What are they doing so far south? What if they come to attack us?' a young mother asked; her child clung fearfully to her, whimpering into her neck. 'We are not wealthy and powerful. Ours is only a small village in the territory of Zebulun.'

'The Assyrians attacked because they do not know the difference between what is good and what is evil,' the fruit-seller said, squeezing juice from a pomegranate. 'I don't believe they know what good is.'

'May YHWH strike them and destroy them,' added his neighbour.

'Amen,' the old woman agreed.

'What can be done?' asked a small fat man in a fine robe as he pulled at his neatly trimmed beard. 'I and the other leaders of the village have met to discuss the attack. We do not have soldiers to protect us.' He accepted a mug of pomegranate juice from the merchant.

'Even if we did, do we want to make the Assyrians mad?' the young mother asked. 'If we were to resist they would overrun our village. They will kill our men and enslave the women and children.' She lowered her voice. 'I have heard that when they capture someone, they remove his skin while he is still alive.'

'I hate Assyrians, and the wicked Ninevites most of all,' the fat man answered as he wiped the dribble of pomegranate from his chin. 'They need to be burnt from the earth, like the evil people during the time of Noah!'

'We can ask Jonah,' the old woman chuntered, turning to the prophet. 'As a prophet of YHWH, you can call upon the Almighty to give us guidance.'

'Jonah . . . does the Creator still speak to you?' the fat man asked. 'Do you hear Him as you once did?'

All those gathered in the marketplace turned to the old man. Every eye stared, needing an answer from him.

The prophet wiped the dirt from his hands. Looking at the people, he slowly licked his lips as he thought. 'It is time for something to be done about the Assyrians,' he spoke slowly. 'But I do not know the will of the Almighty. We must be prepared to do whatever He wants.'

'If it will rid us of the Assyrians, I will do anything,' the old woman stated.

'Is that the will of all of you?' Jonah asked, staring at the crowd.

The people looked at each other, no one daring to speak. Finally, the fat man stepped forward.

'I speak for the leaders of the village,' he said. 'I say we do whatever Jonah asks.'

'Tell everyone in the village to pray,' Jonah instructed. 'All must fast – no one must eat or drink anything. I will go from the village to a quiet place and ask YHWH.'

For the next three days, Jonah and everyone in the village fasted and prayed to the Almighty to deal with the Assyrians.

'Strike them, YHWH,' Jonah shouted from the shade of an olive tree atop a small hill. 'From their great city of Nineveh to the smallest village, destroy them all.'

The men and women and children watched the prophet, Jonah, as he shouted at the sky and danced beneath the tree. A single white dove circled in the sky high above him and when night came, the stars shone brightly down.

At dawn on the fourth day, Jonah was kneeling in prayer when a wind howled around him. It was cold, sharp and needled him with grains of sand. The leaves of the olive tree were ripped from the branches and fell about him like snow. Then came a voice Jonah had heard before. He trembled with fear; it was the voice of the Creator.

'I have heard the cries of the people praying against Nineveh. The city's wickedness is great.'

Jonah smiled to himself, waiting for YHWH to pronounce judgement on the Assyrians and destroy their land.

'Jonah, go to the great city of Nineveh and preach against it, tell the people to repent from their wickedness.'

The wind whipped through the desert, spiralling sand high into the air.

Jonah could not believe what he had heard. '*Preach* to the . . . Ninevites?' he whispered. 'YHWH, surely not? You want me to tell those Assyrian dogs to repent? Why? Do you intend to . . . forgive them? You can't! They're evil! Everyone in the village was expecting You to answer our prayers.' Jonah stood up, clenching his fists. 'I won't have anything to do with this. They deserve to be destroyed, not spared. If I have to run to the ends of the earth, I won't do it. Then, if no one preaches to the Ninevites, they won't repent, and You . . . You will *have* to destroy them!'

Jonah ran down the hill, through the village and to his house. He grabbed a large bag and began filling it with clothes and food. Taking a bag of money, he ran to the door.

'Did YHWH speak to you, Jonah?' the fruit-seller had followed him. She noticed the bulging bag. 'Where are you going?'

'I don't know how long I will be gone,' Jonah answered as he tied the bag on the back of his donkey. He tried to ignore those who had followed the merchant and waited expectantly for an answer from YHWH.

'But, Jonah – what did the Creator say to you?' a man asked as Jonah climbed on the beast and turned it towards the road leading to the coast.

'He asks me to do the impossible,' his face was grim. 'It is something no man should ever agree to. What does the Creator know about me if He can ask me that?'

As the sun crested over the distant mountains, Jonah had left his village and was riding west towards the sea.

'If I leave from a port in Israel, they will wonder why a prophet is going so far away,' Jonah said to himself, and turned the donkey towards Joppa. 'The Phoenicians don't know me and won't care where I am going, as long as I pay the fare.'

By midday, the donkey had carried Jonah all the way to Joppa. The city was bustling with sailors and ships that stood taller than houses. From this seaport, anyone could take passage on a ship and travel throughout the world, which was exactly what Jonah wanted.

After selling his donkey to a caravan train, Jonah walked up and down the port, speaking to sailors and captains, until he found the ship he wanted.

'Tarshish is as far as any captain dares travel,' one captain told him. 'To go farther would be to risk the anger of the sea gods. They would send their monsters to destroy the ship and eat the crew.'

'Tarshish sounds fine to me,' Jonah said, paying the fare. Picking up his bags, he went onboard the ship. Within the hour, the sailors were untying the anchor and navigating out of port and into the open sea. As Jonah looked up, the sails caught the wind, the rigging groaned and ropes tightened.

They sailed for an hour. Jonah then saw each member of the crew go to the side of the ship; they knelt down and bowed their heads. A boy took a talisman from his pocket and threw it over the side of the ship.

'What are they doing?' Jonah asked the captain.

'Each man is praying to his god,' the man explained. 'We don't want to offend the sea gods. Some men give an offering to their gods.' He pointed to one sailor. 'You see that man? Where he comes from, they believe that the god Dagon sends a messenger from the sea. Dagon's messenger would have skin white as lamb's wool.'

'Where is that man from?' Jonah asked.

'Nineveh.'

'Nineveh!' Jonah spat. 'You have an Assyrian dog on board?'

The captain eyed him. 'I do not judge a man by where he comes from. Only the gods know what's in a man's heart.'

'My God has turned against me,' Jonah said. 'He wanted me to go somewhere and do something detestable. I didn't want to, so I decided to go in the other direction.'

'You're a brave man,' the captain answered, 'to run from your god.'

'I would be a fool to do what He asked,' Jonah said under his breath.

As the sun melted into the water, Jonah went below deck. He opened a bag and took out some bread and cheese. The words of the Thanksgiving came to his lips but he bit his tongue. Jonah wasn't sure he wanted to be in conversation with the Almighty just then. It was the first time he could remember eating without first asking the Creator to bless his meal.

After eating and taking a long drink of water, he wrapped a blanket around himself and lay down. He slowly fell asleep to the sounds of the waves gently rocking the ship.

He woke to a hand violently shaking him. There was no light. He couldn't see who gripped his shoulder. Instead of swaying on the water, the ship lurched.

'What is it?' he asked sleepily. 'Who are you?'

'The captain,' the man said in a frightened voice. 'How can you sleep? We are in the midst of a great storm; I've never seen one this bad. The waves threaten to break up the ship. I had the sailors throw the cargo overboard to lighten our load. Better get up and pray to whatever gods you pray to; they're the only ones who can save us now.'

Jonah tried to stand but fell as the boat tilted almost completely on its side. Before he could regain his footing, the ship lurched back, tossing him into the air.

'What shall I do?' Jonah yelled.

'On deck – as fast as you can!' the captain answered.

Jonah felt his way through the darkness to the ladder that led to the deck.

The storm screamed in fury, lightning streaking across the night sky in jagged knives. The ship lurched as waves, nearly as tall as the mast, crashed into its side and washed over the deck. All around, the wind squalled and waves grew like mountains.

The captain handed Jonah a rope. 'Follow me,' he yelled above the storm. 'We're tying ourselves to the mast, to keep from falling overboard.'

Jonah stumbled across the pitching deck, holding on to whatever he could grasp. A bolt of lightning revealed the crew huddled around the mast, ropes tied around their waists. All about the deck were broken wooden crates whose contents the sailors had tossed overboard. Jonah followed the captain's instructions, wrapping the rope around his waist and then tying it to the mast. He tripped as the ship lurched to the left and fell into the lap of a sailor.

'Hang on,' the man screamed. 'I've never seen a storm so fierce.'

'It's the wrath of the gods, I tell you,' the captain yelled. 'Someone did not make peace with his god.' He looked at the men, huddling drenched on the deck. 'Which one of you is it?'

When no one answered, another sailor yelled, 'We should draw lots and see who has angered the gods.'

The captain nodded and reached over to one of the wooden crates. He snapped off several slats and broke them into different lengths. He held them in his hand, with one end covered. 'Whoever draws the shortest one, he is the one responsible for this calamity.'

Each man in turn reached over to select a piece of wood.

Jonah's hand was trembling as he drew his. *It is all my fault,* he thought.

After they all had chosen a piece, the captain yelled, 'When the lightning strikes again, hold up your wood and we shall see.'

A moment later, a massive bolt of lightning set fire to the night sky. Everyone held up his piece of wood. Jonah didn't need to look to know his was the shortest.

'Who are you,' the captain yelled. 'Where do you come from?'

Tell them the truth, Jonah thought. *They should not die because of your disobedience.*

'I am a Hebrew and I worship YHWH, the one true God of heaven, who made the sea and the land.'

A mountainous wave slammed into the boat, turning it nearly on its side. The wood creaked, threatening to break the mast. The sailors screamed in fear until the ship righted itself.

'You have angered the God of the sea,' the captain yelled. 'What should we do to you to make the sea calm down?'

'YHWH brought this great storm because of me. Throw me into the sea,' Jonah yelled, 'and it will become calm.'

'I cannot throw a man into this sea,' the captain yelled. 'Even the best swimmer would drown. Men!' he yelled. 'We're going to try and row back to land. Secure your ropes to the sides of the ship and grab an oar.'

Jonah watched as the sailors untied their ropes and pulled themselves to the oars. After retying their ropes, they grabbed the oars and pulled, screaming under the strain.

Jonah had thought the storm fierce, now it erupted in a wild fury. Lightning streaked without pause, striking all around. The wind howled and screamed as waves tossed the ship. Untying his rope, Jonah pulled himself over to the captain.

'It's no use,' he shouted. 'You have to throw me overboard.'

The captain looked at him for a moment, and then nodded. 'May your God forgive us,' he yelled. Turning to two men near them, he ordered, 'Throw him over.'

Jonah followed the two sailors to the ship's rail. When they hesitated, he yelled, 'You must! Or no one will live!'

'Please forgive us!' one sailor screamed; Jonah recognized the Assyrian.

'I do forgive you,' Jonah yelled.

Looking upwards the two sailors screamed, 'Oh great God, please do not let us die for killing an innocent man, for You have done as You pleased.' Grabbing Jonah's arms, they lifted him over the rail . . . and let go.

Jonah felt the wind whipping him as he fell. He hit the water and sank, his lungs screaming in pain for air. Jonah did not know how to swim, but he began kicking his legs, and reaching upwards. When he broke the surface, the storm clouds were gone and the raging sea was calm. Jonah saw the captain and sailors kneeling on the deck.

'His God is God!' they cried. Then one man – the Assyrian – pointed to Jonah. 'Swim!' he screamed. 'Swim for your life!'

'Behind you,' another yelled. 'It's a great fish!'

Jonah looked over his shoulder. About twenty feet from him, was a gigantic fish. It was taller than a house, with skin like that of an elephant, and a mouth as big as a ship and as wide as a house. Its colossal mouth scooped the water as it came closer and closer.

Jonah beat the water with his fists as he slowly sank beneath the waves. All he could see was a vast blackness that engulfed him. Then all light was gone as Jonah felt himself slipping inside the fish.

'YHWH help me,' Jonah cried. 'I am in the belly of a great fish.'

Then there was nothing. All was as black as death. Without the sun or moon, Jonah did not know how long he had been inside the creature. It could have been hours; it could have been days.

*   *   *

Jonah blinked, trying to focus his eyes against the blinding sunlight. He looked around; he saw sand, seaweed, and hills, palm trees, birds and blue sky. He looked down; he was sitting in a pool of something slimy, floating with fish parts and seaweed, and reeked worse than when he was inside the fish. Shifting his body, he knelt.

'In my distress, I called to You, YHWH, and You answered me,' he prayed. 'In the heart of the seas, when the waves swept over me, I knew that You had rejected me and I would never again see Your holy temple. I sank down into the waters, to the base of mountains in the deep.

'But You brought me up from the pit, Almighty God. When I knew I was dying, I remembered You. People who believe in worthless idols do not know what grace could be theirs. But I do! I will sing to You, YHWH, and give thanks. For however long I live, I will follow You.'

Jonah crawled to the water and peeled off what was left of his robe. With a wary eye on the sea, he stepped into the water to bathe. As he scooped water in his hands, he stopped; the skin of his hands was white. He looked at his arms: white. His legs were white . . . white as a lamb's wool. *Someone might think I am leprous,* he thought, rinsing his robe and cloak and putting them back on.

As he stepped out of the water, a soft breeze blew from the land, swirling around Jonah. The wind was warm and smelled of flowers. From the midst of the breeze, a voice Jonah thought he would never hear again spoke: *'Go to the great city of Nineveh and proclaim to it the message I give you.'*

YHWH had spoken.

Jonah bowed his head and whispered. 'Yes, Lord . . . I will obey.'

*   *   *

He walked nervously through the city gates of Nineveh. The streets were crowded with people. Everyone stared at Jonah. When he reached the marketplace he began to shout.

'Forty more days and Nineveh will be overturned – if you do not repent. You have been judged and shall be destroyed.'

A crowd gathered around him. Fingers pointed. A woman screamed.

'Who brings this news?' a man asked.

'Jonah, a prophet of God,' he answered. 'For what seemed like days, I was in the belly of a great fish that spewed me on the shore. I have come to tell you this. Repent or you will all be destroyed.'

'Why should we believe you?' someone asked.

'Would I be so foolish to come here if God had not sent me?' Jonah asked. 'I have done all that the Creator has asked. Now, it is up to you. Repent or die . . .'

His words stilled the crowd.

Suddenly the mob parted. A file of soldiers marched towards him. Shields, banners, spears clashed together as a trumpet shrilled in the morning light.

'Make way; make way!' the captain of the guard yelled, pushing through the people.

'You . . . need . . . to . . . REPENT . . .' Jonah shouted at the soldier.

The sun glistened on the brass plate that covered the soldier's chest. The captain looked at Jonah, amazed that anyone could speak in such a way. 'You speak to me?' he asked.

Jonah nodded. 'The Creator knows what you do in secret and *you* must repent,' Jonah said.

The captain looked at him, gaping, unable to answer. 'Dagon's messenger,' he croaked and fell to his knees. Seeing his confusion, Jonah explained that it was not Dagon who sent him, but YHWH, the Creator of heaven and earth.

One by one the people knelt.

Jonah walked through the city, past tall buildings and up long streets. All the time he shouted the warning to the city.

The captain of the guard had reported to the king all he had seen. When the king of Nineveh heard that God's messenger warned of the city's destruction, he took off his royal robes, put on sackcloth, and threw ashes on his head.

'From this day, I am proclaiming a fast,' he proclaimed. 'Let no man, woman or child eat anything. Do not let any beast, herd or flock eat or drink. Let the people give up their evil ways and their violence. Let everyone pray. Who knows? Maybe the Almighty will relent and have compassion on us and turn from His fierce anger so that we will not perish.'

Jonah shuddered with anger as he heard the words of the king.

'Don't listen to him,' Jonah muttered under his breath as he walked to the city gates.

A wind blew in from the desert. It circled and swirled in the marketplace and crept under the doors as if it were the eyes of the Creator searching out the hearts of the wicked city.

When YHWH saw what they did and how the people turned from their evil ways, He had compassion on them. All that they had done was forgiven. The Creator did not destroy Nineveh.

Jonah, angry with the Almighty, walked into the desert and slumped to the ground. He folded his arms to blot out the light.

'Even the darkness is as light to You . . .' he grumbled.

Jonah . . . Jonah . . .' said the voice on the wind. *'Have you forgotten who I AM?'*

Without sight or sound, something stirred under the ground. As Jonah sat on the scorching sand, the first shoots of a mighty plant sprang forth. Before Jonah could complain, a bush like nothing he had seen before had sprouted from the desert and shaded him from the sun.

Jonah sighed, knowing that he had no place to hide.

18

The Lions

Candles flickered in the court of the king, casting long, dark shadows over the endless avenues of stone tiles. Every step, every breath echoed through the cavernous room. The walls sparkled as if embedded with diamonds. By the throne stood a tall man dressed in long, fine robes.

'Once again, Belteshazzar, you have advanced my kingdom,' King Darius said, handing the ornate scroll to the tall man.

Belteshazzar bowed, the parchment clasped to his chest, 'It is my pleasure to serve Your Majesty.'

King Darius looked around his throne room. Dozens of administrators and governors who ruled throughout Persia stood in silence. 'Is there anyone in the entire kingdom who is wiser than Belteshazzar?' his voice echoed through the vast chamber.

A murmur rippled as the people in the room crossed their arms and bowed. An older man, Governor Ksathra, who stood in the front of the crowd, turned his head slightly towards the two men next to him. 'Whether or not one believed it,' he whispered, 'it would be at the cost of one's life to disagree with the king.'

His companions grimly nodded their heads.

'I have appointed one hundred and twenty governors to rule the provinces of my kingdom,' the king continued. 'Over these governors, I have placed Belteshazzar, Gazsi and Majeed as administrators. They are to be obeyed as if I – your king – had spoken.'

Gazsi and Majeed raised their heads slightly to bow again in acknowledgement of the king. They smiled to themselves in self-seeking recognition.

'What is more . . .' the king announced, 'the provinces under Belteshazzar have done excellently. Never have I had more gold and fewer problems from any other part of my kingdom.' Darius stepped from his throne to Belteshazzar and grasped the man's forearms. 'Thank you, Belteshazzar. Thank you.' He faced the room. 'Thank you all.'

As the crowd dispersed, Gazsi turned to Majeed and Ksathra. 'We need to talk.'

Gazsi led the other two men through the corridors of the palace. He was taller than most men, a sword-master with grey streaks brushing his dark hair that gave him an air of wisdom. He paused often to speak to a governor here, nodding to another there. At last, he stopped before a carved wooden door, where two guards holding scimitars stood on either side.

The guards bowed their heads; one guard then opened the door and stepped through the doorway while the other scanned the corridor. After a few minutes, the first guard emerged from the chamber and, bowing, held the door open for Gazsi and the two men to enter.

The chambers set aside for Gazsi were opulent, befitting an administrator of the kingdom. Furniture touched with gilt was scattered throughout the room. Colourful tapestries and rugs covered the walls and floor. Ksathra walked to a set of doors carved like lace on the far wall and grabbed the handle with stubby fingers. The doors opened to a private garden blossomed with fragrant flowers.

'We all know that King Nebuchadnezzar built the beautiful hanging gardens for his wife, Queen Amyitis,' the governor observed. Unlike Gazsi, Ksathra was short and fleshy and the grey in his hair lent an eerie cast to his skin. 'Now I see the king adorns his guest chambers in the palace with gardens as well.'

'We are not here to discuss gardens,' Gazsi strode to another side of the room where thick pillows were placed near a low table set with food. 'We must speak of Belteshazzar. I . . . fear him.'

'Ah . . .' Majeed tore a piece of flat bread and bit into it. 'What do you fear from him?'

'Did you not see the regard the king showed him?' Gazsi asked. 'I was surprised that he did not elevate him and appoint him over you and me.'

Majeed stopped chewing. 'He would not,' he said incredulously.

'When have you ever heard the king praise anyone as he did Belteshazzar?' Gazsi asked. 'The man's *influence* over the king grows daily. Some would say it is by magic . . . or by that foreign god he worships.'

'I do not understand your concern.' Ksathra sipped the hot tea, sweetened with honey. 'Belteshazzar is known for being fair and honest.' He looked from Gazsi to Majeed. 'Ah, I understand.' He smiled. 'Both of you have . . . bene-fited . . . from the provinces you have administered. As administrators, you are *the eye of the king*. You're afraid if Belteshazzar turned his eye towards *you*, he might discover some . . . discrepancies . . . in your reports?'

The men's silence confirmed the truth.

'So – something must be done,' Gazsi stated.

'Something must be done,' Majeed nodded. 'But what?

'Discredit him to the king?' Gazsi suggested.

'How?' Majeed asked. 'As Ksathra pointed out, Belteshazzar is known for being fair and honest.'

'We will have to search for something,' Gazsi insisted, turning to Ksathra. 'That is why I asked you here. Finding what people wish to keep secret is a skill of yours.'

Majeed looked at Ksathra with a newfound respect. 'Truthfully?'

The small man spread his hands humbly. 'It is a gift from the gods,' he said with a grin.

'We need you to learn whatever you can about Belteshazzar,' Gazsi said. 'Look into the records he keeps, speak with the men under him. If you cannot find anything in his governmental affairs to bring charges against, then investigate his personal life. I do not care how small or unimportant it seems; *something* must be found.'

'That type of investigation will require gold to help people . . . remember . . . things about Belteshazzar,' Ksathra murmured.

Gazsi looked at Majeed, who nodded. 'You will have whatever you need and, for yourself, you will find that Majeed and I will be most generous.'

Ksathra bowed his head briefly. 'We will all be here for another week, while the king listens to the reports from his governors. Let us meet again in five days.'

'Speak not a word of this to anyone. If we are found in this deed, we will all be dead,' Gazsi murmured as the sweet sound of the evening birds echoed in the garden.

Day followed day, the palace of King Darius was filled with the sound of people. From dawn until late into the night, the king held court. During that time, as he spoke to all the governors and rulers in the land, Belteshazzar was always at his side.

While the meetings between King Darius and the governors continued, Gazsi noticed Ksathra drinking tea with foreign dignitaries in the gardens, speaking with servants and guards at the palace doors.

On the fifth day, Gazsi walked to the palace stable, where servants had his blood stallion saddled and waiting for him. Mounting the horse, he rode out of the palace grounds, up the streets of Babylon, through the famed blue Ishtar Gates – decorated with dragons and bulls – towards the Summer Palace. There, in a garden near the River Euphrates, he met with his two conspirators.

Over the years, Gazsi had honed his ability to read people; a single glance at Ksathra did not make the administrator hopeful. The man looked frail and tired. His hands shook slightly as if his heart trembled.

When they had confirmed that they were quite alone, Gazsi asked for Ksathra's report.

The pudgy man held his hands palms upwards in a sign of defeat. 'I spoke with dozens of men whom Belteshazzar oversees, with the foreign ambassadors he meets, even with guards and servants here in the palace. I could find nothing to discredit him. He is honest and fair in his dealing with the governors, respectful with the ambassadors and even kind to the lowest maid in the palace.'

Gazsi was disappointed, but not surprised. 'So, what of his personal life? What have you learnt?'

Ksathra shrugged. 'Nothing. He does not indulge in food, women, gambling . . . the man reads books and doesn't drink.'

'There must be *something* he does to excess,' Majeed insisted.

'The only thing Belteshazzar spends a lot of time doing is praying to his god,' Ksathra said. 'He prays three times each day.'

'There's nothing then,' Majeed conceded.

'Wait a moment,' Gazsi tapped his lips thoughtfully. 'Maybe there is something we can do. We will need to speak with some of the others, but I think it might work. Come,' he said to his fellow conspirators, 'listen to my plan and tell me what you think.'

The three men met outside the throne room two days later. They had chosen their clothing carefully; if their plan were going to succeed, they would need every weapon at their disposal. Speaking to the steward of the King's Chamber, they waited for admittance. After half an hour, the door to the throne room opened.

The steward tapped his staff on the stone floor and announced, 'Administrator Gazsi, Administrator Majeed and Governor Ksathra.'

The three men looked at each other, took a deep breath, and entered. The throne room was filled with people from the four corners of the world. The only official not there was Belteshazzar; Gazsi had arranged for this meeting when they knew the chief administrator would be at home, praying. He kept his eyes looking straight ahead as they walked towards the throne. When they reached the dais, the three men folded their arms across their chests and bowed from the waist.

'Rise,' King Darius said. 'Welcome, my administrators and my governor. As this is not the scheduled time for your yearly reports, I must assume you are here about something else.' He leaned back in his throne and waited.

Gazsi glanced at the two men at his side and then faced the king.

'O King Darius, may you live forever!' he began with the traditional greeting. 'We know that this yearly meeting comes at the same time as the celebration of the day of your birth. Ah, the earth was indeed blessed on that day,' Gazsi said. He noticed the king's smile broadening and continued. 'The royal administrators, governors and advisors have all agreed that – as part of the celebration – the king should issue an edict and enforce the decree, that anyone who prays to any god or man during the next thirty days, except to you, O King, shall be thrown into the lions' den.'

'Now, O King, we plead with you to issue this decree and put it in writing so that it cannot be altered, in the tradition of the laws of the Medes and Persians, which cannot be repealed.' Gazsi finished his speech with another bow.

The room was so silent Gazsi could hear his heart beating through his chest. *Was it enough,* he wondered. *Will the king fall into our trap?*

He heard Darius shift on the throne.

'Rise, Administrator Gazsi,' the king commanded.

Gazsi straightened and looked at the king.

'I am most flattered by this request,' Darius said. 'It is not often that a king hears himself equated with the gods by his own officials.' He looked around the room. 'I do not see Belteshazzar; what does my chief administrator say to your request?'

Out of the corner of his eye, Gazsi noticed Majeed move his hand behind his back and make a small motion. Suddenly the crowd in the throne room erupted into shouts.

'Long live King Darius!'

'All praise to Darius the Mede!'

'There is no one greater!'

The king rose from his throne, smiling, while the shouting went on for several minutes. Gazsi noticed Darius thrusting out his chest. *All kings are alike,* he thought, *so easily convinced they are like gods.*

After another minute, the king raised his hands to quiet the room.

'I thank you,' he smiled. 'As it appears to be the desire of all my officials, I would be most happy to grant your request, Gazsi.' Turning to a secretary, the king said, 'Attend Administrator Gazsi as he dictates the decree. Then bring it to me. I will sign it, in accordance with the laws of the Medes and the Persians.'

The crowd shouted again. Gazsi, Majeed and Ksathra bowed their way out of the throne room. When the immense door closed with a gush of wind, they looked at each other and smiled.

Within the hour, Belteshazzar returned to the palace; he had heard about the king's decree. Hurrying to the throne room, he ignored the steward and stepped through the doors to see King Darius hold up a document and declare, 'It is done!' amid clamorous applause.

Belteshazzar backed out of the room and walked through the palace corridors. They seemed longer, quieter, colder than they had ever done before. *YHWH,* he prayed, *how did this happen? The Law You gave to Moses said to worship no other god before You. Darius is a good man – and a great king – but he is not a god. I cannot stop praying to You and I will not pray to him.*

Belteshazzar was so intent on his thoughts that he did not notice Gazsi, Majeed and Ksathra following him out of the palace and through the streets of Babylon. He could think of nothing but the words of King Darius.

When Belteshazzar arrived at his home, he climbed the stairs, walked into a room and opened the windows. *I have done this every day since I arrived in Babylon,* he thought, *I will not stop now.*

Thoughts of his life flooded back. Babylon had not been his place of birth. His land was far away, over the mountains. Belteshazzar had been born into Judean nobility; his parents had named him Daniel. He was a young man when King Nebuchadnezzar had invaded Jerusalem. Daniel and three of his friends, Shadrach, Meshach and Abednego, were among the first group of Hebrew hostages sent to Babylon. They had been captured as they played, their hands strapped with leather thongs, and dragged to Babylon.

Many of the hostages tried to remain true to their faith but, in the exotic capital of the Babylonian kingdom, it was difficult. Shortly after their arrival, Daniel and his friends were offered foods from the royal kitchens. Knowing that Babylon was a land of many gods, they had no way of knowing whether the meats had first been sacrificed to pagan idols.

None of them would eat the meat and had requested to be given only vegetables and water. YHWH honoured their obedience: after three weeks on this diet, they were healthier than those hostages who had eaten all the rich palace foods.

Because they were intelligent and showed keen insight, Daniel and his friends were sent to the palace's wise men for training. When King Nebuchadnezzar was plagued with dreams that none could interpret, the Creator of heaven and earth revealed the dreams and their meaning to Daniel.

When he reported YHWH's message to Nebuchadnezzar, the king changed Daniel's name to Belteshazzar, appointed him chief of the wise men, and made him governor over Babylon.

After Nebuchadnezzar died, through each successive king, including the Persian kings who conquered Babylon, the Creator continued to honour Daniel's obedience – until he rose to a position that was considered by some to be second in the kingdom, a position that he kept even when the kingdom was overrun by the Persians. He had gained position and wealth yet, when he built his home, Belteshazzar remembered the source of all his blessings and had a room built on an upper floor with windows that faced Jerusalem. There were no furnishings in the room, only a rug for him to kneel upon. Three times a day, he would return to his home and go into this room. After opening the windows, he would worship YHWH and pray.

What happened? Belteshazzar wondered as he knelt on the thick rug. *Darius would never make such a decision as this on his own.* His face set. *How it came about does not matter. I will not worship Darius or any other man or god.*

Lowering his head to the floor, Belteshazzar began to pray, 'Hear O Israel, YHWH, our God, I pray to You, Almighty God, please help me . . .'

'So, this is how the great Belteshazzar honours the king's decrees.'

Daniel sat up and looked around. Gazsi, Majeed and Ksathra stood at the door, smiling as if they had discovered a secret treasure.

'I did not know you had arrived; my servants did not announce you.'

The three men stepped into the room.

'I saw you enter the throne room as King Darius signed his decree,' Gazsi said. 'I also saw you leave. As we – Majeed, Ksathra and I – had business we needed to discuss with you, we followed you here.' He looked around the room. 'But there are no cushions for us to sit upon. There's only this rug, which you appear to be using in order to . . . pray.'

Belteshazzar studied the other men for several moments. *So this is how it happened.* He knew what his answer to Gazsi's question had to be. Lying was abhorrent to him and – even if he would lie – he couldn't deny it; the others had heard him praying.

'Yes, I was praying, as I do three times every day.'

The other men gasped, their eyes wide.

'I am shocked, Belteshazzar,' Majeed said. 'You knew the king's decree . . . yet you blatantly disobeyed.'

Belteshazzar stared at the man. 'Somehow, I do not think you are shocked, Majeed,' he said. 'I believe that you arranged the decree and planned to catch me praying, although I do not know why, or what you hope to gain.'

'Arranged?' Majeed repeated. 'Planned? They are words of conspiracy . . .'

'All we are concerned about is the good of the kingdom and the king,' Gazsi smiled.

'And as good Persian officials and loyal subjects, it is our duty to report you to the king,' Ksathra sneered. 'However, in the event that you tried to run away, we brought an escort for you.' He turned and pointed towards the door.

Belteshazzar looked to see two guards waiting in the hall. *YHWH help me*, he prayed. Both guards ducked their heads. 'I'm sorry, Lord Belteshazzar,' one guard said. 'We must do our duty.'

'Of course you do,' he reassured him. 'And I will not give you any problems. Let us go now, so I may lay my case before the king.'

Gazsi and his two fellow conspirators found the king in the garden, taking refreshments with the Egyptian ambassador. After apologizing for interrupting the king, he explained they needed to speak with him privately.

Darius turned to the ambassador. 'I am sorry, Your Excellency, but I must speak with my officials. Darius waited until the Egyptian had left before turning to his officials. 'Now, what do you have to tell me that required interrupting my time with a guest?'

'O King,' Gazsi began, 'did you not publish a decree that during the next thirty days anyone who prays to any god or man except to you, O King, would be thrown into the lions' den?'

'I did,' the king said. 'It stands in accordance with the laws of the Medes and Persians which cannot be repealed.'

Gazsi glanced at his two companions and then back to the king. 'We – Majeed, Ksathra and I – are saddened to have to report to you that there is one in the kingdom who has defied your decree. One of the Hebrew hostages who was brought here by great King Nebuchadnezzar. This man pays no attention to you, O King, or to the decree you put in writing. He still prays three times a day.'

Darius stood, his face dark and eyes narrowed. 'Who is this that defies me? On my honour, he will taste my wrath.'

'It is Administrator Belteshazzar,' Gazsi said.

The king's face paled. His knees gave way under him and he fell onto a thick cushion. 'Belteshazzar?' he whispered. 'It cannot be. You are wrong. There must be a mistake.'

'There is no mistake,' Majeed said. 'We found him in his home, praying near an open window. Ask the guards who were with us. Ask Belteshazzar, he openly acknowledges his crime.'

Darius sat stunned.

'We understand how difficult this must be for you, Your Majesty,' Ksathra said. 'To be betrayed by one of your own officials. His punishment cannot be great enough!'

The king looked at him, confused. 'Punishment?'

'The lions,' Gazsi said. 'Your decree states that he must be thrown into the den of lions.'

The king licked his lips. 'They will kill . . .' he trailed off, eyes widening in horror.

'. . . kill him,' Gazsi finished. 'Yes, I'm sure they will. But if punishment is not severe enough or not carried out, what will happen? Other people will believe they do not have to obey laws and soon the entire kingdom will be thrown into chaos.'

'Caught by my own decree,' the king whispered as he realized what he had done. Darius stood and began pacing through the garden, mumbling to himself.

Gazsi looked at his companions and nodded. *Give the king time,* he thought. *He will soon realize that he has no other choice.*

After a time, the king stopped in front of the officials; his face was drawn, his eyes sad.

'Bring Belteshazzar and . . .' he paused, 'prepare the lions.'

The palace was silent. No one believed that Darius would ever give his friend to the beasts. As the guards went for Belteshazzar, the whole of the royal court stood motionless.

As a gift for his coronation, Darius had received six Nubian lions. All Persians knew that lions symbolized the power and glory the goddess Ishtar had given Persia. A special pit was built for the animals and they were treated as royal pets and – when the punishment called for it – royal executioners. Throughout the palace, the lions' roars could be heard, day and night, filling everyone with dread.

With his attendants at his side, the king strode to the room above the lions' pit. The lions roared when they heard Darius enter.

'They are hungry, Your Majesty,' the attendant said, bowing. 'They know you feed them whenever you come.'

The king turned as Belteshazzar was brought into the room. He gestured to the guards to remove his shackles and stepped over to his advisor . . . his friend.

'Belteshazzar, I am sorry,' he whispered. 'I tried to free you, but the law . . .'

'. . . requires it,' Belteshazzar finished. 'And you must obey the law. Just as I must obey the law of my God.'

'May your God,' the king said, 'whom you serve continually, rescue you!'

Belteshazzar smiled at the king. 'Amen.'

Darius stepped back and signalled to the guards, who led Belteshazzar to the edge of the lion's pit.

The great cats grew wild when they saw the men; they roared and lunged, trying to reach the pit's edge. The attendant carried a large piece of meat and tossed it in the far corner of the pit, a practice used to divert the lions so the guards would not be accidently mauled while lowering a prisoner.

As the lions fought over the meat, the two guards grabbed Belteshazzar by his arms then dropped him into the pit. They turned to help the attendant move the immense stone that covered the pit.

Darius watched his friend until the stone was dropped into place. He nodded to his secretary who carried a small box over to the stone. Lifting its lid, he removed sealing wax and a small oil lamp. When the wax was melted, the secretary knelt by the stone and dripped a large pool of the melted wax on the stone, spilling over onto the floor. The secretary stood and nodded to the king.

Darius crossed the floor and knelt. Making a fist, he slammed his signet ring into the softened wax, sealing the stone. 'Anyone breaking the seal before morning will be subject to the same punishment as Belteshazzar.' The king spat and, without speaking to anyone, left the room.

The king hurried down the corridors, not seeing the servants who paused in their work to bow as he passed. A thick, heavy musk of incense hung in the air like a pall of death. When he reached his chambers, he threw off his outer cloak and called for his servant as he tried to hide his tears.

'Tell the steward of the throne room that I will see no one else today,' he ordered, his words cold. 'Explain to my guests that I will not attend them at the evening meal.'

'Yes, Your Majesty,' the servant bowed. 'Shall I have food brought to you here?'

'No,' the king said sharply. 'I want nothing. No food or drink.' He pointed to a curtain that hid a group of musicians playing softly. 'Have them leave as well. I want to be alone.'

As he tried to sleep, he listened to the sounds that echoed through the palace. The lions were silent. They neither roared nor moaned. Despite his brave words, the king knew that his friend was dead.

When the first shaft of sunlight hit the garden outside the king's chambers, Darius threw on a robe and hurried to the lion chamber. The attendant and the guards bowed and stepped respectfully back as the king approached the pit. No sounds came from within and Darius tried not to think of the massive cats sleeping with a full belly.

'Roll back the stone,' he commanded. 'I want to see.'

'But, Master,' the servant replied, 'it will not be good for you to see him this way.'

'He was my friend and I killed him,' Darius answered as he waved his hand for them to obey.

Slowly, the servants rolled the stone away from the lion pit.

Kneeling, the king peered into the murky shadows. Far below, in the dark depths, he could hear the lions sleeping.

'Belteshazzar,' his voice trembled, 'are you there? Did your God rescue you from the lions?'

From the darkness, Darius heard a muffled voice:

'O King, may you live forever!'

'Belteshazzar?' the king gasped.

'My God sent His angel,' Belteshazzar said as he stepped from the shadows in the pit, 'and He shut the mouths of the lions. They have not hurt me. I was found innocent in my God's sight. Nor have I done any wrong before you.'

'An angel saved you?' the king asked.

'He came in to the darkness and brought peace. The lions slept like lambs.'

'Praise be to the God of Belteshazzar. He is God above all gods!' the king cried. He turned to the guards. 'Quickly, help Belteshazzar from the pit,' he ordered, 'and then wake Gazsi, Majeed and Ksathra and bring them here. They set a trap to kill Belteshazzar; now, they shall receive the same punishment they chose for him.'

The guards bowed their heads and obeyed.

'Go and issue this decree, that in every part of my kingdom people must fear and reverence the God of Belteshazzar. For He is the living God and He endures forever: His kingdom will not be destroyed, His dominion will never end. He rescues and He saves; He performs signs and wonders in the heavens and on the earth. He has rescued Belteshazzar – Daniel – from the power of the lions.'

19

The Woman

In the land of Persia and the city of Susa, lived King Xerxes. His hand was mighty and his vengeance swift. All who knew him spoke of his fairness and, in the same breath, would whisper of his justice. His word was his bond and what he decreed would last forever.

Living also in that land was the remnant of the Hebrews who had been captured by Nebuchadnezzar, King of Babylon, and who were now under Persian rule. Though far from Israel, they were determined not to forget their customs or their God. Life in exile had been good, yet there were those who would see them dead. They were seen as outsiders to be chased, persecuted and killed; but the Creator would not forget their faithfulness.

One such Hebrew was Hadassah. She was beautiful and all who saw her fell in love. An orphan, she was cared for by a cousin, Mordecai, an honest man who bowed to no one but his God. He was older than Hadassah and she loved him as a father; Mordecai thought that she was a gift from YHWH.

'Hadassah . . . Hadassah, where are you?' Mordecai called from the front room.

'In here,' she answered as she continued kneading the dough.

Mordecai rushed into the room, eyes wide and breathing hard. 'What are you doing?' he wheezed.

Running was difficult for someone his size and age. Beads of sweat dripped across his forehead and glistened in his eyes, and his heart burst with excitement.

She smiled. 'Making bread.'

'Bread is not important now,' he said dismissively. 'There is news in the marketplace.'

'There is always news in the marketplace,' Hadassah said, 'but only important news would make you forget food. What has happened?'

'King Xerxes has banished Queen Vashti!' Mordecai said.

'What?' she gasped. 'Why?'

'It is impossible to know the truth,' he said. 'All I know is that when the king was giving the seven-day feast for his nobles and guests, he sent for the queen, to show everyone how beautiful she was . . . and she refused to come.'

Hadassah gasped. 'She refused? To obey the king? Why would she do that?'

Her cousin shrugged. 'Rumours run rampant in the marketplace, but none bear the weight of truth. The truth is that the king was furious. He called his seven chief advisors and asked their counsel. All stated that, according to the law, Queen Vashti insulted not only the king but all the men in the land, for – when her conduct is known – other wives will follow her example and despise their husbands. The advisors counselled King Xerxes to issue a royal decree, written according to the laws of the Medes and Persians – which cannot be repealed – that the queen must never enter the king's presence again.'

'Never to see her husband again?' Hadassah whispered.

'Exiled . . . murdered . . . who knows?' Mordecai gabbled.

'So why are you so excited?' she asked.

'There is more,' her cousin said. 'They also counselled the king to give her position to another.'

'One of the king's other wives will become queen?'

'No,' Mordecai said. 'A search is being made for all the beautiful young girls of marriageable age to be brought into the palace. The king will choose one from these to become his new queen.' He pulled Hadassah's hands from the dough. 'You must prepare.'

'What?' she asked.

'The king's men are in the marketplace now.' He paused. 'Your beauty was mentioned.'

Hadassah eyes widened. 'Why me? I am a Hebrew, not a Persian.'

He squeezed her hand. 'You cannot tell anyone you are Hebrew,' he insisted. 'You will have to change your name. Hadassah is a Hebrew name. The king's men might not accept you if they knew.' Mordecai looked into her eyes. 'Hadassah . . . many of our ancestors were brought to this land as captives. Through the years, all our family died,

including my wife and your parents. You are my only rela-
tive. I would see you married before I die. However, I do
not have money for a dowry. Hadassah . . . even if you are
not chosen queen, you would be married and provided for
beyond my wildest dreams.'

Hadassah hesitated. She was not shocked by what her
cousin suggested. A man having many wives was common
even among the Hebrew people. But to become one of the
king's wives meant she would never be allowed to leave the
palace. Hadassah looked at her cousin, his eyes pleading for
her to understand, to accept.

Her heart softened. *Mordecai took me in when I was all alone,*
she thought. *He does not wish me to be left alone again.* Hadassah
squeezed Mordecai's hand and nodded.

'I will do as you ask,' she said, 'but you must send word
how you are keeping – and I will do the same.'

The old man drew her to his chest. 'I promise,' he whispered.

Hadassah had barely wiped the dough from her hands
and straightened her robe and hair when someone knocked
at the door. When Mordecai called her, she breathed deeply
and walked into the front room.

Two men, dressed in fine robes, stood with her cousin.
Their eyes widened when they saw her.

'Ah, Lord Asha, Lord Bahram, this is my cousin,'
Mordecai said. She crossed the room and took his hand, her
eyes lowered, not looking at the men.

'She is as beautiful as we heard,' Lord Asha said.

'As beautiful as Ishtar, the goddess of love,' Lord Bahram agreed. 'Speak; we must make sure your voice is as lovely as your face. Tell us your name.'

'My name?' Hadassah glanced at her cousin. 'Uh . . . my name is –'

'Esther,' Mordecai interrupted. 'Her parents thought her beautiful, but would not use the . . . goddess's name, so they chose one similar.'

'Esther,' Lord Asha said, 'has your cousin explained why we are here?'

'Yes, my lord.'

'And you understand what it means to enter the king's harem as a wife?' Lord Bahram asked.

Hadassah – Esther – looked at her cousin, who nodded his head slightly. 'I understand,' she replied.

'Then please come with us,' Asha said.

'What? Now?' Esther asked. 'I haven't gathered my clothing, my things.'

The king's men laughed. 'You do not need to bring anything,' Bahram explained. 'In the king's palace, all you need will be provided. Now, say farewell to your cousin.'

The two men stepped back, allowing Esther and Mordecai a last moment.

'Hada . . . uh . . . Esther,' Mordecai asked, 'you do understand?'

She nodded. 'I honour you for your care of me.'

'I will come to the palace gate every day to hear how you are.' He lowered his voice, 'May YHWH bless you and protect you.'

Although Esther had walked past the citadel of Susa many times, she had never entered within. Outside it looked like what it was – a mighty fortress. Walls made from dried brick taller than many of the hills surrounding the city, with countless narrow arched windows spaced between towers.

Lord Asha and Lord Bahram escorted her across a bridge wide enough for two chariots abreast and stopped before an iron gate. Guards stood on either side and, near them, a scribe sat behind a small table with a scroll and writing implements.

'Lord Asha, Lord Bahram,' the scribe bowed his head. 'Whom have you brought?'

'One we hope will please the king,' Lord Bahram replied. 'Her name is Esther.'

The man did not look towards her. Before leaving home, Lord Asha had given Esther a long veil that covered her face and hair completely. Once veiled for the king, it would dishonour Xerxes for another man to see her. The man wrote her name on the scroll and nodded to the guards to raise the gate.

Inside, they walked through archways and past spiralled columns rising from marble floors. The walls covered in limestone plaster were painted with sphinxes and the famed blue lions of Ishtar.

After several more turns down several more corridors, the men stopped in front of a large set of double doors with guards stationed on either side. One of the guards

turned and knocked on the door; it was opened by a tall
man, with heavy rolls of fat, dressed in a robe of red
trimmed with gold. He bowed.

'Whom have you brought?' he asked.

'One we hope will please the king. Her name is Esther.'

The two lords turned to Esther.

'May you find joy here, Esther,' Lord Bahram said.

She didn't know what to say, so she merely nodded her
head. The men bowed and left. The tall man opened the
other door and stepped to one side.

'I am Hegai,' he told her. 'I am in charge of the king's
harem. Please be welcome to the place of women.'

Esther bowed her head and walked past him. The heavy
door closing behind her sounded permanent.

YHWH, she prayed silently, *I believe You sent me here. Be
with me and show me how to serve You here.*

Days and nights became weeks and months as Esther
learnt the ways of the harem. She had many teachers, as all
the females in the palace – from the king's mother, sisters,
aunts and cousins to the newest arrivals like Esther – had
rooms or apartments in the place of women. Esther's kindness quickly made her one of Hegai's favourites and he
moved her into the best rooms and assigned servants to
tend her.

Esther had obeyed Mordecai's instructions and never
revealed her heritage to anyone. Each day, when the others
were resting, Esther walked to the edge of a courtyard near
the palace gates. There, a stone wall cut with scrollwork,

provided privacy while still allowing cool breezes. Mordecai sat on one side and told her news of their neighbours and Esther told him of her lessons. Before he left, he would whisper a prayer, asking God to protect Esther and give her favour in the house of the king.

His prayers were answered. One day Esther told him, 'King Xerxes has chosen me to be queen.'

Through the scrollwork wall, she heard Mordecai clap his hands. 'YHWH be praised, this is wonderful news!' he laughed.

'King Xerxes is planning a coronation for me. There will be a holiday throughout the land and a great banquet,' she said. 'I will ask that you be invited.'

'I will be honoured.'

'I am moving to another part of the palace, but I will still come here to meet with you.'

'I know that YHWH will use you to bless this land and our people.'

The day before the coronation, Esther was late arriving.

'I have spent the morning preparing for tomorrow's ceremony,' she explained.

'Esther, something has happened,' Mordecai sounded anxious.

'What?'

'While I was waiting for you, I heard voices. They sounded angry and I heard one of them say, "Kill". I slipped behind a bush. They called each other Bigthana and Teresh.'

'They are royal officials,' Esther said.

'Esther, these men are planning to assassinate King Xerxes.'

Esther gasped. 'Tell me what you heard, that I may warn the king.'

The next day, Esther reported that the two officials had been arrested and hanged.

'It is to be recorded in the Chronicles of the King that you discovered this plot,' she said. 'And you are to become one of the royal officials.'

Shortly after her coronation, Mordecai told Esther that Haman – the king's new vizier – had been given a special honour. 'The king has commanded that all kneel to Haman,' Mordecai said. 'That I will not do.'

'Why?' Esther asked.

'Haman wants more,' Mordecai fumed. 'He wants people to grovel before him. And that I will not do!'

'Be careful, cousin,' she said. 'The vizier is powerful.'

Day after day, Mordecai refused to kneel to Haman and, soon, Esther heard of this. She was resting in a secluded spot in the palace garden, when two maids walked near.

'I heard this man Mordecai refused to bow to Vizier Haman,' one girl said.

'I heard too,' the other maid said. 'What is more, I heard that the vizier discovered Mordecai is a Hebrew. I feel sorry for him and his family; the vizier has an evil temper.'

The next afternoon Mordecai did not meet Esther. Certain something terrible had happened, she returned to her rooms and fell on her couch, weeping. One of her maids, Lo-Ran, pleaded with the queen to tell her how she could help.

'My cousin Mordecai has made an enemy of the vizier,' Esther said, 'and I fear for his life.'

'Mordecai the Hebrew?' Lo-Ran gasped. 'That means that you are . . .'

Esther nodded. 'Send for my servant Hathach. He can leave the palace and seek out my cousin.'

When he returned, Hathach said that Mordecai would not come into the palace because of the king's decree.

'What decree?'

'Vizier Haman has told the king that the Hebrews refused to obey the laws.' Hathach said. 'The vizier convinced the king to issue a decree – on the thirteenth day of the month of Adar all the Hebrews are to be destroyed. Majesty, your cousin urges you to plead for your people.'

Esther grew pale, her eyes widening. 'I cannot do this. Tell Mordecai it is forbidden to approach the king without being summoned. Anyone who does so will be put to death, unless the king extends his sceptre.'

Esther was in agony waiting for Mordecai's response; she paced through her apartment, refusing to eat any of the food or drink that Lo-Ran offered. When Hathach returned, she barely acknowledged his bow.

'What did my cousin say to my message?' she pleaded. 'I must know!'

'Majesty,' Hathach said, 'your cousin said, "Do not think because you are in the king's house you will escape. If you do not speak out, deliverance will come from another place, but you and all your father's family will perish. Who knows but that you were given your royal position for such a time as this?"'

Esther could not allow her people to be destroyed. She thought of what she could do and how she could save her people. 'Tell my cousin to have all the Hebrews fast and pray for three days. I, and all my servants, will do the same. After that, I will go to the king. If I die, so be it – then I die!'

On the third day, Esther put on her royal robes and walked to the throne room. The guards opened the doors for her, bowing. She tried to calm her breathing, praying for YHWH's protection.

King Xerxes was sitting on his throne, talking to Vizier Haman. When he saw Esther he smiled and extended his golden sceptre; he was letting her approach him.

Esther walked the length of the hall and when she reached Xerxes, she touched the tip of his sceptre.

'Let Queen Esther be seated next to me,' the king commanded. Entranced by her beauty he smiled at her. 'Only something important would cause you to risk entering my presence. Whatever it is, I will give you, even to half my kingdom.'

'I ask that you come with Vizier Haman to a banquet I have prepared.'

'We shall come,' the king responded.

Haman preened like a peacock. 'I am honoured, Majesty,' he bowed.

Xerxes stood and extended his arm to Esther. They left the throne room, Haman following. They walked to a fragrant garden where a low table with three couches was set with food and goblets of wine. The king escorted Esther to one of the couches.

After they had eaten, the king asked Esther, 'My Queen, tell me your petition?'

Esther looked at Haman. He had eaten little and spoken less. *I need him to be comfortable, to be off his guard.* Esther smiled at her husband.

'My petition tonight is this . . . let the king and the vizier come tomorrow to another banquet. Then I will answer the king's question.'

The king smiled. 'Mystery and food; Esther, you know the path to a man's heart.' He laughed and nodded. 'Haman and I will come to your banquet.'

Esther smiled. 'Thank you.'

Haman left the palace and made his way to the city gates. There, shadowed against the walls was a wooden gallows. A soldier of the palace guarded the narrow, wooden steps.

'Is it built as I instructed?' Haman asked.

The guard bowed. 'It is tall enough to hang a giant.'

'Then it will be good enough for the Hebrew Mordecai,' Haman said as he walked back to the palace. 'If he had bowed to me, he would live. Now he and all his people shall be killed.'

In the palace, the king went back to his chamber but could not sleep.

'I wish to hear something read,' he told his servants. 'Bring the Chronicles of the King.' When he heard the story of the assassination plot of Bigthana and Teresh, Xerxes asked, 'What honour did Mordecai receive?'

'None.'

'None?' the king was incredulous. 'Something must be done. Who is in the outer court?'

The guard opened the door. 'Vizier Haman.'

'Let him come in.' When Haman had bowed, the king asked him, 'Vizier, what should be done for a man the king wishes to honour?'

Haman smiled. 'This man should wear a royal robe and ride one of the king's horses. He should ride through the city with someone proclaiming, "This is what is done for the man the king delights to honour!"'

The king nodded. 'Yes, this is what needs to be done. Haman, get the robe and the horse and do this for Mordecai. Then attend me at the queen's banquet.'

Haman's throat constricted, as he listened to the King. Gulping, he bowed and rasped, 'As Your Majesty commands.'

As the king had commanded, Haman led Mordecai through the city. Then, beating his chest and screaming with rage, he ran back to the palace.

The banquet Esther had ordered was even more lavish than the previous night. Oil lamps lit the room; soft winds blew in from opened doors.

'All your favourite foods have been prepared, my King,' she said when the men arrived.

'Ah, my Queen,' Xerxes smiled, 'you are worth more than rubies. Haman – what do you think of her – has anyone one like this ever been born?'

Haman tried to smile.

Xerxes was the only one to enjoy the meal. Esther was too nervous to eat and Haman appeared distracted. After they had finished eating, Xerxes asked, 'Queen Esther, now tell me, what is your petition?'

Esther slipped her hands nervously under her veil and grasped them.

'If it pleases Your Majesty, my petition is for my life and the life of all my people. We have been sold for destruction.'

The king slammed his cup down, spilling wine on the table.

'First men try to kill me, now someone dares to kill my queen? Who is this man?'

Esther pointed towards the vizier. 'Haman.'

Haman rose trembling, shaking his head. 'Majesty –'

'Quiet!' Xerxes roared and stamped out of the opened doors into the garden.

'M . . . m . . . my . . . Queen,' Haman wheezed. 'I do not understand. Why would I wish to kill you?'

Esther faced the vizier. 'Because,' she said icily, 'I am Hebrew and Mordecai is my cousin.'

'It cannot . . . I did not . . . Please!' Haman stumbled and fell on the queen's couch. He grasped her hands, 'Please, you must . . .'

'So, it is not enough that you wish to kill my queen,' Xerxes stood in the door, rage contorting his face, 'you dare molest her while I am near?'

Trembling, Haman pushed himself to his feet, his mouth opening and closing like a fish.

'Guards!' the king roared.

Two guards entered the room as soon as they heard the king; one grabbed Haman's arms, the other covered his face.

'Majesty,' Harbona, the king's personal servant had followed the guards into the room, 'Haman has built a gallows seventy-five feet high to hang Mordecai, the man who revealed the plot to kill you.'

Xerxes wrenched his signet ring off Haman's hand. 'Hang him.'

Haman collapsed in the guards' arms as they dragged him from the room.

Then, Xerxes crossed to the queen and embraced her. 'Did he harm you?'

'No,' Esther said, and told the king that she was related to Mordecai.

'I was wrong to trust Haman,' the king said, 'but I will correct that mistake. Harbona,' he told his servant, 'summon Mordecai.'

The king turned back to Esther. 'I will make Mordecai vizier. And whatever has to be done to protect your people, will be done! I swear it!'

20

The Prophet

The darkened room made no difference to the old man lying on the bed. Age had faded his vision so he could only tell apart the brightest sunlight from the darkest night. His frame, when he stood, was tall and his muscles still hinted of a time of strength. The skin on his hands was as thin as the finest parchment and creased with countless lines, as was his face. Only his voice, deep as a cavern and strong as an elephant, still had the power to inspire fear and awe.

'Helah,' he called.

The woman sewing by the light of an oil lamp laid aside the cloth and needle and crossed the room to kneel by the bed. 'I am here, Isaiah,' she said, taking his hand.

He lifted his other hand to feel the contours of her face. 'Ah, my beautiful wife,' he smiled.

'How would you know?' Helah smiled. 'You're nearly blind.'

Isaiah laughed. 'I'm a prophet.'

'And I'm a prophetess,' she reminded him, 'but that doesn't mean I know why you called me.'

Isaiah's smile faded. 'Our sons, Jashub and Maher,' he said. 'Call them to me. I must continue.'

'I will get them,' Helah stood and crossed to the door. 'Sons,' she called, 'your father is awake.'

Two men entered the room. Tall in stature, with strong features and a steady gaze, they were a near copy of their father.

'My sons, please bring chairs and a table and place them near the bed,' Isaiah asked. 'Helah, bring parchment and writing implements.'

Several minutes later, his sons had placed the furniture as Isaiah had requested while Helah gathered all they would need.

'I will leave you to speak with our sons alone,' Helah said, placing a cushion behind Isaiah's back. 'I must prepare the evening meal.'

Isaiah nodded in his wife's direction. After he heard the door close, he leaned back. 'My sons, we must continue. I have little time left and would have you write down the prophecies the Creator gave to me.'

Jashub spread out the parchments on the tabletop. Shalal selected two bone pens from the box of writing implements and handed one to his brother. They dipped the tip of the styluses into a dish of water and rubbed them across a cake of dried ink.

'We are ready, Father,' Jashub said.

Isaiah nodded.

'Good, good,' he said. 'Of all the prophecies the Almighty has spoken to me, there is one greater than the rest. It tells of the coming of a redeemer. Jashub, you heard part of this prophecy, when YHWH sent you and me to meet King Ahaz.'

Isaiah's older son lifted his chin and squinted his eyes as he thought.

'I remember,' he nodded. 'We met the king at the end of the aqueduct of the Upper Pool, on the road to the Washerman's Field.'

'That's right,' Isaiah said. 'Three of the king's enemies were marching their armies against Ahaz and YHWH sent me to tell the king to not be afraid of them. Yet, part of the prophecy was not for that time, nor for our lifetime, but for a time yet to come.' The prophet straightened on the cushion, his fading eyes seeing into the future, and when he spoke, his voice echoed as if another spoke through him. *'Therefore the Lord Himself will give you a sign: The virgin will be with child and will give birth to a son, and will call Him Immanuel.'*

'I remember, Father,' Jashub said. 'At the time, it confused me. How can a woman who has never been with a man conceive a child?'

'I know not,' Isaiah said. 'Prophets do not always understand what they are told to speak. I believe that the Creator of the Universe can make a virgin to bear a son.'

'Call . . . him . . . Immanuel . . .' Shalel whispered as he wrote. He looked at his father, 'What does "Immanuel" mean?'

'It means, "God with us",' Isaiah said. 'Another time YHWH spoke to me about this child and His name. Write this; '*For to us a child is born, to us a son is given, and the government will be on His shoulders. And He will be called Wonderful Counsellor, Mighty God, Everlasting Father, Prince of Peace. Of the increase of His government and peace there will be no end. He will reign on David's throne and over his kingdom, establishing and upholding it with justice and righteousness from that time on and forever.*'

'Do you not see?' Isaiah grew excited. 'This child will be Almighty God!'

'YHWH . . . will become . . . a man?' Jashub's eyes widened.

Isaiah nodded. 'So it would appear.'

'Will there be any signs to let us know when this will happen?' Shalel asked.

The old prophet nodded. 'There are signs. YHWH spoke to me of some, others I have learnt from the prophets before me. Do you remember how Balak, King of Moab, had brought the prophet Balaam to curse the Israelites?'

Jashub laughed. 'And all Balaam could prophesy was a blessing.'

'Yes,' Isaiah agreed. 'But one of his prophecies was about this child. "*I see Him, but not now; I behold Him, but not near. A star will come out of Jacob; a sceptre will rise out of Israel.*" You see, He might not come in our lifetime.'

'I understand the sceptre means He will be king,' Shalel said, 'but what is this star?'

Isaiah shrugged. 'I am a prophet. I was not trained in the science of the stars like the magi of the Medes and

Persians. Perhaps, if I live long enough, I can write to them of this star. Maybe they can explain.'

'So, a child and a star,' Jashub said. 'What else do you know of this, Father?'

'I spoke to Micah,' Isaiah said. 'He, too, has received a message concerning this child. He said the Almighty told him, *"But you, Bethlehem, though you are small among the clans of Judah, out of you will come for Me One who will be ruler over Israel, whose origins are from of old, from ancient times."'*

'Bethlehem is where King David was born and lived as a shepherd boy,' Shalel said.

His father nodded. 'And YHWH spoke to Micah of shepherds and this child too,' Isaiah said. 'In that same prophecy, the Almighty said, *"He will stand and shepherd His flock in the strength of the Lord, in the majesty of the name of the Lord His God."'*

'He will be a shepherd?' Jashub asked.

'Again, I know not,' Isaiah said. 'YHWH has often referred to our kings as shepherds, watching over the people day and night, just as sheep in the fields. I believe mankind will see Him as many things. A babe, a child, Immanuel, a shepherd . . .'

Jashub and Shalel had been busily writing all of their father's words and looked up when he stopped speaking.

Isaiah was still, his chest barely moving under breath. His eyes – glazed with age – stared at nothing, but his sons recognized the signs; at that moment, their father was hearing from YHWH. They dipped their styluses in the water, rubbed them across the cake of ink and held them poised over the parchment. Should their father speak the prophecy aloud, they were ready to write down the Creator's words.

Isaiah, prophet of the Almighty, spoke, his voice tinged with the echoes of eternity:

'Who has believed our message and to whom has the arm of the Lord been revealed? He grew up before Him like a tender shoot, and like a root out of dry ground. He had no beauty or majesty to attract us to Him, nothing in His appearance that we should desire Him. He was despised and rejected by men, a man of sorrows, and familiar with suffering. Like one from whom men hide their faces He was despised, and we esteemed Him not.

'Surely He took up our infirmities and carried our sorrows, yet we considered Him stricken by YHWH, smitten by Him, and afflicted. But He was pierced for our transgressions, He was crushed for our iniquities; the punishment that brought us peace was upon Him, and by His wounds we are made whole. We all, like sheep, have gone astray, each of us has turned to his own way, and YHWH has laid on Him the wrongdoings of us all.

'He was oppressed and afflicted, yet He did not open His mouth; He was led like a lamb to the slaughter, and as a sheep before her shearers is silent, so He did not open His mouth. By oppression and judgement He was taken away. For He was cut off from the land of the living; for the transgression of my people He was stricken. He was assigned a grave with the wicked, and with the evil-doers in His death, though He had done no violence, nor was any deceit in His mouth . . . because He poured out His life unto death, and was numbered

with the rebellious. For He bore the sin of many, and prayed for the transgressors.'

Isaiah sat, nearly blind, but seeing beyond the veil of time. He clenched his fist, gasping, 'His hands . . . His feet . . .'

'What are they doing to him?' Shalel asked his father. It was as if he knew Isaiah stood on the edge of time and looked in to the future.

'It is too much . . . they are madmen and fools . . . they kill Him . . . the Son of YHWH . . .'

His breathing grew ragged and he swallowed.

'Thirsty . . . so thirsty,' he rasped. He shook his head.

'So much blood,' he cried, tears streaming down his face. 'The blood of the Almighty's sacrifice.

'For me . . .' He turned his head towards his sons; the glaze from his eyes was gone and he could see them clearly.

'For you.' He rose from his bed and lifted his hands.

'For all mankind.'

What's the **BIG** idea?

Now you've enjoyed reading YHWH
why not let us help you understand the original...

A REFRESHING WAY
FOR ADULTS TO SEE
THE WHOLE BIBLE

www.Bible.org.uk

Helping you understand your Bible

BIBLE EDUCATION
FOR PRIMARY SCHOOLS